MW01612737

Give Her
the World

Give Her the World

Copyright © 2022 by Delaney Lynn, Lady Bookers Press

This is a work of fiction. Names, characters, businesses, places, events, locales, and incidents are either the products of the author's imagination or used in a fictitious manner. Any resemblance to actual persons, living or dead, or actual events is purely coincidental.

All rights reserved. No part of this publication may be reproduced, distributed, or transmitted in any form or by any means, including photocopying, recording, or other electronic or mechanical methods, without the prior written permission of the publisher, except in the case of brief quotations embodied in critical reviews and certain other noncommercial uses permitted by copyright law. Please do not participate in or encourage piracy of copyrighted materials in violation of the author's rights.

Editing by The Pro Book Editor
Interior and Cover Design by Murphy Rae

Paperback ISBN: 978-1-7378753-2-1

1. Main category — Fiction/Romance/Contemporary
2. Other category — Fiction/Romance/New Adult

First Edition

To the hopeless romantics.

Chapter One

Hayes

"Another round!" my teammate shouts from the other end of the bar.

It's the first day of syllabus week, the first week back to school when teachers assign no homework and we spend approximately fifty minutes in each class simply reading the syllabus. It's pointless really. It's not like we don't have access to our syllabus through the campus portal. There's no reason to even go to class this week, and most students don't. Unfortunately for myself and the rest of the East Valley baseball team, if our coach caught wind of us skipping class, even on syllabus week, we'd have extra sprints to run after practice.

"Murphy!"

I turn to find my best friend Jason holding up another shot of Jameson for me. I pull back the shot, and a collective cheer sounds throughout the bar as we finish our ninth shot of the night. It's tradition for the senior class baseball players to take one shot for each championship East Valley has taken home the previous years—our own tribute to all the great players who have made it to the big leagues. Thanks to our undefeated

1

season last year, East Valley has officially won sixteen championships.

"Fuck, dude. We shouldn't have pregamed before this," Jason says.

"You," I correct. "*You* shouldn't have pregamed. I feel great." I give him a teasing nudge.

"How many more?" he asks.

"Seven. Come on, next rounds on me."

I walk to the bar to order a shot of Jameson for each of the eight seniors participating in this year's championship shots. "Eight shots of Jameson, please," I ask the blonde bartender, grinning.

Even in the dark lighting of the sports bar, I can see her cheeks blush. She's cute—cute enough that I can hopefully flirt my way to a few of those shots being free, seeing as I don't have much extra cash to spare. I'm here on a full-ride scholarship, which was the only way I was ever going to be able to attend college. We're not supposed to work during the season, though I've kept my job since freshmen year and Coach hasn't said a thing. As long as it doesn't interfere with my stats, he doesn't mind me pocketing a few extra bucks a week. My parents especially don't mind. In fact, it was their idea.

The cute bartender returns with a tray full of Jamo. Looks like my charm worked. I count ten shots, so that's two free. Jason and I will be ahead by one round, and he'll be one shot closer to finding his head buried in the toilet.

After the guys each grab their respective shots, Jason and I look at the four remaining.

"Ready, man?" I ask as he eyes the liquid like it's poison.

The bar is packed, but the bartender is staying close by, making eyes at me like she wants to strike up a conversation.

"Hey," I call out to her. "Think you can take one of these for my friend here? Just don't tell the guys. He won't hear the end of it."

She smiles as she leans against the bar, pushing her perky tits on full display. Jason's gaze moves from the shots to her chest, but her eyes stay on me. "Sure," she says.

I pick up two of the shots, Jason and the bartender each taking one for themselves.

"And what is the name of my savior?" Jason asks, still eyeing her chest.

Her gaze flickers to Jason for a moment before landing back on me, her focus on my lips. "Natalie."

"Natalie, it is a pleasure to meet you," Jason says, then he downs his shot.

Natalie holds up her shot glass to mine in cheers.

I oblige and down the first one, followed by the second.

Natalie is making it a point to blatantly check me out, and I know if I want to get laid tonight, this will be a sure thing. I mean, who the hell am I kidding? Of course I want to get laid. But even still, I know nothing is going to happen between us. It's never been my thing to sleep with the girls who practically throw themselves at me. I pass her a wink and walk away to the other side of the bar where the rest of the baseball team has pulled together a few tables.

Another round of shots has already been brought to the table. Damn, am I going to be fucked up tonight.

"Shut the hell up, everyone! I'm going to make a toast!" shouts our catcher, a short and thin guy named Tony, but we all call him Bony. It doesn't matter how many calories the guy eats or how hard Coach works him in the gym, he doesn't beef up. But he's one of the fastest guys on the team and can throw one hell of a baseball. He's also a damn good catcher.

"Atta boy, Bony. Let's hear it!" shouts Kevin, mine and Jason's roommate and our second baseman.

"This one's for you, Hayes Murphy, for leading us to another East Valley victory and the reason we're all getting extra fucked up this year! You're the best goddamn pitcher I've ever had the privilege of catching for. Let's do it again, brother."

I hold up the shot someone passed me and give Bony a head nod. I don't need to get sentimental with him right now in the middle of this bar, but he's the best catcher I've ever had. After I down my twelfth shot of the night, I find Bony and give him a one-armed hug. Jason's arm falls to my shoulder from behind, quickly pulling me back from Bony.

"You gonna hit that?" Jason asks, nodding toward the bar.

"Who?"

"The bartender. She's been making eyes at you. You gonna hit that?"

I shrug. "I don't know. Night's still young."

Jason rolls his eyes. "Come on, dude. I've known you your whole life. Why do you always do this?"

"Do what?" I play dumb.

"Let the easy ones go. Don't you want to get laid?"

"No shit, I want to get laid."

"Then why are you letting Natalie go to waste? Not that I mind. I happily take the rejected women off your hands each time. But look at her. She's hot as fuck."

I shake my head and laugh. "She's all yours," I say, though I might regret that later when I'm rubbing one off in the shower.

"Dude, come on. You haven't brought a girl home in months."

"Are you keeping track of my sex life now?" I chuckle.

He rolls his eyes. "Fine, man. Fuck you. I tried to help. I apologize in advance when you hear Natalie screaming my name through the walls later." He winks before he walks away, straight to Natalie who still has her eyes on me.

Having been the star player on my baseball team since before I could properly fuck, I have no shortage of women who are willing to sleep with me. Problem is, most of them just want to be able to say they slept with Hayes Murphy, East Valley's star pitcher and soon to be MLB rookie of the year. No one doubts I'm going to get drafted this year and likely head right for the big leagues because my stats are better than most of the guys in the minor league. In high school, the attention was cool, but I got bored of it quickly. Once I realized I would be playing pro one day, I gave myself some standards. It's not like I would be taking advantage of these girls. Like I said, they willingly throw themselves at me. I know they want to sleep with me, but I find it way more attractive when a girl could give two shits about who I am.

Two hours later, I finally take my last championship shot. Jason sat at the bar talking to Natalie up until twenty minutes ago when her shift ended and he walked her out to her car. He got inside, no doubt having her take them back to our place. She eyed me yet again on her way out, but I looked away, pretending I hadn't seen. Even though I'm not interested in Natalie, I am, however, interested in the bombshell that is walking into the bar alone. Her hair is pulled back in a long ponytail, her brown hair swaying when she walks. Her bright blue eyes noticeable from across the bar, they are the perfect contrast to her dark hair and tan. She's petite, with grabbable hips and perfect breasts. Her lips have to be my favorite thing on her though, plump and naturally pouty, causing my dick to stir in my jeans. I'd put her in her mid-twenties, probably only a year or two older than me, though you'd never guess with my six-foot-three build and lean muscle from years of playing ball.

She doesn't so much as glance my way when she walks in, clueing me in that she has no idea who I am. Anyone from around here knows the East Valley baseball team, doesn't matter their age. They like to acknowledge our winning records and congratulate us on the most recent championship. We're well-known in this small town, especially me as the pitcher. This chick though, I already know she doesn't have the slightest clue who the rowdy bunch in the corner is.

I eye her as she takes a seat at the bar and another bartender appears quickly to take her drink order. She glances around the bar, taking in her surroundings and completely missing my eyes on her.

Damn. She doesn't even notice me. And I love it.

I slam the rest of my beer and set the empty glass down. Sixteen shots and a couple beers deep, I'm in no way feeling shy. Not that I'm ever shy. I slide into the bar stool beside her, careful not to show my interest too soon. The bartender drops off her drink before switching her gaze to me. Her eyes widen as she notices who I am, though I have no desire for her to let

5

this mystery woman know. For tonight, I just want to be a random guy at the bar who can hopefully get the beautiful woman sitting beside him to notice him.

"What're you havin'?" the bartender drawls, her southern twang a noticeable change to the midwestern accents that are prominent here in Timbers, Michigan.

I nudge my head toward the drink she just set down. "I'll have what she's having."

The bartender walks away, and I instantly feel the woman's eyes on me like heat in a fire. Her gaze is burning through my skin as she slowly scans over my body.

"What if you don't like what I ordered?" she asks.

I tilt my head to face her, locking gazes with her blue eyes for the first time. I have never seen eyes like hers. I'm not even sure that they're blue anymore. I can see flecks of dark blues and greens, giving her eyes the most rare tint of turquoise. Damn, are they beautiful.

"You look like you have good taste. I'm not worried," I quip.

"Hmm. So, you'd be alright with a tequila-vodka mix on the rocks?"

My eyebrows arch. "You've gotta be shittin' me. You ordered a tequila and vodka? Who does that?"

Her face remains serious for one...two...three seconds before she bursts out laughing, and damn it if she doesn't have a beautiful laugh too. "I kind of wish I did order that. But no. It's tequila and sprite." She holds up her glass and takes a sip through those plump, kissable lips.

Is everything on this woman perfect?

The bartender reappears with my tequila-sprite. "Wanna start a tab or are ya'll together?" she asks with a sinister look.

"Yeah, just put them both on my tab." I hand the bartender my card, and she takes it with a disappointed sigh.

"You don't have to pay for my drink."

"It's no big deal." Though I already spent way too much on booze tonight and my bank account is going to be hurting until my next paycheck, something tells me a few drinks with this woman will be worth it. "So, you're not from around here, are you?" I ask.

"How can you tell?"

I smile. "I just can."

"No," she admits. "Just moved to Timbers a few days ago. I start my new job tomorrow and couldn't sleep. Figured this might calm my nerves a bit. How about you? What brings you to..." She eyes the drink menu with the sports bar's name spread across the top. "Off Base this time of night?"

I can't tell her that its tradition for the baseball team to come here every year to celebrate our championships, because that would give away who I am. She doesn't seem like the kind of girl who would chase a guy based on his future status as an MLB player, but they often never do. So, I lie. "Met up with a few buddies. No reason other than to throw back a few."

She looks around the bar, stopping at the table in the corner that houses the last remaining seniors of the night. She might have seen me come from that way, though I hope none of them give away who we are.

Her eyes meet mine again. "Well, thanks for the drink." She takes another sip, and I follow suit.

"Where'd you move from?" I ask, eager to learn more about her and keep the conversation flowing.

"Chicago. It wasn't cold enough for me in the winter, so I figured I'd move up north," she jokes.

"Ah, not a fan of the snow? You've definitely been living in the wrong part of the country then."

"No kidding. Luckily, we have a few months still before the hibernation begins."

"Cheers to that." I raise my glass. "How about another?" I ask, eyeing her near empty glass.

She looks to her drink for a moment, contemplating before her turquoise gaze meets mine. "Sure, let's have another."

"Normally I at least find out a woman's name before I buy them their second drink," I joke.

She laughs, that beautiful fucking laugh that I could listen to for hours and never grow tired of. Fuck. That must be the alcohol talking. I'm not usually this much of a sap, though her laugh is enthralling.

She holds out her dainty hand to mine. "Rayna."

Even her name is beautiful. I don't stand a chance with this woman. I smile, shaking her tiny hand in my callused pitching one. "Hayes."

I call the bartender back over, ordering two more of Rayna's drink of choice. Truth is, I should probably stick to beer. The mix of tequila, beer, and Jameson isn't going to feel so great in the morning.

"Here ya'll are. Let me know if I can get ya'll anything else. Last calls in about twenty or so," the bartender says, setting down our drinks.

Rayna looks at her watch. "Shit. I didn't realize how late it was."

"Bar closes early during the week. Don't worry, still plenty of time to get a full eight hours in before the big day tomorrow."

She smiles, and my eyes drop to her lips. I can't help it. They move delicately over the straw as she takes a sip of her new drink. I'd give anything to trade places with that straw right now.

She gives me a knowing smirk. "I live down the street, if you want to continue this at my place. I make a mean tequila and vodka. You shouldn't knock it 'til you try it."

Damn. A woman not afraid to get right to the point. She's checking off all my boxes tonight. I definitely won't be walking away from Rayna anytime soon.

My gaze moves to her chest briefly, where her swollen breasts are being held beneath her fitted shirt. I take the new drink and down it in a few gulps before leaving the empty glass on the bar and waving over the bartender to close out my tab. Rayna laughs, sipping casually on her drink. The glimmer in her eyes is telling. We both know where tonight's going to lead. She needs a distraction, nervous to start at this new job of hers. Me? I just need someone who doesn't know who the fuck I am. It's almost no use trying to get laid unless I'm on the road traveling somewhere. Luckily, Rayna is from Chicago, just

8

moved here, and is the hottest chick I've ever laid eyes on. I think my night is going to end just fine.

Once the tab is paid, I lead Rayna out to the parking lot, my hand grazing the small of her back. If she minds, she doesn't let on.

"I parked over here," she says. "Wanna just ride with me?"

"Sure." Not that I had another choice. My car is back at my place since I got a ride over with Kevin. It's not like I could even drive right now anyway, given the night I've already had and I have no desire to fuck up my future.

Rayna stops beside a 2001 red Toyota Camry. "It's not much, but it gets me around," she says.

"Looks just fine to me." I drive my dad's 1992 Dodge pickup. It probably has twice as many miles as her little car but also gets me around just fine. These kinds of cars last if they're well taken care of. When I get inside, I can tell that she takes care of it. It may not be a new car, but you wouldn't be able to tell with the all-black leather interior being in pristine condition.

There's a unique smell in the car, and I quickly familiarize that scent with her. "Your car smells like vanilla and cucumbers."

Rayna's eyebrows raise. "Impressive." She opens the glove box in front of me and pulls out a bottle of hand lotion that pictures a vanilla bean and cucumber on the front. "Quite the sniffer you got there," she teases, laughing as she tosses the lotion back into the glove box and starts the engine.

Five minutes later, we're pulling into an elegant housing complex lined with storefronts on the first level and five stories of condos above, which comes as a surprise after seeing the kind of car she drives. She has to be rich to live here.

Rayna parks in the enclosed parking lot before shutting off the engine and looking at me. "We're here," she says softly, seeming nervous.

I didn't know this about myself before, but suddenly this shy and innocent version of Rayna seems even sexier than the one who got straight to the point, asking me to her place. *Just keep ticking off those boxes, Rayna.*

She gets out of the car slowly, and I follow her lead as she shuts and locks her doors. Her car looks odd in this complex. I could tell by the engine knocking as we drove here that her bearings are beginning to wear out. She may take care of the car the best she can, but there's nothing she can do to prevent the engine from getting old. She'll have to take it in soon.

Rayna doesn't speak as we enter the complex through a side door. I follow her to the elevator and wait with her quietly until the elevator dings its arrival. She hits the number three as the elevator doors close. The tension in the air is thick. We both know what I'm doing here. She must be attracted to me if she invited a stranger back to her place after only two drinks. There's no doubt in my mind that I'm downright attracted to her. If the strain in my jeans isn't giving it away, then the dirty thoughts about her lips on my body sure are.

My thoughts are interrupted as the elevator jolts to a stop. The doors glide open, and Rayna quietly walks to a door labeled 32 C. She scans her keycard and walks in.

"It's all rather extravagant for my taste, but my brother insisted if I was going to be living alone that I find the safest place in Timbers. And well, this place was deemed the safest." She hangs her keys on a hook near the door. "But a little over the top, in my opinion."

I glance around. She's right, it's fancy as hell. The all-white marble counter tops, white cabinetry, white trim, and cement flooring all scream money. So, she's rich. But she drives an old Camry.

"Show me around?" I ask, hoping to calm her nerves.

"Right," she says. "Well, this space is pretty self-explanatory. Kitchen, living area. There's a bathroom through that door." She points to a door near the far end of the living room before she walks toward the hallway. "There's an extra bedroom I converted into a study, so my desk is in there, and then the bedroom is right there." She swallows, her voice sticking at the last few words.

10

She's still nervous. I get the feeling she doesn't do this often. With my pickiness, I guess I don't either. It's been a few months since I've been with a girl. And I've never been with a girl like Rayna. Frankly, I think she's out of my league.

"Can I make you a drink, Rayna?" I ask, backing away from the bedroom and toward the kitchen. I'm in no rush for this night to end, and I'd like to make her comfortable before I take all her clothes off.

She laughs to herself. "I'm sorry, I should have offered. I don't do this sort of thing."

I reach for her hand, squeezing it gently in mine. "Neither do I."

I can see her shoulders relax ever so slightly, her turquoise eyes studying my face before they lock on my lips. I can't help but pull her in closer to me, desperate to calm her nerves by making her comfortable with me. Her body is tense as I wrap my arms around her slender body. I tower over her petite frame, but she somehow melts into me perfectly. I can feel her body relax as I gently stroke her back. I settle my head on top of hers and get a whiff of that vanilla-cucumber scent again.

"Your hair smells like your lotion," I mumble.

Her laugh vibrates against my chest. "I like the scent. I use the same brand for my shampoo, conditioner, body wash, and that lotion in the car."

I take a deep inhale. "I like it too."

She smiles as she looks up to me. Her eyes have softened, and I can tell she's warming up to me, to the thought of me.

I brush a loose strand of hair away from her face and tuck it behind her ear. She has long, soft hair. Even with her hair pulled back, it falls well below her mid-back. I move my hand until it's cupping her cheek. Her skin is silky smooth, not a blemish in sight. She is the most beautiful woman I've ever seen, and I can't believe I have the pleasure of sharing a night with her.

Her breath hitches as I gently brush my thumb over her cheek, my gaze fixed on her eyes while hers are on my lips.

11

"Rayna," I whisper and her eyes flicker to mine. "Is it okay if I kiss you now?"

All the alcohol from the night hardly phases me as I'm about to lean in and kiss the softest lips I've ever seen. I sure as hell wasn't sober when Rayna walked into the bar, but over the hour or so I've been with her, I've sobered up greatly, despite her drink of choice. I'm more alert to her every sound, to the rapid beat of her pulse, to her breathing, to her tense and relaxed stature. I've studied this girl more tonight than I've studied during the last three years of college.

Her head nods only slightly, and if I wasn't paying attention, I'd probably have missed it. My lips fall slowly to hers, almost timid in their descent to finally feel those pouty lips on mine. The moment they touch, their softness brushing against mine, I already know this night is going to be better than I ever imagined.

She opens for me quickly, allowing my tongue to explore hers with a deeper kiss. I pull her body closer to mine, one hand settled at her waist, the other reaching up to her long, silky hair. As our kiss grows deeper, Rayna becomes more comfortable. Her arms reach around me until they're gripping my back, trying with all their little might to pull me even closer to her.

I lead Rayna backward until her back is against the wall. I lift her, and her legs automatically wrap around my waist, inviting the bulge in my pants to press firmly against her. Her hands find my hair and grasp at it with desperation. I keep one palm firmly gripping her tight ass as I hold her up, the other pressed against the wall. We're going to have to make our way to the bed soon because I'm not sure how much more of this woman's soft moans I can take before I'm desperate to be inside of her. I still haven't seen her bedroom, though I know which door it's behind, thanks to her little tour.

I take my hand off the wall and hold onto her so she doesn't fall, then carry her to the door she claimed as her room, our lips locked the entire way. She reaches behind me for a light switch as I enter the threshold. Bright lights capture us as I get my first glimpse into her bedroom with the unfortunate loss of her lips on mine.

I eye the giant king-sized bed with dark orange bedding that is a stark difference to the bright whites of her living space. The rusty orange color might be that rare touch of Rayna in this place, leaving me to appreciate the color contrast all the more. I gently place her on the bed, kneeling in front of her so that we're at eye level.

"Is this okay?" I ask. The last thing I want to do is pressure her into something she doesn't want, though by the way she was kissing me, I'd guess she wants this just as much as I do.

"Yes, Hayes," she answers softly.

I stand up, lifting my shirt over my head and exposing my muscular figure, thanks to nearly nineteen years of baseball.

Her gaze drops over my chest before falling even lower, to the V that disappears beneath my pants where a noticeable bulge urges to break free. Her eyes quickly flicker up to mine, perhaps embarrassed that I caught her staring at my junk. I can't help but chuckle.

Right now, I'm thanking my lucky stars I didn't settle for that bartender earlier tonight. Jason can have her. All I want right now is Rayna and her turquoise eyes; her pouty lips; her soft, silky skin; and that long, dark brown hair. I don't need to see her naked to know her body's going to be a homerun. Those grabbable hips have been easily on display in her tight jeans, the ones she's unbuttoning right now. She shimmies out, clad only in a skimpy pair of underwear and a formfitting tee. I'm dying to see her breasts.

I cup my dick over my jeans in anticipation. The damn thing hurts with how hard it's straining against the fabric. Just the thought of her nearly naked, sitting in front of me, is enough to do me in. But I hold it, eyes focused intently on her breasts as she slowly removes her top. And fuck if I didn't think she was perfect before, her flawlessly, petite yet curvy frame is on display for me. Her breasts are the perfect size, perky and just waiting for my touch. Her matching bra and panties combo is so sexy, yet also an unwelcomed barrier to the real treasures that lay beneath.

"Fuck, Rayna."

I quickly remove my jeans in my haste to start touching her, to explore her body and her perfect curves. There's nothing graceful about the way I slip out of my pants, my dick still hidden behind my boxer briefs, though there's much more give in the elastic material. I quickly dive for her, my mouth finding her perfect lips for another deep kiss. My hands roam over her breasts, down to her waist, until they find that sensitive spot between her legs. She's so wet for me already, my fingers stroking above the soft cotton material as I continue to kiss her.

Her bra and panties fall to the floor, eventually followed by my briefs. I don't know where tonight will lead, I don't know how tonight will end, but one thing's for certain, I can't get enough of Rayna no matter how hard I try.

Chapter Two

Rayna

The first thing I hear is the dull sound of a bell repeatedly chiming in my deep slumber. It starts off faint, like simple background noise that grows louder and louder as I approach it. Though, I'm not moving. I'm in a peaceful rest, my body sprawled across the bed haphazardly as it tries to ignore the imminent bell.

Why is it still ringing? Will someone just turn the damn thing off already?

I roll over in search of where the obnoxious bell continues to alert me to its presence. My arm falls over something firm. A body. A warm body. My eyes fly open as I realize the scene I'm in. My alarm is going off, it's my first day at my new job, I had a one-night stand, and that one-night stand slept over and is now lying next to me in my bed.

Shit.

First things first. I need to find my damn phone to shut off that alarm. I scan the room, seeing our clothes sporadically thrown awry. I eye my jeans, realizing the sound is coming from somewhere beneath them. I slide out of bed, the cold air of the condo biting my skin, causing sudden goose bumps to emerge. And that's when I realize I'm still naked. I glance over to the bed where Hayes is still sound asleep. How can he sleep through that annoying alarm?

I shuffle toward the bathroom to throw on a robe before finding my jeans and shutting off the damn alarm. Luckily, it was my first of many. I still have time to get ready, eat a quick breakfast, and leave so I won't be late on my first day. I peek over to where Hayes still lays, wondering if I should wake him up and tell him he needs to go. But his face looks so peaceful, relaxed. That dark, messy hair on top of his head is in disarray, no doubt from my fingers brushing through it countless times last night.

Thoughts of the night stir an ache in my core. That man knows what he's doing. After two rounds of incredibly hot sex, we both must have passed out, completely worn from the intensity. Flashes of our night together play in my mind. His stubble grazing over my thighs. His kind green eyes as they took in every inch of my body. His tongue skillfully playing with my nipples. And the feeling of him inside me is not one that I'll forget anytime soon, or ever. I admitted to him that I didn't do this, one-night stands. He told me he didn't either. But what does that mean? Could our night together turn into anything more than what it was? Would he be interested in sleeping with me again? Because I'm not holding out hope that there's anything better. I've never had a man make me feel like *that* before.

I turn on the shower, eager yet also dreading to wash away last night's sweat. And, boy, did we work up one hell of a sweat.

I slide off my robe and step into the tile shower, the water head from above raining down on my body as I rinse Hayes from my skin. I reach for my vanilla-cucumber shampoo, the smell Hayes was so keen to. It's always been my favorite, ever since I was a little girl.

As I lather in the shampoo, repeat with the conditioner, and end with the body wash, I try to ignore the disappointment I feel that I may never see Hayes again after today. Just as I'm about to begin rinsing off the body wash, the sound of the bathroom door opening startles me. The shower is enclosed with a glass door, and I can see Hayes's perfectly sculpted torso as it eases into the bathroom, heading directly for the shower. When he opens the shower door, he's smirking, those adorable dimples that I noticed last night on full display.

"Mind if I join you?" he asks, eyes moving down from my lips to my breasts and then to my legs rather slowly.

"I was just finishing up," I answer honestly, moving to switch places with him so he can shower and I can finish getting ready.

He reaches for my hand as I work to move past him. "Stay. Please."

My eyes lock with his, and suddenly there is no possible way I can say no. "Okay."

He closes his eyes and inhales deeply. "I could smell the vanilla-cucumber from the bedroom," he says, a soft smile on his lips.

I grab the shampoo bottle and hold it out to him. "Now you can smell like it too."

He squeezes a little in his hands and then lathers it into his dark, shaggy hair. "You know I'm not going to be able to stop thinking about you all day now, right? Not when I'm going to smell you everywhere I go."

I smile. "Maybe that was the plan."

His hands settle on my waist and he pulls me closer to him, his hardness now firmly pressed against my belly. "Was it now?" he asks, his voice gruff. "Then I ought to do something for you, so you can do the same."

I can only manage a nod before his lips find mine again. In a matter of minutes, he has me pinned up against the shower wall as he moves ever so slowly, but with just enough force, inside me.

17

Sitting at my island, enjoying a cup of coffee with Hayes and the waffle toast he made us, I can't help but laugh at the weird, delicious masterpiece I'm chewing.

"So, you just put one of those frozen waffles in the toaster, add some butter, and sprinkle it with cinnamon sugar? That's your secret?" I ask.

He smiles, his mouth full of waffle toast. "That's it. Pretty fucking good, right?"

I laugh. It's so hard not to laugh with Hayes. He seems to bring out the giddy schoolgirl in me with his comforting demeanor and smooth moves. I know he said he doesn't normally do what we did last night, but I can't help but think about how many other girls he must pull these moves on.

"Yeah," I agree. "Pretty fucking good."

I grab our empty dishes and leave them in the sink. It's only eight in the morning, though it feels more like six. Hayes and I hardly got any sleep last night, what with all the rolling around in the sheets until the early hours of the morning. But I'm not complaining. I haven't felt this lively in a long time. I'm ready to crush it at my new job. I really hope this won't be the last I'm seeing him.

"Hey, listen, I've gotta head to work now. Can I give you a ride somewhere? Or...shit." My phone starts ringing, and I see my brother's name flashing across the screen.

If I don't answer it, I know he'll just call back again and again until I pick up. The last thing I need is to be with a guy I just met last night while talking to my brother. He'll know something's up, then he'll start to ask questions, and they're likely going to be questions I don't have an answer to.

I blurt out, "I have to take this. The doors will lock behind you when you leave. There's some cash in that drawer if you need to call an Uber. I'm so sorry." I scribble my number on a loose sheet of paper and hand it to Hayes.

It might not be a good idea to leave a stranger in my condo, but I know it's a worse idea to talk to my big brother with a random guy I just met only a few feet away. And the money in the drawer, hell if he really wants to steal it all, then he needs it

18

more than I do. There's only a couple loose bills in there, saved for the numerous times I've had pizza delivered over the last three days.

The call from my brother already went to voicemail and the phone is now ringing for a second time. Damn tenacious brother.

I lock gazes with Hayes, praying it's not the last time I'll get lost in those beautiful green eyes of his. "Last night was...well...I really enjoyed it. Sorry to be leaving you like this. Call me if you need anything." I walk out of the condo, cursing myself with those parting words. *"Call me if you need anything."* Really?

And then my damn phone rings for a third time.

"Yes. I'm here. Sorry, I was getting my things together for work," I say.

"Well, hello there, little sis, and good morning to you too! Aren't we sounding chipper this morning," my brother says. He's back in Chicago, a time zone behind, though he sounds like he's been awake several hours longer than me, which is probably the case. He works for our dad's law firm downtown, making a more than okay living, but together, they work more hours than any other two people I know.

"Good morning, Sam," I say in my most friendly morning voice, though I can't hide the bitterness behind my tone for how he just caused me to walk out on Hayes. "How are you today?"

"No need for the sarcasm, Rayna. I just wanted to wish you luck on your first day."

I open the door to the parking lot, walk to my car, then manually unlock the doors. There are no automatic locks for this old thing, but I'll drive this car until it's no longer a working vehicle, all because it belonged to my mom. "Thanks. I feel good. I'm prepared."

"We knew you would be," I hear my dad's voice in the background.

I must be on speakerphone. It's definitely a good thing I left Hayes in my condo. The last thing I needed was to be interrogated, not only by my protective brother but by my overbearing, overprotective dad who can't accept the fact that I'm a grown twenty-seven-year-old woman who can make her own damn decisions.

"Hey, Dad."

"Hi, honey," he says, his voice always taking on a softer tone with me. "Have a good day. Good luck. I love you."

"Love you too. I'll call you both tonight, let you know how it goes."

"Sounds good," Sam says. "Talk to you later, Rayna."

"Bye." I hang up.

Minutes later, my phone rings again, this time an unknown caller. I almost ignore the call, but then hesitate, because what if it's Hayes? What if something happened at the condo and he needs to get ahold of me?

"Hello?" I answer.

"Rayna," he says.

I can almost hear the smile in his voice. "Hayes," I return, unable to stop my own smile from spreading across my face.

"You left in a rush, so I wanted to call and tell you that I also *really* enjoyed last night. And this morning. You have the best tequila-vodka I've ever had. Might be my new favorite drink," he jokes.

I never made him a tequila-vodka, and anyone who drinks those two in combination should immediately seek a therapist. Or maybe they'd deserve an award. Either way, I used the drink as an excuse to invite Hayes over last night, though we both knew what I was really asking him for. Is tequila-vodka our new code name for sex? That was the best tequila-vodka I've ever had.

I can't help but laugh. "Sorry I had to leave so abruptly. My brother and dad were calling and if they found out I was with a guy I just met last night, well, they'd probably be on their way to Timbers faster than a cheetah can pounce on a limping alpaca. It doesn't matter to them that I'm a twenty-seven-year-old woman. They treat me like I'm still a child who needs to be told which direction to go in." I realize I'm carrying on far too long than I should. Is he still even on the phone?

20

But then I hear a deep, throaty chuckle on the other end of the line. "A *cheetah* pouncing on a *limping alpaca*...haven't heard that one before."

"*That's* what you got from all that? Not that they'd likely show up at your doorstep asking a million questions. Or the mere fact that *you'd* be the limping alpaca in this scenario?"

"I'm great with parents. And brothers."

I shake my head. If only he knew *my* dad. And brother. "Believe me, they'd automatically hate you if they found out the things we did after only knowing each other for a few hours."

"And what things did we do exactly, Ray?"

Ray? Now we've got nicknames. Alright, Hayes. I'll play. "Well, *Hay*. If you need me to refresh your memory, you can come back tonight. I'm sure I can figure out something that'll jog that ol' memory of yours." I have no idea where this confidence is coming from, but the thought of spending another night with Hayes is thrilling.

His laughter leaves me smiling even wider than before. "I'll be there. What time?"

"Seven good for you?"

"Seven's great. I'll see you tonight, Rayna. I look forward to the refresher."

Chapter Three

Hayes

I walk around Rayna's empty condo after hanging up the phone with her. That woman must really trust me to leave me alone in her condo like this. And letting me know about a drawer full of money? It's not like I'd ever let a woman pay for me, though I know Rayna isn't short of cash if she's living in a place like this.

I take one last look around the condo, glancing at the hallway and remembering what it felt like to hold her in my arms, to feel her walls being broken down as she learned to trust me with her body. The feel of her pouty lips on mine. Her smooth, soft skin that laid tangled in a mess of sheets with me.

I haven't slept that good in months. And when I woke up to the smell of her vanilla-cucumber scent lingering, accompanied with the sound of running water, I couldn't stay in that bed alone any longer. I knew what I would find behind the bathroom door. That woman is addicting, and I'm already looking forward to another night with her.

Twenty-seven. She had said on the phone that she was twenty-seven years old. I figured she might be a little older than me, with the way she carries herself and then this condo she has to herself. I wonder if she will care about the five-year age difference. It sure as hell doesn't bother me. Nothing about her bothers me.

I call Jason to see if he's awake yet. We have a lecture together in about an hour and I need a ride home so I can change, unless I want to show up to class in the same clothes I was sporting last night.

Jason answers the phone after five rings, the hangover evident in his voice. I'm actually surprised I don't feel worse. That waffle toast and coffee, along with the incredible shower sex, brought me back to life.

"Yeah," Jason says into the phone, and it sounds like his face is muffled in a pillow.

"I need a ride."

"Fuck you."

"Come on, pick me up. We've got class soon."

I hear shuffling on the other end, his voice coming out clearer. "Where are you?"

"I'll send you my location."

Fifteen minutes later, I'm standing in front of one of the shops that make up the first floor of Rayna's complex. Jason pulls up in the brand-new Dodge Ram his mom just bought him. It's safe to say that his family isn't short of money like mine is.

"Who the hell lives here?" he asks as I climb into the passenger seat.

"Girl I met last night."

He grins. "You decided to get your dick wet after all. Atta boy."

I roll my eyes. "Shut up and drive. I need to change before class."

He pulls away without another word, the smirk on his face still firmly in place.

"So," I start. "How was your night with Natalie?"

His smirk breaks into an all-out grin, showing off his perfect thousand-dollar smile. *Literally*. I think his mom paid big money to fix his teeth after he got hit in the face with a baseball our freshmen year, knocking out three of them and leaving him with the fattest purple lips I've ever seen. "Let's just say it was a good thing you didn't come home last night."

A few minutes later we pull into the driveway of our three-bedroom house that we rent off campus. I jump out of the truck and hurry to the front door. We have to leave soon if we want to get to class on time, seeing as it's a good twenty-minute walk to campus.

"Hey, Murphy!" Jason yells from behind me.

"Yeah?" I turn as I push open the door.

"Natalie's still here. Do me a favor and don't ruin this one for me. I think I might actually like her."

My eyebrows shoot up, the surprise impossible to hide. I'd never intentionally hinder my best friend's chances at a girl, but I know what he means. Natalie was making eyes at me the entire night until she finally left with Jason. She's the perfect example of someone who only wanted my attention because of my status as the best college pitcher in the country. If Jason actually feels something for this girl, then there must be more behind her clout chasing ways because he's never admitted to liking someone before. Or maybe she's just a good lay. Either way, I have no intentions of ruining this for him.

I nod before I enter the house, then head straight for the stairs and into my bedroom. Jason's room is directly across the hall, and I notice the door shut, Natalie likely still in his bed. I quickly change into a different pair of jeans and a new shirt, already catching whiffs of that vanilla-cucumber body wash on my skin as I change and instantly thinking of Rayna. I'll never be able to smell vanilla or cucumbers again without envisioning that beautiful woman in my arms.

I slip on my gym shoes and run back downstairs, noticing Jason's bedroom door now open. Natalie stands in the kitchen with her arms around Jason's waist as I approach. Kevin's sitting at the kitchen table, eating a bowl of cereal. He's in our morning lecture too.

"Morning," I say to Kevin as I pass by him to grab my backpack.

24

His nose scrunches as he fills his mouth with a giant spoonful of cereal. "Why do you smell like that?" he asks.

I grin. "Trying something new. You like it?"

"Dude, you smell like a chick."

I laugh. "You almost done, fat ass?"

He picks up his bowl and dumps the remaining milk in the sink, looks to me, then to Jason, who still has a very clingy Natalie wrapped around him. "You two lovebirds walking with us?" Kevin asks.

"Nah, Natalie's gonna give me a ride," Jason says.

"I can give you guys a ride too," she offers quickly, eyes locked on me.

I don't answer, careful not to accept anything from this girl that she might assume means something more than it does. Instead, I look to Jason, but Kevin answers for us all. "Hell yeah."

I guess that means Natalie's driving us to class. I don't say anything as I follow behind the three of them to Natalie's Subaru Outback. Kind of a big car for such a small girl. I climb into the backseat with Kevin, Jason in the front, and Natalie in the driver's seat.

"Where's your class at?" she asks, eyeing me in the rearview mirror.

Again, I refrain from answering, letting Jason give her the directions. I keep my eyes focused outside the window until we're pulling in front of Chestnut Hall.

"Thanks for the ride!" Kevin shouts as he jumps out and shuts the door.

"Yeah, thanks," I murmur, because I can't completely ignore her like an asshole.

Jason reaches across the center console and kisses Natalie before he exits the car, whispering something in their private moment as I get out and start walking toward the building with Kevin. He soon catches up with us as we walk into the building toward the lecture hall.

"Jason, are you already pussy whipped by that girl? Normally you can't kick them out of the house fast enough," Kevin remarks.

"Shut up," Jason says as we take our seats near the back of the empty auditorium. We're the first students to show up, earlier than normal, thanks to the unexpected ride from Natalie.

"And where were *you* last night?" Kevin asks, turning to me.

"With a friend."

"A lady friend?"

I can't hide the smile on my face. Rayna is definitely a lady friend.

"So that's why you smell like a girl. Did you steal her perfume or something?" he asks.

"Took a shower," I answer.

"Oh, *hell yeah!*" Kevin beams. "So, I'm the only one who didn't get laid last night? That's it. You're both going out with me tonight for night two of syllabus week. My dick feels left out."

"No can do," I answer quickly. "I've already got plans."

"What plans?" Jason jumps in.

I give them a knowing smirk. Plans I have no intentions of telling them, though they can reach their own conclusions and figure out that it's with my new *lady friend*. My sexy as all hell, twenty-seven-year-old lady friend. Whatever plans I have with Rayna tonight definitely don't include these two idiots.

"Sorry, guys, I'm out." I focus my attention to the front of the room.

The lecture hall begins to fill with people. We're taking a Sports Nutrition elective, a class most of the baseball team takes at some point during their four years at East Valley. Coach finds the topic of particular interest and says it will help us not only with our potential future careers in sports, but also in our daily lives. I've heard the class is hard as hell. I know a hell of a lot about sports, and I know how important nutrition is to stay strong and energized, so I don't really see how it can be that hard. All I know is that most guys save the class for their final year at East Valley, where it hardly matters if you end the course with a big fat F when you're potentially getting drafted in the next few months anyway. Not all of the baseball players here get drafted, but we're the best Division 1 school in the Midwest with a high rate of players making it to the big leagues. One F our last year isn't going to keep us from playing professional ball. With all that said, this is the one class I've been dreading this semester. Luckily, it's only two days a week and today's class should be nothing more than reviewing the syllabus.

The rest of the students file in until we're left with a lecture hall filled with minds eager to learn. Those eager minds do not include the rest of the senior baseball team that waited until the last second to take Coach's one required course. Some guys on the team quit their senior year playing ball if they know they're not going to get drafted, all because they don't want a failing grade affecting their GPA and chances of finding a good job or a graduate program. The students who major in this shit are some of the smartest at the university, graduating to become doctors or some other position in the health field. The thought of even taking a course that could essentially qualify you to help save lives is enough to leave me scared shitless of the upcoming semester. It's not like me to fail, and despite my inevitable draft into the MLB, I don't want to leave East Valley with anything less than a passing grade.

I notice a petite woman with long, dark hair enter the lecture hall through a door at the front of the room that likely leads to her office. My breath hitches when she first walks out from behind the podium, the familiar sway of her hips and lumps of her breasts nearly impossible to ignore.

"You have got to be shitting me," I mumble under my breath.

Kevin nudges me. "I heard there was a new professor this year who took over for Dr. Arnold. I didn't know she'd be hot as fuck. Did you see her ass when she turned around?" he whispers, followed by a low whistle.

This has got to be some sick joke. There's no fucking way that *Rayna* is my new professor.

I sink back in my seat, hoping she can't see me. With no such luck, I listen as she introduces herself as Professor James to the class, eyeing each student across the lecture hall until her gaze lands on me. Her face pales with recognition.

Rayna James. My new professor. This is so fucked up.

Chapter Four

Rayna

I just stopped talking in the middle of my introduction, my face no doubt white as a ghost. The room spins as my gaze is locked on the shocked pair of green eyes staring directly at me. There's no way he knew I was his professor. And there's no way in hell I would have guessed he was still in college. The man towers over me, his strong and muscular build, the short stubble on his face. I hadn't even thought to ask him how old he was. This class is full of students of all ages. What if he's a freshman? What if I slept with my eighteen-year-old student? Not that his age really matters at this point. The fact that I slept with my *student* is damaging enough.

I clear my throat, a hundred eyes on me, waiting for me to continue. "As I was saying, my name is Professor James. As most of you probably know, Dr. Arnold retired last year after having taught at East Valley for an incredible thirty-two years. From what my colleagues say about him, I know he will be dearly missed."

I walk to one side of the room, making sure to meet the gazes of each of my students. I always found it to be important when I was in school, for teachers to talk *to* you, not *at* you. By maintaining eye contact with my students, I hope to gain their attention and interest in the subject matter so they will better succeed.

"I've heard the rumors about this course. I know the material can be challenging. I've specifically lined up office hours each day of the week, excluding Sundays, that I encourage all of you to take advantage of. This course is not easy. If anyone has signed up for my class with the intentions of earning an easy A, then I suggest you drop out right now because it will be anything but easy."

I wait a few moments, surprised when no one stands to exit the lecture hall. Then I make my way to the other end of the room, the side where Hayes focuses intently on my every word.

"I have to say, I'm pleased with how many of you decided to show up to lecture today. I know it's syllabus week and we're supposed to simply review the syllabus today, but as I previously stated, this course is challenging. There is a lot of material to get through and only one semester to get through it. I trust that each of you will read the syllabus at home and become fully cognizant of my attendance and coursework policies."

The remaining forty minutes of class, I try to ignore the heat of Hayes's presence as he takes notes attentively. The lecture today focuses mainly on the B vitamins, though we will study the rest of the vitamins come Thursday's lecture.

After I dismiss the class, I notice Hayes dragging behind. Only when the auditorium is emptied and Hayes and I are alone do I ask to see him in my office. He follows quietly behind me as I lead him through a side door on the main level of the lecture hall.

My office is a decent size, equipped with a standard oak desk and two chairs facing the desktop. I requested there be a sizable table placed in the corner of my room for office hours, and there are four chairs surrounding the table in hopes that my students will take advantage of my generous availability to them.

Hayes lingers near the desk, clearly uncomfortable and unsure what to do, his hands tucked in his pockets.

"Take a seat," I instruct him as I shut the door to my office so we can have some privacy.

He hesitates before sitting in front of my desk.

I take a seat next to him, not wanting to use the intimidating factor of being his superior while discussing his sex life. *Our* sex life. "Hayes," I start. I can already see the dread in his eyes. Last night and this morning was obviously as good for him as it was for me. But this *can't* work, for more reasons than one, and I need him to know that.

"I know," he says before I'm able to finish what I was about to say. "I know it can't happen again. And I'm not going to tell anyone."

My shoulders sag in relief, not that I thought he would tell people he slept with his professor, but that he understands how wrong this would be if it continued.

"I had no idea you were a student here," I say.

"And I had no idea this was the new job you were starting," he says back. "You're good, by the way. Great, actually. You did great in there. I know you were nervous."

I can't hold back the smile. He's right, I was nervous. And he's a big reason why I made it through the night without having a panic attack. His reassurance means more to me than it probably should. "Thank you, Hayes." I stand up, nervous about the question that's been making me sick since the moment I saw him sitting in the lecture hall. I hesitate, fidgeting with my hands before I just come out and say it. "How old are you?"

His eyes search mine, probably sensing my fear. "Twenty-two."

Twenty-two. Okay, not so bad. He's probably a senior, graduating soon. At least I won't have to see him every day for the next four years. At least the five-year age gap isn't larger, or illegal. Oh my God, what would I have done if he was seventeen? The thought makes me queasy. Anyone could look at Hayes and guess that he's well into his mid to late twenties.

It was a simple mistake. It's not like I showed up to that Off Base bar in search of a one-night stand. I only wanted to take the edge off, my nerves getting the best of me as I sat alone in my condo.

"For what it's worth, I didn't want this to be a one-time thing. You're incredible, Rayna....er...Professor James."

"This can't be *anything* anymore, Hayes."

"I know."

"Ever."

He dips his head, and I notice him swallow once before he stands up, his size towering over me. He doesn't say anything as he walks to the door. I can't help but admire his muscular back as his T-shirt clings to him in the same places my hands wandered just hours ago.

"Shit," I mumble. I can't believe this is happening to me.

I must have said that louder than I intended because Hayes turns around, one hand on the doorknob, his eyebrows furrowed as his eyes once again search mine. "I can drop your class," he offers.

"Why would you do that?"

His hand falls from the door before his fingers rake through his dark and disheveled hair. Hair that air dried in a perfect mess after his morning shower with me, his professor. I don't know," he says. "Then maybe this would be okay? Maybe we could pick up where we left off? Maybe I could still show up to your place tonight and just forget that this is fucking happening?"

"No." I don't mean to sound harsh, but everything he's saying is exactly what I want to happen, even though I know it can't. "Drop the class if you want. It won't change anything." I open the door behind him and usher him out. "I have to get ready for my next lecture."

He leaves without another word.

I close the door behind him and melt away in my desk. I was so excited for this job. A chance to teach at a large university, one with so much recognition for their academic scholars who go on to collect Nobel Peace prizes and work in the most well-known clinical facilities in the world. I always knew I was intelligent enough to teach at a university of this stature, I just didn't think I'd ever in a million years find myself in a situation like this.

Chapter Five

Hayes

Just my fucking luck. If the guys on the team found out that I spent the night with the new Sports Nutrition professor, they'd be singing my praises to the high heavens. I'd do just about anything for Rayna to not be the sexy new professor every man on campus has been talking about since she first walked her tight ass into the lecture hall this morning. *Fucking hell, man.*

After my little chat with Rayna in her office, I skipped out on the rest of my classes, fully aware of the punishment Coach would have for me at practice tonight.

As I drive my shitty pickup toward the field, Jason in the passenger seat and Kevin in the back, it takes everything in me not to pull over and beat the shit out of Kevin. My knuckles grip the steering wheel in a pathetic attempt to keep my hands off my teammate and friend.

"She has the nicest ass I've ever seen. I already gave my hand a little workout earlier thinking about it. *Fuck*, dude. And how about those lips?"

Jason rolls his eyes as he texts on his phone, likely talking to Natalie.

"Don't act like you guys weren't drooling over Professor James like fucking dogs. You know she's hot as fuck."

"Yeah," I agree, careful not to give anything away. "She's hot." More like beautiful and sexy as hell. Kevin sees her as a piece of meat. I see her as a damn beautiful woman. I know the sounds she makes when she comes. I know the exact shade of pink her nipples are, and how they pebble under my touch. I even smell like her damn body wash right now.

I pull into the student parking lot before we walk over to the field. It's the off-season, though there's technically no off-season when you're a Division 1 athlete. Practices are year-round, summers filled with strength and agility training. Fall mostly consists of IOs where we separate into infield and outfield positions before a full team batting practice, ending the night with weight training. Then for me, and anyone else who decided to miss out on any lectures without a valid excuse, sprints.

A half hour later, we're standing in the outfield, stretching to loosen our muscles before two hours of hard work. I'm lying on my back as Jason lifts my leg and pushes it as close to my head as he can, all while keeping my knee straight. The stretch pulls at my hamstring, allowing for a little more flexibility each day. We switch to the other leg, Jason's eyes roaming around the ballpark. He's not acting like his normal self today. I remember the silence in the car as he texted on his phone while Kevin went on and on about Rayna.

"What gives?" I ask. "You good, man?"

He shrugs.

"Come on. What's going on?"

"What's going on with me?" he asks. "What about what's going on with *you*, bro? You skipped the rest of your classes today and have been hiding out in your room. You know Coach is going to make you run, right?"

"Yeah," I sigh. "Look, I don't want to talk about it. The girl I met last night isn't who I thought she was. That's all."

"Damn."

I stand up, running in place to get my body warm.

"She find out who you really are?" he asks.

"Something like that. Now it's your turn. Tell me what's up. Does it have anything to do with Natalie?" I ask, eager to shift the conversation back to him.

"Yeah. I don't know what it is about her that I like so much, but I think it's safe to say she's obsessed with you and I don't stand a chance. She keeps asking me about you, about if you'd be home tonight."

"I'm sorry," I say, because what else can I say? She's the kind of girl who's going to marry a man for his money, not the kind of girl my best friend deserves. Jason has a good shot of getting into the minor leagues, though his chances of playing professional ball ended there after his Tommy John surgery in high school. His right arm hasn't been the same since, and all the scouts know it. If it hadn't been for that damn surgery, women like Natalie would be throwing themselves at him. "You don't want a girl like that anyway," I remind him.

"Yeah. Whatever. Just another notch in my belt. I probably just couldn't get enough of her pussy and mistook that for something more."

I chuckle. Only Jason could use the word pussy and not sound like an asshole. Unlike Kevin. "Maybe we should go out with Kevin tonight after all. Looks like we both could use the distraction."

After two hours of practice and an extra half hour running sprints with a sophomore who also skipped out on class today, I'm finally leaving the locker room, ready to head home. It's been a long fucking day.

Ready to get their night started, Kevin and Jason caught a ride home with one of the other guys on the team since I had to stay late. I'm cutting through a small parking lot on my way to the student lot where my pickup sits when I hear the familiar sound of a car engine failing to turn over. I know that sound all

36

too well, which reminds me of my upcoming shift at the Auto Repair in the morning. I can't let Kevin get me too fucked up tonight — my bank account sure can't take another hit like last night and I need tomorrow's paycheck more than usual.

I continue walking, the noise growing louder as I get closer. When I turn the corner, I finally see the source. What are the odds that the 2001 red Toyota Camry sitting in this lot stalling *doesn't* belong to Rayna? I watch as her slender body steps out of the driver's seat, clearly frustrated by her car that "gets her around" but now won't start.

"Car trouble?" I yell as I walk up to the hood, my eyes immediately drawn to the engine.

"It's nothing. I just need to get jumped."

"It's not your battery. It's the engine. I heard it clicking last night. You'll have to take the car into a shop."

"Great. I guess I'll call a tow then," she mumbles as she reaches for her phone from somewhere inside the car.

I try so hard not to stare at her ass as she bends over, but I'm a guy and she really does have a great ass. I clear my throat. "Come on, I'll give you a ride home."

She ducks her head to look at me from inside the car, her brows furrowed. "It's fine. I'll call for a ride. Or the tow truck guy can take me home."

I look around the lot, her car the only one left. It's dark out, dark enough that I can use that as an excuse to give her a *safe* ride home. "You'd really rather get a ride home alone from a stranger at night? Don't be stubborn. It's just a ride. For all anyone knows, I'm an Uber driver." I pull out my phone and call the shop. "Hey, Bill. I need a tow for the 2001 red Toyota Camry in the teacher's lot at East Valley." I finish explaining what I suspect is wrong with the car and end the call. "They're sending someone over to tow your car in a half hour," I tell Rayna. "I'll look at it in the morning and try to fix the problem. Like I said, I think you need a new engine. Might be a good idea to look into buying a new ride. Not sure the car is worth as much as it'll cost to fix it."

"It's worth it," she blurts.

Obviously, this car means something to her, so I don't argue. "Alright. Well, I'll take a look at it tomorrow."

"How'd you do that?" She gestures to my phone. "And why are *you* going to look at my car?"

"I work at the Auto Repair a few miles down. And we have a towing service, so I figured it was the least I could do."

"Oh," she says. "Well, thanks."

"Offer still stands," I say. "Can I give you a ride home?"

She looks to her car, then back to me. "Okay, let me just grab my things."

I wait near the curb as she bends inside the car, reaching for a bag while giving me another incredible view of her ass. I turn around and focus on something else before she gives me a semi that I can't hide in these baseball pants.

The car door shuts, and she joins me on the sidewalk. "Okay. All set."

I turn to face her and see that she has a giant bag thrown over her shoulder, a purse in her left hand, a laptop case in the other, and a traveling coffee mug tucked beneath her armpit.

"Here, let me take something." I reach for the heaviest item thrown over her shoulder, but she jerks away.

"I'm fine. Let's just go."

I pull my hands away and throw them up in surrender. "Alright." I reach for my baseball bag on the ground and start walking toward the student lot.

We walk quietly, her heels clicking against the sidewalk the only noise breaking the silence as we head toward my pickup. There's no backseat, so I open the bed to throw my baseball bag inside and then try to take her things to put in the back, but she refuses, saying she'll just keep them at her feet. I walk around to the passenger side of the truck, opening the door for her and standing there in case she can't get in by herself. Of course, she's stubborn enough not to let me help her, first throwing her stuff to the floor, then using both hands to lift her tiny body into the seat. I shake my head and laugh underneath my breath before I shut the door. I take my seat on the driver's side and start the engine, the truck roaring to life.

38

"It's not much, but it gets me around," I say, using her words from last night.

She doesn't so much as crack a smile as I turn out of the student lot and head toward her complex. She lives about fifteen minutes, give or take, off campus. If I have to spend the entire fifteen minutes with her in silence while the tension between the two of us nearly suffocates me, I think I'll lose my damn mind.

"Say something, Rayna," I whisper.

She's looking out the window and hasn't looked at me once since we walked away from her car.

"What do you want me to say?" she says softly.

"Anything."

"Thanks for the ride."

I sigh. "No problem."

She must hear the frustration in my voice because her head finally turns. Her beautiful turquoise eyes study my face before looking down to my practice gear. I hadn't thought of it, but I probably smell like shit. The smell of her vanilla-cucumber body wash long since dripped off my skin.

"You play baseball?" she asks.

I nod once, looking into her eyes as I do. There's not a glimmer of hope in those eyes, not like there is with most girls when they realize who I am, if they didn't already know. Hope that I might be their sugar daddy. Hope that they won't have to work a day in their life. Hope that I might bring them about some status of fame. She must have some idea that if I'm playing baseball my senior year at a Division 1 school, there's a chance I could get drafted.

"You any good?"

I smile. "I'm okay."

"Why are you taking my class? You're an athlete. Aren't you supposed to take all the easy classes so you can just party and play your sports?"

I laugh at the way she says, "play your sports." I have a feeling that she was a total nerd in school and doesn't have the slightest clue about the first rule in baseball. "Coach says it's good for our future, and our life. He makes the entire team take the course before we graduate."

"Hmm. Good to know. I'll have to have a word with this coach of yours. I like the way he thinks."

"Some guys end up quitting the team," I say. "Because they're afraid of failing the class. They'd rather quit than suffer a failing grade."

She frowns, her perfect lips pouting and drawing all my attention to them.

I turn to focus back on the road.

"Well, they shouldn't quit. That may have been Dr. Arnold's MO, but I don't intend to allow any of my students to fail. Not if they truly want to pass, anyway. If they put in the work, then so will I. You let your team know that, okay?"

I smile. "Okay."

I turn into her complex, passing the store fronts before I pull up to her entrance. I glance at the clock, knowing full well that it's past seven and if she wasn't my new professor, we'd be enjoying each other's company for the second night in a row.

She doesn't move to unbuckle her seatbelt as we both sit in my truck in utter silence.

I turn off the engine, it's loud grumbling distracting me from the conversation I know we're about to have. I already know what she's going to say, though I can't help but give this another shot.

"Rayna, listen, I know you don't know who I am, and that's honestly what made me approach you in the first place last night, other than how insanely beautiful you are. I haven't been able to stop thinking about you since you left this morning, and I don't *want* to stop thinking about you. I'm going to get drafted into the MLB after this season. I could've been drafted last year, but I decided to stay to finish my degree and play one last year with my team. Had I accepted a position in the majors last year, I wouldn't be your student and this wouldn't be a problem. I'm old enough to date you, if that's something you want. It's not a crime to date someone older than you, or younger than you, in your case. I'll drop the class. No one has to know about us.

Coach won't drop me from the team if I don't take your class. I'm too valuable a player." I shut my eyes, fearful of rejection. I can't even believe I'm willing to make these sacrifices for a woman I just met yesterday.

"Hayes…"

"Please don't say it. I don't want to have to stare at you for fifty minutes twice a week knowing what's beneath those clothes, wanting you more than I've ever wanted another woman in my entire life, and not be able to do a damn thing about it."

"I can't date one of my students."

"It's not illegal, Rayna. We're both consenting adults. And I already told you, I'll drop the damn class."

"Don't drop the class. I mean, not if you don't want to. Like I said, it won't change anything if you do." She gathers up her things and opens the door.

I hurry out to help her, rushing to the other side of the truck.

She sits in the passenger seat, her arms full of all her belongings and her turquoise eyes filled with sadness. "I wanted this too, Hayes. I really did. But I can't risk my job, my reputation. This is my *dream* job. I'm teaching some of the smartest students in the country."

She won't risk her job for me, and I don't blame her. I'd never give up my career in the MLB for someone I just met either. I guess I'll be seeing her twice a week in a lecture hall full of other students, left only with the memory of our one night and morning together.

She hops out of the truck, her small frame standing in front of me.

"Not even one last night?" I beg, having no idea what the fuck is wrong with me. I'm acting desperate.

She gives me a sad smile. "Have a good night, Hayes. Thanks again for the ride."

Chapter Six

Rayna

Walking away from Hayes tonight was harder than it should have been. I was more than tempted to invite him back into my condo. We had sex this morning, what the hell difference would it make if I spent one last night with him? But my conscious got the better of me. I didn't know Hayes was my student this morning—*that's* the jarring difference between then and now.

I call my brother on the way up to my floor, eager to get this conversation over with and sulk in bed. I can't believe Hayes is my fucking student. And that my damn car is having engine problems *again*.

Sam picks up after the second ring. "Hey, sis."

"Hey. Just getting home now. My car took another shit. I'm getting it looked at in the morning."

He sighs. "Rayna, I know what that car means to you, but maybe it's time to let it—"

"No," I cut him off. "Not until it's not drivable. I'm keeping it as long as I can. It's the only thing I have left of her."

"Is that Rayna?" my dad asks in the background.

"Are you guys still at work?" I ask.

42

"Hi, sweetie," Dad cuts in. "Yes, we're working on a big case. It's going to be a late night. How was your first day?"

I smile, remembering just how good my first day was despite the little hiccup in my morning lecture. "It was great. A student even said I did a great job today." I leave out the part where I slept with said student for obvious reasons.

"Of course, you did, Rayna. Did you ever doubt you could?"

"Only a little. This is one of the best schools to teach at in the country."

"And they're lucky to have you," my dad says, his voice soothing.

"I just wanted to catch you guys before I went to bed. Don't stay up too late. And don't work too hard. Even the two James boys need a break sometimes."

"Talk to you later, Rayna," my brother says, followed by my dad's soft goodbye.

I hang up the phone and crawl right into bed. I don't have the energy to do anything tonight. Tomorrow's a desk day, meaning I teach no lectures, though I've already got several eager students lined up to meet with me in the afternoon, during office hours, wanting to stay on top of their studies, especially in their hardest class.

When I shut my eyes, I try not to think about the moments I last spent in this bed. But it doesn't work. I fall asleep thinking about Hayes's hands on me, the way his lips felt on my warm skin, the way his body held onto me while we slept.

My alarm rings at six the following morning, same as yesterday, though I'm less confused this morning thanks to the full sober night's sleep I got. I jump in the shower, then slip into a pair of black dress slacks and a short-sleeve button-up blouse. I walk into the kitchen, searching the cabinets and fridge for something to eat for breakfast. When I open the freezer and eye the frozen waffles, I can't help but smile and think of Hayes and his silly waffle toast.

Opting for just coffee this morning because thoughts of Hayes made me lose my appetite, I ride the elevator down to the first floor and walk into the enclosed parking lot in my building. I freeze when I don't see my car before I remember that it was towed last night from the school.

"Shit," I mumble, searching for my phone in my purse. I'll have to call an Uber.

The loud roar of an engine echoes in the enclosed space, an old pickup pulling out from around the corner and stopping in front of me.

You've got to be kidding me.

Hayes jumps out of the truck and takes my bags.

I'm not even able to resist this time, still in shock that he just appeared out of nowhere. "What the hell are you doing?" I finally manage to ask.

"Putting your bags in the truck," he says like it was a dumb question.

I eye his dark blue jumpsuit and remember that he has work at the Auto Repair this morning. "And where are you taking them?"

"I'm taking *you* to work?" he says like it's a question.

"What about my car?"

"I'll call you when it's finished. I stopped in early this morning. It's definitely the engine. I already called in for all the parts I'll need. Should be ready by this afternoon."

My eyebrows raise. It's awfully nice for him to be doing this for me after I turned him down not once but twice yesterday and basically reprimanded him in my office. "That's...nice. Thank you."

"You're welcome. Now get in."

"How'd you know what time I leave?"

"You left at the same time yesterday," he says matter-of-factly.

"Right," I mumble as I climb into his pickup, noticing his outstretched hand available to me for help should I need it. The truck is high up and it's hard for me to get in, especially with heels, but I manage.

Once I'm settled, Hayes climbs in and drives us away.

"It's nice of you to be doing this for me, but no more rides after today. Once my car is fixed, this can't keep happening." If someone were to see us… I don't want to think about what would happen. Or what they might say.

"Okay."

My gaze shifts to the window, trying to ignore the knots in my stomach that seem to appear every time I'm with Hayes.

"You teaching at all today?" he asks.

I shake my head. "No, I have desk days Monday, Wednesday, and Friday. Office hours too."

"Ah, yes. Those generous office hours of yours. I have a feeling a few of my teammates might be frequenting those, and it's *not* because they're wanting a good grade."

I roll my eyes. I can't help but wonder if Hayes will be coming to my office hours at all. I know I'm not going to be able to avoid him the rest of the year, especially if he stays in my class. But how will he act when there are other people around? Will he let on what's happened between us? I know he said he wouldn't tell anyone, but the way he looks at me, it's like I can tell he's seen me naked. Or maybe it's all in my imagination.

"Did you decide if you're going to stay in my class or not?"

He turns to meet my regard, studying my face as if trying to figure out what I want his answer to be. "Didn't seem worth the hassle of getting on Coach's bad side for dropping the one class he requires." He looks back to the road. "Unless you want me to. Then I will."

"No," I say too quickly. "It's not necessary. And he's right. It is beneficial to your future career and your life. You'll learn a lot. I promise."

He nods.

The rest of the ride is silent. Soon we're pulling in front of Chestnut Hall.

"Thanks again for the ride."

He doesn't move to get out of the truck like he always does when I'm getting out, though it's probably for the better. He must figure I don't want anyone to see us together like this. And he figured right.

"I'll call you when your car's done."

"Thanks."

I shut the door and walk toward the building, ready for another day at my dream school.

Chapter Seven

Hayes

It's almost eight o'clock at night by the time I get the parts and finish putting the new engine into Rayna's car. Wednesday is one of my few days off from baseball, so I purposely schedule my classes around the day, leaving it open to work a double shift. Rayna's car took me the entire two shifts and some, way longer than I thought. Finding an engine and replacing it in a car nineteen years old is no easy task. Luckily, my dad's been teaching me how to work on cars since I was old enough to pick up a bat. If I wasn't going pro, I'd have a future in the auto mechanic's industry should I choose that route.

I give her phone a ring, not expecting her to still be on campus with how late it's gotten and wondering how she got home.

"Hello?" she answers.

"Just finished up. She's running good as new. I still have the old engine, looks like someone tried to re-build it. You might want to take it back and get a refund. This thing is a piece of work."

I can hear her heavy breathing on the other end of the line. "You're shitting me," she finally says.

"No. Uh, do you need a ride over? Where are you?"

She's quiet for a moment. "No. I'm still on campus. I'm on a run. I can be there in an hour?"

"You're going to *run* here?"

"Yeah."

"No," I argue right away. "I'm leaving now. I'll be on campus in twenty minutes. Where should I meet you?"

She sighs. "Hayes, you've already done enough for me."

"I'm not letting you run here this late at night. I'll meet you at Chestnut Hall." I hang up before she has a chance to argue.

I grab my keys, pathetically giddy that I'm going to see her again soon. Unfortunately, after this, I'll only be seeing her in the front of a lecture hall. No more private moments. No more phone conversations. No more rides home. She'll just be Professor James to me.

Exactly twenty minutes later, I'm pulling up to Chestnut Hall. Rayna's standing on the sidewalk, glistening under the streetlight from the run she was on. She's wearing skintight workout pants and a sports bra, showing off her toned arms and abs. Fuck, does she look hot.

I hop out of the car, knowing full well she won't let me help her into the truck but still wanting to try. There's no one around this late at night, so I know no one will see us. I purposely didn't try to help her when I dropped her off this morning with all the students roaming around.

"Good run?" I ask, unable to hide my smirk as I take in her beautiful sweaty body.

She nods, hopping into my truck right away with all her things. She's getting better at that, or maybe it's because this is the first time she's getting in without her heels.

I walk back around to the driver's side and get in, pulling away once I get settled. "How was your desk day?"

"Fine," she says, adding nothing more to the conversation.

I take that as a hint. She wants to ride in silence. Fine. I drive us the rest of the way to the Auto Repair, parking in front of the door. I had to lock up the shop before I left, since everyone else left when the shop closed at five.

"You guys are closed?" She jumps out and walks toward the door where our business hours are displayed. "You closed *over* three hours ago?"

I shrug, pulling the keys out of my pocket and unlocking the door. I flip on the lights while I hold the door open for her.

"What the hell, Hayes?"

"What?" *Did she not want her car finished today?*

"Why are you doing this for me? Driving me around. Calling me a tow. Working on my car for..." She looks at her watch. "Over *twelve* hours."

"I didn't get started on your car until closer to ten. I had to wait for the parts."

"That's beside the point, Hayes!" she practically yells. "Why! *Why* are you doing this?"

"Because you needed help. What's the big deal? You just moved here, and I don't see anyone else stepping up to help you."

"That doesn't mean that *you* need to. I could have handled this on my own. What do you think I would have done if you didn't happen to be walking through the parking lot yesterday? Or if I hadn't shown up to that damn bar the other night? Where do you think I'd be then? In this same situation, taking care of myself!"

I try to ignore the tremor in her voice as she tries to yell at me, clearly angered over something other than my willingness to help her. "Rayna," I say softly.

She holds up one hand. "Don't."

I take one step toward her, but she takes one step back, not allowing me to get any closer. "What's the real reason you're upset?"

Her head falls, her fingers gripping the space between her eyes. "You know why."

"I don't, Rayna," I lie. I have a feeling what's been on my mind all day is the same thing that's bothering her.

She finally looks up at me, our eyes locking. "You're making this harder. *Yes*, we slept together. *Yes*, it was great. *Yes*, you're an annoyingly good guy and if things were different, I would want to keep seeing you. But things *aren't* different. I'm your teacher. You're my student. This is the situation we're in, and it's not going to change. You being nice to me? Coming to my rescue? It doesn't make it any easier. I have the most attractive guy in the world bending over backward to help me, and it's not making this any easier!"

I release a tired breath, not even able to enjoy the fact that she thinks I'm attractive. "I'll stop. I'll pretend you don't exist outside of class. Outside of you being my teacher. I'll stop." It's the last thing I want to do, but I don't want to risk her losing her job or tarnishing her reputation when she's only been working at her dream job for two days. "Let me grab your keys."

"How much do I owe you?" she asks, sounding tired.

"The parts cost three grand."

"And what about the labor?"

I wave my hand. "Nah, don't worry about that."

"Hayes."

"I didn't give you a choice on where to take your car. I get paid for working today either way. I'm not charging you labor."

She sighs. "I have the money."

"I don't doubt you do, Rayna. I've seen where you live."

"Can I at least tip you?"

"I don't want your money. Now drop it," I warn. I know she said no more favors, no more helping her, but I really don't want her fucking money. Right now, I just need her to go because the feistier she gets, the sexier she is.

I ring her out at the register and hand her the keys. She takes them but doesn't make to move. Instead, we stand there in a staring match, her breathing noticeably heavier from our argument. I know she wants me. She knows I want her. If she doesn't walk away, I'm not going to be able to resist her any longer.

50

"You should go," I say, first to break the silence.

"Right. Yeah. I should go." But she still doesn't move.

I walk around from behind the register until I'm standing close enough to her to get a whiff of vanilla-cucumber. It takes everything in me to not reach out and touch her, to not tangle my fingers in her long ponytail or pull her body closer until it's flush with mine. I take a deep breath and walk around her, opening the door to let her out.

Her shoulders relax and she lets out a lung's worth of air.

I know in that moment that she wanted me to make a move, to kiss her, her body tense with anticipation. And I'd be lying if I said I didn't want to do that too. But I know she would have regretted it after, regretted whatever that simple kiss turned into. She already said this can't work. I'm giving her what she wants. I'm going to act like Rayna James is nothing more to me than the professor in my hardest class. The class I'll dread going to twice a week. And the professor who every guy on my team wishes they could fuck, unaware that I'm one lucky son of a bitch for having already had a night with her.

Chapter Eight

Rayna

I walk out of my office Thursday morning to an auditorium filled with students. Noticeably absent is Hayes Murphy, the apparent star of the East Valley baseball team and projected first round draft pick this upcoming spring.

I left the Auto Repair last night after almost throwing my body at him and begging for another night together. When I got home, I did a quick google search to find that he did indeed turn down the MLB last year. He's also apparently a pretty big deal here in Timbers, Michigan, though he doesn't have the ego I'd expect from a star athlete.

As the last of the students settle into their seats, I greet the class with a warm welcome, eyes still scanning the room for signs of Hayes. Maybe he ended up dropping the class after all?

"Good morning," I begin. "I'm happy to see each of you have returned for day two and that I haven't scared you away yet. Several of you took advantage of my office hours yesterday. I'm already impressed with the minds of those I was able to work with. I want to continue—"

Hayes walks into the lecture hall late. He doesn't even look at me as he finds an empty seat in the back, pulling out his notebook and laptop.

I clear my throat, trying to pick up where I left off. "I want to continue to encourage all of you to sign up for whatever office hours work with your schedules. If you need individualized attention with me, please shoot me an email, and I'd be more than happy to schedule a time to meet. Alright, let's get into chapter two."

After fifty minutes of discussing the rest of the vitamins and other essential nutrients, I dismiss the class. Hayes doesn't hang behind, his coldness exactly what I asked for, though not at all easy to take. I spent another night last night envisioning his hands on my body, his lips on my skin. It's not getting any easier to see him, and I'm afraid it never will.

After he and the rest of the students exit, I let out a deep exhale and return to my office.

The following two lectures go the same way. Hayes walks into the auditorium and finds his seat, not making eye contact with me once. His eyes remain focused on his laptop or his notebook as he takes notes. Once class ends, he walks out with the rest of the students, usually accompanied by his friends from the baseball team.

While dismissing the students today, I urge them to study hard this weekend, their first exam already coming next Tuesday. Moans and sighs fill the lecture hall when they realize we've already discussed enough content to cover the first five chapters in our coursework. I warned them this class wouldn't be easy, and this first test is going to be the deciding factor on whether my students will stay and work for a passing grade or drop the class, opting for the easy way out. My office hours are slammed for the next few days leading up to the exam on Tuesday. Each of my four lectures follow the same schedule, leaving several students requesting individualized attention before the exam. I'm even coming into the office on Sunday to meet with a few students who work full-time jobs while maintaining full-time student status. I told Hayes that I would be willing to help my students in any way I can if they're willing to put in the effort, and I meant every word.

After settling into my desk to get ready for the next lecture, I hear a knock at my door.

"Come in!" I yell.

The door opens slowly, and a handsome man pokes his head inside.

"Can I help you?"

He steps all the way in, leaving the door ajar as he takes a few steps toward my desk. "Professor James, I just wanted to introduce myself. I'm Dr. Stevens. I teach Biochem and Physics. My office is just down the hall. We haven't had the pleasure of meeting yet, and I've been meaning to poke my head in here. Have I caught you at a bad time?"

I immediately stand up. and stick my hand out. "It's a pleasure to meet you Dr. Stevens. Please, call me Rayna." I've met a few of my colleagues, though they're mostly old, snooty professors who have been here for as long as I've been alive. Dr. Stevens looks around my age, likely a little older, given away by the doctor title in his name.

He takes my hand. "Dan," he says with a soft smile.

Dan is a good-looking man. Pale skin and a clean-shaven face, his dirty blond hair sitting pleasantly on the top of his head. He's in shape, my guess a runner by the lean muscular shape of his legs. He's not even trying to hide the fact that he's checking me out, his hazel eyes lingering down my body, stopping on my chest for a moment too long. When he realizes he's staring, his eyes dart quickly to meet mine.

"How have your first couple weeks been?" he asks, genuine curiosity in his tone.

"Great. The students are great, though I learned quickly that a lot of people are scared to take my class. Dr. Arnold has quite the reputation around here."

Dan chuckles. "He was very play-it-by-the-books. Didn't believe in individualized attention. He felt he gave the students what they needed to pass during lecture and had no intentions of giving them anything more."

"Damn."

"Damn is right. I took his class when I was in undergrad. Wasn't easy, but it wasn't impossible."

"You went to East Valley?"

"I did." He smiles. "Best four years of my life."

"I can imagine. It's a great school. I feel so lucky to teach here."

"Well, if you're teaching here, teaching *this* class, then you must be damn smart."

My lips curl at his praise. I don't get complimented on much other than my appearance. Sometimes it seems like the only people who notice my brain are my dad and Sam.

And Hayes.

Forget about Hayes, Rayna. Dan notices too.

"It was nice to meet you, Dan."

"You as well, Rayna." He turns to walk out of my office, hesitating for a beat before turning back around. "If you're free tomorrow night, a couple of us from this department are meeting at a bar after work. I can give you my number if you're interested in going. Maybe meet a few more of your new colleagues?"

"Yeah." I smile. "That'd be nice."

He scribbles his number on a piece of paper before walking out of my office. I can't help but think about what Hayes said last week. About how there wasn't anyone else around to help me with my car trouble. I'm alone here, Hayes being the only person who was trying to get to know me, and I pushed him away. Granted, it was for a good reason, but still. I need to put myself out there. Make some friends.

I smile as I look at Dan's number. Maybe he'll be my first new friend.

Chapter Nine

Hayes

After baseball practice Friday night, the guys and I decide to meet up with the rest of the team at Off Base. I haven't been back since the night I met Rayna. Not for any reason in particular, I just haven't. The second I walk in, my eyes are drawn to the barstool where she first sat when she walked in nearly two weeks ago.

I didn't drop her class, not so much because I didn't want to deal with Coach's bullshit but more that I just couldn't stand the thought of not seeing her at all. It's pure torture sitting in that lecture hall, listening to her gentle voice as it spews off shit I've never even heard of. She somehow makes things make sense, though a lot of the material is still hard to grasp. I'm fucked for Tuesday's exam. Jason and Kevin signed up for Monday's office hours with her, but I made some bullshit excuse for why I couldn't go. I'll see how the first test goes. I'd rather not have to ask her for the extra help. It's hard enough sitting with her in that auditorium while a hundred other bodies are present. I don't want to step foot into her much smaller office. Being that close to her and not being able to touch her, would be too damn hard. I know from experience.

We pull a few tables together in our usual corner. The bartender with the southern accent asks what we'd like to drink, eyeing me and not being the least bit subtle about it. When she walks away after taking each of our orders, her hips sway with just a little more force than they did at first.

I don't need to tell Jason I'm not interested in this chick either, it's already a given after the way he's been commenting about my sulky mood since I told him the girl I spent the night with wasn't who I thought she was. What I left out was that she was damn near perfect, smart, beautiful, the chemistry off the charts. But she's also our professor. AKA she's off limits.

The bartender hands me a beer, her fingers brushing over mine in the exchange and lingering for a second too long.

"Thanks," I say flatly.

"Sure thing," she drawls before she smiles and walks away.

Jason pulls up the seat next to me, beer in hand. "Natalie's working tonight," he says.

I scan the bar. Sure enough, Natalie is standing there, eyes glued in our direction. On me. "Ignore her," I warn.

"Yeah. Not making that mistake again. She has asked me for your number three different times since that night."

I scoff. "That's not creepy."

Jason laughs in an attempt to brush off the hurt. "How's work been?"

My eyebrows furrow. Weird change of subject, but alright. I'll bite. "Fine, why?"

"Just checking in. You good on cash?"

"I'm fine, Jason."

"Alright. You know you can always come to me if you're short. You're my best friend."

"Yeah, I know. Thanks. Where's this coming from?"

"Someone said you were at the shop working overtime last week. Thought maybe it was because you needed the extra cash."

Last week. When I was putting in a new engine for Rayna. "Nah, it was nothing man. I was just helping out a friend."

Jason frowns. "What friend? I know all your friends."

"Just a customer at the shop." He does not need to know that I was working on our professor's car. He'd find it suspicious that I hadn't mentioned it.

He gives me a funny look before his gaze focuses on the door. "Oh shit."

It's my turn to frown. "What?" I turn around to see what he's looking at, only to find a handful of the staff from East Valley walking in.

But that's not the real kicker. The thing that makes a quiet *fuck* slip from my lips is Rayna, in her tight blue jeans and fitted top. Her eyes look worried as she scans the bar, only for that fear to be validated when they settle on me.

I break eye contact with her immediately, turning back around and chugging my beer. It's one thing to not make eye contact in class, to pretend that her presence doesn't faze me when she's talking about mineral absorption and the benefits of vitamins. It's an entirely different thing to pretend she doesn't exist when she's in the very bar I first met her in, wearing clothes like that.

"Should I go buy Professor James a shot?" Kevin asks, appearing out of nowhere.

I roll my eyes and continue to drink my beer.

"No, dude. Don't be weird," Jason answers.

"Her ass looks even better in jeans," Kevin adds.

Jason shakes his head.

I remain quiet.

"What?" Kevin looks to Jason, then me. "Don't act like you guys didn't just check out her ass."

I sigh. "I have to take a piss." I stand up and make a bee line for the bathroom, careful not to make eye contact with Rayna as I pass the table where she sits.

I walk into the stall and find a urinal. I don't actually have to piss, but it would be weird if I came in and didn't go about my business as usual. A few minutes later, I walk out of the bathroom, having had those few extra moments to process and calm down about Rayna being here. Those minutes no longer matter though, the second I run into her perfect body in the secluded hallway that leads to the restrooms.

"Sorry," she mumbles before she looks up and realizes it's me. "Shit."

"I was just leaving," I say, having decided just now that this is the last place I want to be. I'll head home, tell the guys I'm not feeling well.

"Hayes, stop. You don't have to do that. I'll go."

"No. You should stay. It's important you make some friends, you know, just in case you need *help* with something else."

She sighs with reluctance. "I didn't know this was where they were meeting. Had I known before, I would have declined the invitation."

"It's fine, Rayna. Really. I was heading out anyway." It's not the truth, but what does that matter? She doesn't want me to act like she affects me, like I still think about her every fucking second of the day. "Have a good night."

I brush past her, making my way to the table and pulling out my wallet. I leave a few bills on the table to cover my beer. "I'm heading out," I say to Jason.

"What? Why?"

"Not feeling great. Call me if you need a ride later."

His eyes scan the bar as if they're looking for someone before they settle on me again. "Alright. Feel better."

I nod and walk out, feeling the heat of Rayna's gaze on my back the entire time.

Chapter Ten

Rayna

I don't know what I was thinking. I didn't have to go to the bathroom. I only saw Hayes walk that way and hoped to run into him. I mean, not literally, though that's what happened. He didn't even look phased by my presence. Not how my stomach was turning inside out with anticipation after I found out this was where we were meeting tonight. I wondered if he'd be here again. I wondered if he'd say anything, if he'd be drunk enough to try and have a repeat of the last night we were here. Or if I'd get drunk enough that I would no longer care about our teacher-student relationship and ask him to take me home.

The truth is, I haven't even had a drink yet and I'm staring at his back as he walks out, wanting to follow him.

I reach for my purse without realizing it, and before I know it, I'm walking out the door, only steps behind Hayes. This could be the biggest mistake of my life, but right now I don't even care. All I care about is being near him again, not getting his cold shoulder everywhere we turn. I want him to notice me again, to look at me like he did before, like I am the most beautiful girl in his eyes.

I search the parking lot, looking for him, for his truck. I don't see either. I round the corner of the building, to the lot that's in the back, and spot him.

"Hayes, wait!" I yell.

His body freezes, then he turns around slowly, no doubt questioning what the hell I'm doing approaching him in public like this.

I catch up, slightly out of breath, not because I'm out of shape but because Hayes is literally taking my breath away. I'm so nervous for what I'm about to say, for what I'm about to do. It takes me a few moments before I can form the words.

"Meet me at my place," I say quietly. "I'll be there in twenty minutes."

His eyes study mine, likely searching for the truth behind my words. That's all he'll find there because I sure as hell need him tonight even if I regret it in the morning.

After a long stretch of silence, he finally speaks. "Okay." He turns around and gets into his truck, the engine roaring to life before he pulls out of the lot.

I turn around and walk back into the bar, finding Dan ordering a drink at the bar. "Hey, Dan?"

"Rayna, there you are. What do you want to drink?"

"Actually, I'm pretty tired. I think I might just head home. Raincheck?"

His disappointed smile does not go unnoticed. "Raincheck," he agrees.

I park my car in what's now become my spot at home. It's always open for me, and I always take it. I see Hayes sitting in front of the entrance, unable to get in without a key. I feel a sense of relief that he actually came, but that relief also comes with nerves. I'm more nervous right now than I was when he was a total stranger and came over for a one-night stand, which was pretty damn nervous.

I step out of my car, my heels echoing in the enclosed lot.

Hayes stands up immediately when he sees me. He looks nervous too, probably wondering what the hell changed my mind about us and why I decided to ask him to come here tonight.

I scan my key, and the door clicks. Hayes opens it, allowing me to enter first and then following closely behind. We walk to the elevator in silence. He presses the button, and we wait for its descent. The overhead bell chimes as the elevator arrives, opening its doors to invite us in. Hayes waits for me to walk in before him. Again, he follows, pressing the third-floor button and standing on the opposite end of the elevator. Once we reach my floor, I step out and walk directly to my door with my key ready. I open the door to my condo, holding the door open to allow Hayes in. He follows, stopping near the kitchen table. I hang up my keys, set my purse on the island, and walk down the hall to my bedroom. It takes a few seconds before I hear his heavy footfalls moving to meet me. My heart thumps rapidly in my chest as I think about what I'm about to do, what *we're* about to do.

I sense his presence in the doorway, my back to him as I stand facing the bed. I slowly pull my top off over my head, tossing it to the side. I can hear his breath hitch in the eerie quiet. I unbutton my jeans next, pushing them down and over my knees, stepping out of them once they've reached the floor. I didn't see my night going like this, so I didn't bother to wear a matching bra and panties set. Not that it matters. There's no use for either article of clothing in this situation. I reach behind my back and unsnap my bra, dropping it at my feet. Lastly, I loop my thumbs inside my panties before I push those down too. Only once they've reached the floor and I'm completely nude do I dare turn around to face Hayes.

His green eyes are laser focused on me, on my body, and that it only makes my heart beat faster. I hadn't realized just how badly I wanted him to see me, to acknowledge me again, until this moment. The bulge in his pants can't go unseen. I silently praise myself that I did that to him.

Hayes doesn't move, his eyes scanning my body ever so slowly. I notice his heavy breathing as he waits for me to make the next move.

"I don't want you to pretend that I don't exist, Hayes. I do exist. I'm here. I'm standing right here," I say, my voice cracking with the vulnerability of my actions.

"You could never not exist to me," he says.

I swallow before I dare speak again, his lack of movement making me nervous. He could still turn me down, tell me this isn't a good idea. And he'd be right. I know this isn't smart. I know that he's my student and if anyone found out what I was doing right now, it wouldn't look good for me.

"I'm your professor," I say.

He nods.

"I'm in a position of power over you," I clarify.

He shakes his head. "No, Rayna. I would never do something that I didn't want to do. The only power you have over me is a night we spent together that I can't forget. Fuck that you're my professor. I didn't know it then, and it doesn't matter to me now." He takes powerful steps toward me, stopping unexpectedly a few feet away. "I want to do this, Rayna."

"I want to do this too."

And with those last words, he closes the remaining distance between us, his lips smashing against mine in a desperate kiss that we've waited weeks for. His hands roam my body, not leaving a single inch untouched. His lips part from mine only to leave a trail of tender kisses across my jaw, to my neck. We step backward until the backs of my knees hit the bed. He holds my body, laying me down carefully, his falling with me. I reach for the hem of his T-shirt, lifting it over his head. His muscular form takes over my small and slender frame. My hands wander across his chest, down until they reach the deep V that leads to the bulge in his jeans. I work to undo his button, but he takes over, quickly ridding himself of his jeans and boxer briefs and letting his hardness spring to life.

His mouth finds mine again, kissing me tenderly, his palm cupping my cheek. "I've missed these lips," he whispers.

I smile as he kisses the corner of my mouth, then my cheek, working his way down until his tongue flicks over a pebbled nipple. He moans softly, the sound sending vibrations to my core. His hand wanders farther down as his mouth continues to pay special attention to my breasts, his fingers sliding between my legs.

"God, you're so wet," he mumbles.

My hips involuntarily move against his hand. Not being able to see Hayes, to talk to him, having to act like he isn't anyone other than my student is cause enough for the tension that's built between my legs, ready to explode any moment.

"I need you inside of me, Hayes," I beg.

His eyes flicker to mine, soon followed by his lips, where he kisses me more passionately than I've ever been kissed.

I spend the rest of the night memorizing the feel of Hayes inside of me, the feel of his lips on mine, and the soft noises he makes as he thrusts into me, sending us both over the edge and into oblivion.

It's Saturday morning when my eyes open again. No alarm. No hangover. No confusion over whose body I'm waking up next to. I fell asleep, a mess of tangled limbs with Hayes. I wake up the same way, my head relaxed on his chest, one arm wrapped around his waist, and a leg thrown haphazardly across his thighs. His arms wrap around me as if trying to bring me closer than I already am.

I don't regret last night, not like I had expected to. I know that this thing between us can't be like a normal relationship. I can't hold his hand on campus or go out to dinner with him where other students or faculty might see. He said it himself — no one has to know. He graduates next semester and then he'll be off to play in the MLB. Who's to even say we'll still be sleeping together by then? For now, whatever this is will stay between us. At least that's the idea I came up with in my head on my drive home last night, fully aware of what my plan was and where I intended it to lead. Hayes didn't seem to mind. He showed up, happily consenting to another night tangled in the sheets with me.

Hayes stirs beneath me. "Good morning," he says, his voice full of sleep.

I smile against his chest. "Good morning."

His hand begins to move softly down my arm, and we lay quiet for a long time before he breaks the silence. "So," he says quietly.

"So," I repeat. I know what's coming. We have to talk about last night, about what it means.

"Last night was unexpected."

"It was," I agree.

"Do you regret it?"

"No. Do you?"

"Hell no."

I laugh. "What do you want this to mean?"

He sits up, maneuvering us so that he's able to look at me.

I pull the blankets up to wrap around my naked body, the morning air in the apartment making me chilly.

"I don't want this to be the last time I see you," he answers.

"It won't be."

"Outside of the classroom," he specifies. "Do you know how hard it is to sit in that lecture hall and listen to how smart that damn brain of yours is, Rayna? It's sexy as hell."

I laugh like a giddy schoolgirl. *God, what is this man doing to me?*

"Every guy on the team wants to fuck you."

"Well, that's....flattering." Honestly, it's weird. I see all my other students for exactly what they are, students. Had I met Hayes on that first day of class, I'm not sure there'd have been any sexual chemistry there. The fact that we met under different circumstances makes it hard to not want to continuously *fuck* him.

65

"Honestly, it's annoying as hell."

"It's not like that would ever happen."

"I didn't think *this* would ever happen again," he confesses.

"Hayes, this is different. You know it's different."

"I know."

"So, back to my question. What do you want this to mean?"

He thinks for a moment. "I want to see where it can go. I want to give it a real shot. I like you a lot, Rayna. More than I should, obviously." He gestures toward the prominent tent that's formed between his legs.

"Okay."

His eyebrows shoot up. "Okay?"

I smile. "Yes, okay. But there are some things I'm not comfortable with. Nothing at school. Ever. Don't look at me like you've seen me naked. You tend to do that. Or you did. And no going out together in public places anywhere in Timbers."

He nods. "For how long?"

"How long are you expecting this to last, Hayes?"

He smiles. "I don't see myself growing tired of that sexy brain of yours anytime soon."

I laugh. "Right. Because it was my *brain* that made you approach me that first night."

He shrugs. "And those lips." He leans in, brushing his lips with mine and smiling. "What about when I finish your class? Does it matter to be seen together when you're not my professor anymore?"

"I think it would be best if we waited until you graduate, if we last that long."

His arms surround me in a giant bear hug as he pushes me onto my back, his entire body hovering over me. "Oh, we'll last that long." He kisses my cheek, my neck. "I'm not worried." He moves the blanket as he kisses his way down my stomach, stopping between my legs.

A soft moan escapes my lips. I just hope I don't fall in love with my student.

Chapter Eleven

Hayes

I call Rayna's cell immediately after class Tuesday morning. "Your test was hard as shit," I say instead of the usual hello.

She laughs. "Oh, come on. It wasn't that bad."

"Of course, you'd say that. You're the one who wrote it. Everyone thinks they failed."

"I'll have them back to you by Thursday." She pauses for a moment. "You really think you did that bad?"

"I know I did."

"Should've came to office hours with your friends."

"I think I might do that next time. I don't like failing. At anything."

"Don't worry. I told you, I won't let anyone fail if they put in the effort. You've completed all your assignments on time so far. It's just one bad test. It's not the end of the world."

I smile, thankful she's teaching this year and not that heartless Dr. Arnold. I'd stand no chance with him behind the lectern. "What time is your last lecture?" I ask, eager to see her again. I haven't spent time with her since Sunday morning after having spent Friday and Saturday night in bed with her.

Yesterday was filled with classes and practice, and tomorrow I'll be working another double. I need to see her again tonight.

I can picture the smile on her face as she sits in her office, phone pressed against her ear. "I'm out of here by five-thirty at the latest."

I grin. "Great. Practice is over at six. I'll bring over dinner?"

"No. I'll have something delivered. Just come straight from practice." I hear shuffling of papers on her end. "What do you have a taste for? Thai? Italian? Oooh, there's this Mexican restaurant on fourth street I've been dying to try."

My grin hasn't faded. "Sounds perfect. I'll see you tonight."

"See you tonight."

Stuffing my phone back in my pocket, I catch up to Jason and Kevin walking ahead of me. I trailed behind them so I could give Rayna a ring.

"Who was that?" Jason asks.

"No one."

"Same no one you were with Friday and Saturday night?" he asks.

I roll my eyes. "Did office hours with Professor James help at all with that exam? I'm pretty sure I failed it."

"Helped with some material for my spank bank," Kevin jokes. His remarks are getting really old, really fast.

Jason just shrugs. "I think it helped on the mineral absorption section. I didn't understand that shit for the life of me, but she did a good job of explaining it in layman's terms."

"I'll probably go with next time," I say. "That test ripped me a new asshole."

Jason chuckles.

We approach the house, stopping at the sight of a familiar Subaru Outback sitting in the driveway.

"You've gotta be shitting me," Jason murmurs.

"What the hell is she doing here?" I ask.

"No idea."

Kevin has no clue what we're talking about until he sees Natalie step out of the driver's seat. Then he mumbles, "Shit."

Natalie saunters toward us, stopping in the middle of the front yard as we approach. I feel her heavy stare on me, though I ignore her and head straight for the front door. I don't give a fuck what she wants. I just hope Jason's smart enough to not fall for her shit.

Twenty minutes later, Jason knocks on my open bedroom door.

Sitting at my desk, I look up from the assignment I've been trying to finish up for one of my afternoon lectures. "What's up?"

"You busy tonight after practice?"

"Hanging with a friend."

"A friend. Do I know this *friend*?"

I shrug. Technically, he does.

"Same friend you did a favor for at the shop?" he asks.

"Why does it matter, dude?"

"No reason. Just wondering why you're being so secretive about this new chick you're seeing. Is it the same one you told me about before? The one who had you mopping around like a four year old?"

I shake my head, annoyed. "What did Natalie want?"

"Same shit."

I give him a questioning look, urging him to elaborate.

"Her sorority is throwing a social next weekend and she asked me to be her date."

"Please tell me you told her no," I scoff.

He smiles, a wicked smile. "I did. Even better, I told her I'm already going with one of her sorority sisters."

I let out a deep bellied laugh. "Hell yeah. Who?"

"That's the thing I wanted to talk to you about," he says hesitantly.

Again, I shoot him a questioning look. Why would he want to talk to me about who he's going with to a sorority social?

"It's Emily."

Ah. Now it makes sense. "Emily," I repeat.

"We'd go as just friends," he continues. "Unless you don't want me to, then I won't. She didn't have a date and knew I wouldn't be creepy and hit on her. I told her I'd make sure it was okay with you first, though. I honestly didn't think you'd mind. Whoever your new *friend* is, I think she's got you by the nuts."

I shake my head. "No, you're right. I don't care. And even if it wasn't as friends, it's water under the bridge, man. She's free to date whoever she wants. As are you."

"But you're my best friend," he argues.

"Jason, I could give two shits if you fuck her. Emily and I have been over for a long time. Doesn't matter to me, dude. Swear."

"Alright." He walks out of my bedroom, seemingly unconvinced that I wouldn't care if my best friend fucked my ex-girlfriend.

Emily and I dated most of Junior year. She had just transferred here from a school in New York. She's pre-law and one of the smartest people I've ever met. She's also very attractive and the new face of Chi Omega as their recently elected chapter president. But Emily and I have been over for several months. We had a good run, but when I almost entered the draft, I realized she wasn't someone I could see myself with long-term. Especially not with the way my life is going to change drastically once I start playing for the MLB. There's no way to know what team I'll play for, where I'll have to move. Emily and I were never a forever thing, and I'm glad I realized that sooner rather than later.

I never considered she might want to date one of my friends. Specifically, not Jason. But if there's one thing I know about Emily, it's that she isn't going to be with a guy just because of his social or economic status. Jason's a good guy, he deserves someone like her.

Damn, I haven't thought about her in ages. Not since a certain professor came storming into my life like a damn tornado. She's constantly on my mind, and I want to constantly be in her bed.

Thoughts of seeing her again tonight leave me smiling like a damn fool. It's not even that I want to just be in her bed. I think I realized that those two weeks I had to ignore her, ignore the feelings I had unknowingly developed for her. I've never enjoyed someone's company as much as I enjoy being around Rayna.

Chapter Twelve

Rayna

Three classes down, two to go. I've heard mixed things about my first exam. Some students say the exam wasn't as hard as they expected it to be, while others, like Hayes, say the test was "hard as shit." Majority of my Wednesday will be spent grading, though I already began shuffling through the lot of them from my morning lecture. I happened to come across Hayes's, and while he didn't do as well as I would have liked, he didn't fail. I smiled as I graded his answers, excited to tell him tonight that he's smarter than he thinks. Had he come to my office hours, he probably would have done even better.

I step out of my office, on my way to the only teacher's lounge in Chestnut Hall, and pass by Dan. I haven't seen him since my shady exit from Off Base the other night. I offer him a friendly smile.

"Hey. How are your exams going today, Rayna?" he asks politely.

"I've only managed to grade a few, but so far, no failing grades. That's a good sign, right?"

He chuckles. "I'd imagine so."

I busy my hands by fidgeting with a ring on one of my fingers. "Look, about the other night. I'm sorry to have bailed on you like that. I did appreciate the invite. I just hadn't realized how exhausted I was."

He rests one of his hands on my shoulder, the other holding what looks to be a cup of coffee. He must be coming from the teacher's lounge. "Don't worry about it. I happily took the rain check. I'll be sure to cash in on it soon." He winks and then continues down the hall, disappearing behind a door that I assume to be his office.

By the time five-thirty rolls around, I'm four coffees deep and more than exhausted from a long day of exams and last-minute sessions with students. I walk to the teacher's lot, heels clicking against the sidewalk, as I eye the baseball stadium where I know Hayes is practicing right now. A soft smile spreads on my lips as I think about that strong body of his in those tight baseball pants.

I get in my car and drive home. Once inside my apartment, I dig through my carry-out drawer filled with tip money and menus, pull out the menu for Casa Margarita, and place a delivery order before heading for the shower.

Hayes hasn't been here since Sunday, after having spent most of the weekend with me and leaving here with his own key to my apartment. I quickly found it a nuisance to have to ride the elevator down to the parking garage entrance to let him into my building. Now, he's able to let himself in. I didn't want to make it a big deal, because it isn't one really, but I was afraid that giving him a key to my place might scare him away. If it did, he didn't let on. He happily took the key card before placing an intoxicating kiss on my lips and leaving to study.

I'm rinsing the rest of the body wash off when I hear the door to my condo open, followed by Hayes's foot falls in the distance.

"Rayna?" he yells.

"In the shower! Just finishing up."

His steps carry until they're just outside the bathroom door. He softly pushes the door open, poking his head in. "You want

73

some company?" he says, his sweaty hair sticking to his forehead.

I grin. "As much as I'd love some, the food will be here soon." I shut off the showerhead. "But it looks like you could still use a shower." I open the door, grab the towel on the hook, and wrap it around my wet body. After the towel is securely fastened and I've used a second towel to dry off my hair, I place a soft kiss on his lips. "I'll get the table set."

"*Fuck*," I hear him mumble under his breath.

As I'm stepping into my bedroom I yell out, "Something the matter?"

He chuckles. "I think you have a pretty good idea."

I do. Those baseball pants hide nothing.

I walk to my closet, slipping on a pair of leggings and a loose sweater, when the showerhead turns on. I can't help but wonder if he's going to take care of his problem, visions of me swirling in his head. The thought is enough to send an ache directly to my core.

The buzzer in my condo rings, announcing someone's here to see me. I grab some cash from the drawer and head down the elevator, meeting the delivery man just outside the glass door entrance. I hand him some bills in exchange for the food, the smells of spices quickly overpowering my senses. When I get back to my condo, Hayes is standing near the set table wearing only a baggy pair of sweatpants.

"Now who's the tease?" I quip.

He chuckles as he steps toward me. I place the food on the counter and slip into the embrace of his muscular arms wrapping around me, pressing the front of me into the island, enclosing me in his giant frame. He nuzzles his face into my neck, sending chills down my spine.

"Hi, Professor James," he purrs.

"Hello, Hayes Murphy."

He takes a big inhale. "Mmm, you smell good."

I take his hand and leave a soft kiss near his knuckles. "So do you."

He kisses my neck tenderly, melting me into him as he consumes me with his touch.

"Let's eat," I say, trying to break away from his affection. As much as I love his lips on me, I can't ignore the fact that I'm starving. And he has to be too, after a couple hours of running bases and hitting balls.

He releases me after one last sloppy kiss on my neck, groaning as I step away. The loss of his warmth is noticeable.

I put the food on the table, separating the sides of rice and beans and the variety pack of tacos I ordered. "There's shrimp, chicken, and steak tacos. Figured you were bound to like at least one of those."

"You did great. Thank you for dinner. Next time it's on me," he says.

I wave my hand. "Don't be silly."

His brows furrow in frustration as he pulls out the chair across from mine and takes a seat. "I can afford to buy you dinner, Rayna. Just because I work as a mechanic doesn't mean I'm poor."

"I never said it did. But you're still in college, and I remember what it was like to not work or have my own money. Really, it's fine. I don't mind."

That doesn't seem to appease him because the look of frustration doesn't fade. "I have my own money."

"Of course, you do." This is starting to feel like an argument. I didn't mean anything by what I said. I just wanted him to know that I don't mind picking up the tab. Especially while he's still in school.

He reaches for a couple steak tacos, then scoops a side of rice and beans on his plate. I fill my plate with shrimp and chicken tacos, saving the rest of the steak for him, seeing as that's what he likes.

"How was practice?" I ask, hoping the topic of money is now off the table.

"Decent. Coach has me working with the new freshman pitcher, hoping I can shape him up to take over the team next year once I'm gone."

"He any good?"

Finally, Hayes smiles. "Not as good as me."

"Humble," I say through a mouth full of food.

He shrugs. "Anyone else complain about that exam today other than me?"

I smile. Now I can tell him the good news. "Mixed reviews. But guess who didn't do as shitty as they thought?"

His eyebrows raise. "No way."

My smile only grows. "Yes, way. C minus. Not bad, Murphy. Now imagine the grade you would've gotten if you came to my office hours!"

He drops his fork as he stands, and it clatters loudly against his glass plate. "We have to celebrate!"

I giggle. "Celebrate a C minus?"

"Hell yeah. I *didn't* fail!" He examines the contents in the fridge. "You have anything to drink?"

"Bar cart near the window."

"Right." He closes the fridge and walks toward the picture windows. He pulls out a bottle of champagne. "Mind if I pop this?"

"Go right ahead."

He grabs us two champagne flutes and pours a generous amount of bubbly into each. He hands me my glass, holding his up as he takes his seat. "To my sexy, intelligent professor who somehow made my brain understand nutrient absorption."

I blush. "You're smarter than you think. You don't give that pretty little head of yours enough credit."

He smiles and takes a sip. We enjoy half the bottle and most of the tacos, soon leaning back in our chairs, stuffed.

After dinner, Hayes and I settle on the couch, a white sleeper sofa from my dorm room in college. How it's managed to remain white all these years is beyond me, though I haven't been able to part ways with it yet because of how ridiculously comfortable it is. It could have a giant red wine stain and I don't think I'd get rid of it.

Hayes has his arm wrapped around me, my body tucked into his. He places a gentle kiss on my hairline as he watches the tail end of the Chicago Cubs vs. Milwaukee Brewers baseball game. I've never watched an entire game of baseball before. Sure, I've been to a few of the Cubs games at Wrigley with my dad and Sam, but I drank beer and ate Ballpark Franks. I didn't pay attention to who was running the bases. I know the basics about the game. You hit the ball, then run around the bases. If the other team catches the ball, then you're out. That sort of thing.

"Oh!" Hayes yells, his eyes lighting up as the people in the stands all erupt in cheers and rise to their feet. Something good must have happened.

"Did someone score?" I ask.

"Kris Bryant just hit a game winning two-run homer!"

"So, the Cubs won?"

"Hell yeah, they did." He kisses my head again.

"Are you a Cubs fan?" I ask. I grew up in a family of Cubs fanatics. The worst thing he could say is that he's a White Sox fan, though I suspect he's more of a fan for whoever plays in Michigan. I don't even know the name of their professional team here.

He looks down to me, his eyes lingering on my lips before his gaze locks with mine. "You're from Chicago. Your family likes the Cubs?"

I nod.

"How do they feel about Tigers fans?"

"As long as you don't root for the Sox."

He laughs. "I like the Cubs. They're the ones who were scouting me last year. I was in talks with their head coach for a few months. Obviously, it would've depended on how the draft turned out, but they had their sights set on me."

Huh. I hadn't even considered the possibility that Hayes could play for the Cubs.

"That'd be an automatic in with your folks, yeah?" he asks.

I frown. I haven't told him about my mom yet. How would he know it's only been my dad, Sam, and I for the last ten years?

"My dad and my brother Sam, yeah. My mom passed away."

His smile fades. "When?" he asks softly.

"When I was seventeen."

"Damn." He moves to press his forehead against mine.

My body stiffens, the loss of my mom still difficult. I don't like to talk about her much, the wounds still too fresh, though I know if Hayes asks, I'll tell him everything.

"Your car," he says. "It was hers?"

He is smarter than he gives himself credit for. I smile a soft smile, remembering when my mom first gave me that shitty red thing. "She didn't come from a family with money. Actually, she really didn't have much money at all. My dad's side is well-off. He comes from a long line of lawyers. My brother's one now too. My mom said it was important that we learn to appreciate the little things in life, not always expect to get the nicest or newest thing. She wouldn't be caught dead buying her kids a brand-new Maserati or something expensive like my dad had insisted. Driving around when you're that young, that's when you're supposed to make your mistakes. Ding a few mailboxes, maybe hit a parked car or two. Anyway, that's the car she picked out for me. It was even shittier then, believe it or not. I've put a lot of money into that thing to make it drivable. All new interior, *a new engine*." I give him a playful grin. "After she died, I couldn't get rid of it. It reminds me too much of her."

I look around my condo, at the expensive light fixtures and flat screen TV. "In a world where you can have all these things, all this money to buy these things, that shitty car is what means the most to me. I'd give it all up to have her back."

Hayes cups my face, his thumb wiping away at the slow tear that trickles down my cheek. "Now I understand why you wanted me to fix it," he says, his voice soft.

After a few silent moments, he speaks again. "My parents don't come from money. Sounds like I grew up a lot like your mom did. My whole life, they tried to give me everything I ever wanted, even when they couldn't. I grew up on food stamps, shopping at Goodwill. My first baseball glove was a hand-me-down from a friend I met at school after his dad bought him a brand-new one. The thought of owning a brand-new baseball

78

glove just seemed like something that would never happen to me. I was happy just to have my *own* glove. My parents had to take a second mortgage out on their home when I started playing travel ball. They were hesitant at first because it's a shit ton of money, but my coach at the time called them up, let them know I had a real future as a ball player. A future that would make money never be a problem.

"My dad has worked at a mechanic's shop my whole life. He started teaching me things when I was real young, letting me change oil and tires with him. Easy stuff. As soon as I was old enough to start working with him, I did. Started making extra money to help with bills and stuff. Luckily, that coach was right about my future in baseball. I finished at the top of my league that year, earning my team a Little League World Series Championship. Eventually, teams started paying for me to play with them, so that made the financial burden of the sport go away. I was able to continue to play ball without worrying what it was doing to my parents. I'm here on a full-ride. I only continue to work so I can afford to buy tequila-vodkas for pretty girls at the bar." He winks.

I smile, happy he's sharing this with me. Happy he *wants* to share this with me. "Where are your parents now?" I ask.

"They live in a small town about an hour south of here."

"Do you ever visit them?"

He smiles. "I do. When baseball allows it. They've been up here a few times too."

"They must be so proud of you."

"Not nearly as proud as I am of them. I didn't grow up with much, but I always had everything I needed. I owe my life to them."

I press my lips against his, thinking it's not possible for this man to get any more amazing. I don't know how I kept myself away for those two weeks. "Let's go to bed," I whisper against his lips.

"You're tired?"

I smirk. "Not at all."

Chapter Thirteen

Hayes

I carry Rayna in my arms to her bedroom, to the bed I've become accustomed to sleeping in with her next to me. Her long, dark hair lays over my arm, falling into a long waterfall of silk below. I gently set her down at the foot of the bed, kneeling in front of her to meet at eye level. I tuck away a loose strand of hair behind her ear, all the while staring deeply into her mesmerizing turquoise eyes.

"You are so beautiful, Rayna," I whisper softly.

She's more than just a beautiful body though. In her world, she can afford anything. She admitted to me that of all the things she owns, that shitty red car means the most to her. If that doesn't show how big her heart is, then I don't know what does. It pained me to see the sadness in her eyes as she spoke about her mother. I don't know what happened to her, but I suspect she'll tell me when she's ready. She's already given me so much of herself, risking her reputation, telling me a little bit about her past. It was all I could think to do to tell her about my past, my family and the struggles we've faced. She didn't look at me differently. I didn't see pity in her eyes. There was something more, something I couldn't read...not yet. Then she asked me to go to bed. Everything I've learned about Rayna in these few short weeks of knowing her is what makes her so beautiful to me. The sharp curves of her body, the perky lumps of her breasts, they're just an added bonus to this already beautiful human. That's not what I see when I look at her, not anymore. She's not just a pretty face to me. She's Rayna. She's smart, and strong, and has a heart of gold. She loves her family and misses her mom dearly. I want to know more about her, know everything there is to know. Then I want to make her feel special, the way she makes me feel just by being around her, especially in this way.

I kiss her softly at first. She rests her hands on my shoulders as I try to express through this kiss just how much it means to me, how much she already means to me.

Our kisses grow hungrier, as does my need to be inside her. I lift up her baggy sweater, exposing her bare chest. Slipping one pebbled nipple into my mouth, I loll it around with my tongue as goosebumps appear across her chest. Her fingernails brush through my hair and she pulls me closer to her. I grasp her tiny waist, lifting her farther onto the bed and moving swiftly above her. I slide down her leggings, followed by her panties, until she's left lying nude beneath me, her beautiful hair sprawled across the pillow.

I stand beside the bed as I remove my sweats, my gaze lingering slowly over her striking body. "I'm so glad you walked into that bar."

She smiles. "I'm so glad you were there."

She sits up, maneuvering herself to the side of the bed and sitting in front of me, then wraps her arms around my hips. She kisses my stomach, soft and delicately. She teases me with her tongue as she trails farther down, my need for this woman only growing stronger as the seconds pass. She takes me in her mouth, and my head falls back from the unexpectedness of the moment. Her warm mouth, her pouty lips, move over my length. Her tongue swirls in that same teasing way it did just a few moments ago, this time over my tip. This woman is going to be my undoing. I've never felt anything so good.

My hands find her long hair and I fist the strands behind her head. It takes everything in me not to push myself farther into her, trying to ignore the pure male instinct that is urging me deeper. I can't last another second, not with the way her tongue moves up and down my length. I pull her head away, finding her mouth immediately. She falls onto her back before I slide myself between her legs, her soft moans pushing me farther.

I move my hand between her legs, rubbing at that little bundle of nerves as I continue to push myself in and out of her. She breaks away from my lips and tips her head back, a moan escaping her lips.

I know I'm not going to last much longer. My fingers work frantically, hoping I don't come before she does. My prayers are answered because her body tenses as her eyes squeeze shut, the moans growing louder as her body rides out this wave of pleasure. It's enough to push me over the edge with her as I quickly pull out, using my free hand to aim the cum on her slender stomach.

She takes birth control, I've seen the pills in the bathroom, but I won't come inside of her, not until she gives me permission. I was surprised last Friday night when she said not to bother with a condom, the skin-to-skin contact amplifying the explosion that was inevitable.

Once we've both had a moment to catch our breath, I stride into the bathroom, grabbing a towel to clean her up with. Afterwards, we lay together entangled in the sheets, our warm bodies coiled together, the room smelling of sex. She rests her head on my chest as I draw circles on her shoulder.

"How was someone like you still single?" I ask.

Her head turns to meet my gaze. "Someone like me?"

I press a soft kiss on her forehead. "You're not just a beauty, Rayna. You have brains too. Even you must know what a catch you are."

"Says the future MLB player."

"That's exactly why I was single," I state.

"What do you mean?"

82

"Some girls are hungry for the fame, or the money. Take your pick. They want to sleep with me just so they can say 'I slept with Hayes Murphy, the star pitcher at East Valley.' "

"I slept with Hayes Murphy the star pitcher at East Valley," she teases, her eyes twinkling.

I grin. "I slept with Rayna James, the sexiest college professor there ever was."

She slaps my chest playfully. "Seriously though, anyone who would want to be with you because of your future profession is missing out on a kind, emotional, and sentimental guy who would literally do anything for the people he cares about."

I tighten my grip around her body, pulling her closer to me. "You really make me sound like a man, Rayna," I say sarcastically.

"Oh, you also have a huge dick. Need me to stroke your male ego some more?"

I let out a deep bellied laugh, her broad smile making her that much more beautiful. I give her a wink. "Nah, but I know something else you could stroke."

This time she laughs. "Already? Again?"

I lift the sheet covering us to give her a peek of the growing hardness between my legs. "He's always ready for you."

"*He?*" she mocks. "Now he has a separate identity? Does he have a name too?"

I bring my hand to my forehead in fake disbelief. "Rayna! First, I'm emotional and sentimental, now you want me to name my dick? You're trying to take my man card away, aren't you?"

"Believe me"—she trails kisses along my chest—"your man card is fully intact."

I groan as her head disappears beneath the sheets and her warm mouth takes me yet again. This time, she doesn't stop and I don't pull her away. This time I discover what it feels like to come inside that hot mouth of hers.

Pure. Fucking. Ecstasy.

Chapter Fourteen

Rayna

When I wake up, it's to the sound of Hayes's phone alarm. The room is still dark, no evidence of the sun in its morning glory.

"What time is it?" I moan, turning over and wrapping my arm over his chest, trying to pull him closer. His warmth is comforting. The last thing I want right now is to be in an empty bed without him.

"Four-thirty," he mumbles. His arm that's slung around my shoulder squeezes me. "I'm sorry. I have to get up for work."

I moan again.

Hayes presses a kiss to my forehead before he shuffles out of bed. He heads for the bathroom, shutting the door behind him to keep the light from escaping. A few seconds later, I hear the showerhead turn on.

The next thing I know, he is standing over me on the side of the bed, kissing me softly before he leaves. I must have fallen asleep again.

I reach for his hand, tugging him closer to me. "Will you come back tonight?" I whisper, my voice full of sleep.

His free hand brushes a few strands of hair off my face. "It'll be late."

"I don't care. I like having you in my bed."

I can hear the smile in his words. "Sure, Rayna. I'll see you tonight."

He places one more tender kiss on my lips before stepping out of the room.

Desk days lately have been anything but. I haven't had a chance to sit at my desk the entire day, and its nearly dinner time. Instead, my time has been spent with students, reviewing their exams and making sure they're on track for the next lecture. The hardest part about my class is that each exam pours over into the next. If a student doesn't understand the basic content from exam one, it puts them behind for the rest of the semester.

Dan walks into my office sometime between five and six with two Starbucks coffees in hand. "Thought you could use another one. There's been students coming in and out of here like crazy today," he says.

I smile at his thoughtfulness. I think it's safe to say that Dan is my first friend in Michigan, outside Hayes of course. "Ahh, thank you." I take one of the cups and put it to my lips, letting the warm caffeine slide down my throat. "You're a lifesaver."

"That's the exact same thing I've been hearing about you. The students are really taking a liking to you, Professor James."

"What can I say, *Dr. Stevens*. I enjoy what I do. I enjoy it even more when my students aren't falling behind."

He chuckles. "Have you been able to get any work done?"

I shrug. "Not much. I'm sure it's a lost cause at this point. I've got one more session in a half hour, then I'm calling it a night."

"Has anyone ever told you that you work too hard?"

"As a matter of fact, no. If you knew my dad and brother, you'd know why. I don't work nearly as hard as them."

Dan takes a seat in one of the chairs in front of my desk. "I think you could use a break. How about this Saturday? It's our school's first home football game. It's a big deal. East Valley is College Gameday's featured game of the week. A couple of us have a tailgate spot outside the stadium. It'll be fun."

"Tailgating?"

He smiles. "Yes, Rayna. Tailgating. We eat, drink, and watch football. Come on. I swear you'll have fun."

"I've never been to a tailgate. Or a football game."

"We don't have to go to the actual game. The fun part is the tailgate itself. If it's not for you, I swear I won't give you a hard time about leaving."

I think about it for a second. Strangely, my first thoughts go to Hayes. What if we were going to spend this Saturday like we did last? Tangled in the sheets together, Hayes only leaving my bed for a few hours for practice. But this is another opportunity to make friends here, and I bailed on Dan the last time he showed me this kindness. If I plan to teach here long-term, which I do, then I suppose I should get in the school spirit.

"Alright, I'll give it a go. What time should I be here?"

"Let's meet in the parking lot at noon. We can walk over to the tailgate spot together. You won't be able to park anywhere near the stadium on game days."

"Okay. Thanks, Dan. I'll see you Saturday."

He stands to leave, his smile broad. "I'm looking forward to it."

Once I'm finished meeting with the last group of students, I change into my workout gear and go for a run around campus. After a swift five miles, I'm sweating, out of breath, and in desperate need of a shower.

I get home around seven, another late night for me. One hot shower later and I'm sitting on my couch with a glass of red wine and Thai takeout, glancing at my phone every few minutes, wondering when Hayes is going to show up. The shop closed at five, though he told me it was going to be a late night

86

when I asked him to come back. Maybe he was staying late to work on another friend's car like he had mine? He hasn't called or texted all day, so I have no idea what's keeping him later than his normal hours.

I find myself in bed at ten o'clock, wondering if he's even going to show up. I still haven't called him. The last thing I want to be is one of those clingy, needy girls, though a call from him would have been nice.

I eventually fall asleep and wake up to the familiar sounds of his heavy footsteps on my wood floors. I stir in bed, glancing at my phone to see what time it is. It's after midnight. What the hell could he have been doing this whole time? And what kept him from calling?

I sit up in bed, flicking on the lampshade near my side of the bed. Hayes opens the door slowly, trying not to wake me. He looks surprised when he sees that I'm already awake. He isn't wearing his work clothes. Instead he's looking sexy as hell in a pair of dark denim jeans and a gray T-shirt.

"I'm sorry," he says right away. "I knew it was going to be a late night, but I didn't know it was going to be this late." He walks over to the bedside and plants a soft kiss on my lips.

I can taste beer on his breath. At least now I know where he's been. "You couldn't call?" I ask softly.

He sighs. "I should have."

His lips find mine again, and soon he's lying on top of me, pressing his hardness against me. I can't tell if he's drunk, having no idea how much he actually had to drink, but I feel weird about the way he's throwing himself at me.

"Hayes."

"Yeah?" he mumbles before he dives in for another deep kiss.

I scoot him off me, sitting up in bed until my back is pressed against the headboard. My breaths are short, like I'm winded after going for a run.

"What's wrong?" he asks.

"I just wish you would have called," I say, unable to hide my annoyance.

"I'm sorry."

"You were at the bar."

He nods.

"You could've just told me that?"

He nods again.

"I don't want to be upset. I don't want to care, but I do. Then you show up drunk and just throw yourself at me. Why? Why did you do this? Why did you leave me waiting?"

"I had to work late," he says. "Then Jason showed up and dragged me to a bar with the rest of the team. He was giving me a hard time about being MIA lately. He took my phone and wouldn't give it back until I had a couple drinks with him. I had a couple and it turned into more. When I finally got my phone back, I saw how late it was. I couldn't drive at that point so I either had to sit there and sober up or leave my truck and get a ride. I got a ride so I could get here faster. I'm sorry, Rayna. Jason's my best friend. He's not an idiot, and he knows something's going on with me. And it fucking sucks not being able to tell him. Having to keep you a secret. I mean, are you even my girlfriend? I don't even know what the fuck we are."

My eyebrows furrow as I look at a now seemingly angry Hayes.

When his eyes find mine, the anger dissipates as sadness takes over. "I'm sorry, Rayna. I care too. I wanted to be here. I still showed up."

"Yeah," I say. "You still showed up."

I slide out of bed and walk into the kitchen, grabbing a cup of water for Hayes. When I get back to the bedroom, he's sitting on the side of the bed, his feet on the ground as his elbows rest on his knees.

"Here," I offer. "Drink some water."

"I'm not nearly as drunk as I was the first night we met."

"Good, because I want to tell you something."

His head turns to meet my gaze as I take a seat next to him.

"I was married," I start.

His eyes flash to an emotion I can't yet read, though his eyebrows dip low like he's feeling something between confusion and sorrow.

"You asked me last night how I was single. It's because I got a divorce last year. I was married for almost four years. Married right after undergrad. He was the love of my life, or at least that's what I thought. I met him my freshman year at Northwestern. He wanted to be a teacher too, like me. We had a lot in common. Our relationship was easy. It made sense to marry him when he asked. I did love him. After three and half years of marriage, I caught him cheating on me. I'll spare you the details, but he broke my fucking heart and I haven't been with anyone since. Not until you. Not until that night."

"You deserve so much more than that, Rayna. He's a piece of shit for doing that to you."

I smile a sad smile. "I know. That's why I left him. Even after he tried to convince me it was a one-time thing, that it would never happen again. He suggested counseling, but I had already made up my mind. After my divorce was finalized and I moved back in with my dad and Sam, I started applying for jobs out of state. I needed a fresh start, a change of scenery. That's how I ended up here. East Valley has always been where I wanted to end up one day, but my ex had no intentions of leaving Chicago, ever. So here I am. I was single because I had just gotten divorced. I have no friends here because I left all of mine behind. What family I have left is four hundred miles away."

"You have me," he says softly, grabbing my hand and squeezing. "You'll have me for as long as you want me."

Chapter Fifteen

Hayes

East Valley's first home football game is today. Tailgates here are wild and the baseball team has been known to throw some of the best pregame parties in our school's history. Jason, Kevin, and I have the biggest off-campus house, so we're hosting. The backyard is set up with folding tables fit for several games of beer pong while the front yard has a couple corn hole games set up. Jason and I are carrying in the last of the many kegs we ordered for today. It's only eight in the morning, but I know the guys are going to start strolling in any minute.

I slept at Rayna's again last night, waking up early to meet Jason at the liquor store and fill our truck beds with the kegs. She's tailgating with some other professors today and promised me that we could meet up after the game at her place.

Wednesday night was a turning point for us in our relationship. I still don't know what we are, if she's my girlfriend, or if we're just casually seeing one another. But I do know that she opened up to me about her failed marriage, trusting in me not to hurt her the way that asshole had. I had no idea she was married before, but it explains how a catch like Rayna was single when we met.

I can't get enough of her. I've never felt this way about any of my past girlfriends, even Emily who had never done anything wrong. I want to spend every minute with Rayna, even if those minutes are spent cooped up in her condo.

My thoughts are broken from Rayna as the guys start trickling in. Kevin hands me a red solo cup filled to the brim with beer.

"To the first of many, Murphy," he says.

I take a sip, planning to take it slow today. I don't want to be blacked by the time I finally see Rayna tonight, though the chances of me staying even a little bit sober are slim to none. If I have to bail early, then I will. I don't want to leave her waiting for me all night like I did Wednesday. It was an asshole move, even if it wasn't intentional.

A couple hours later, our house is packed shoulder to shoulder with East Valley students. I spot Jason talking to Emily by one of the pong tables. It probably should be awkward at the very least, but it's not. I walk over to them, hoping to make my best friend feel comfortable enough to pursue whatever it is he wants to pursue with her.

"Hey, Emily, how've you been?" I ask, roping one arm around her in a friendly hug.

Her small body relaxes against mine in a familiar way before she pulls away. "I'm good. You?"

I smile. "Couldn't be better." And it's true. Thanks to Rayna.

Jason still looks awkward as shit, so I level with him. "Get that look off your face, dude. This isn't weird. At least not for me." I pat him on the shoulder. "Relax."

Emily laughs. "Told you."

He throws his arms up in surrender. "Alright, alright."

Jason has always been one to take advantage of his status on the baseball team. He doesn't care if girls sleep with him because of it, or if they're only sleeping with him because I wouldn't, like Natalie, but him and I both know Emily isn't going to do anything with him just because he's a baseball player. If he really is pursuing this thing, it's because he wants more than just a quick lay, and I can respect that. Emily deserves more than that.

I leave them to enjoy each other's company, walking back into the house and upstairs to my bedroom. Wanting to call Rayna before she gets to the tailgate, I find her number in my contacts and give it a ring.

"Hello?" she answers, her soft voice like music to my ears.

"Hi, Rayna."

"Hi, Hayes."

"Are you all decked out in your blue and white East Valley gear?" I ask.

"*What*? I have to wear the school colors?"

I laugh. "It's a tailgate, Rayna. You're supposed to wear the colors of whatever team you're rooting for."

"Oh," she says. "I'm wearing blue jeans."

"And I'll bet your ass looks amazing."

She laughs. "Cut it out. I don't have any EVU clothes. I'm wearing a yellow shirt right now. Should I change?"

Now it's my turn to laugh. She really doesn't know anything about sporting events. "Yes, Rayna! Blue and white! No yellow!"

"Fine." She sets the phone down, and I hear shuffling on the other end. "I have an all-white shirt I can wear. It's plain, and my jeans are blue. Is that okay?"

"Yes, that's better. I'll bring you one of my T-shirts so next time you can wear appropriate tailgating attire."

She giggles. "How thoughtful of you." There's more shuffling and then. "Wait, Hayes? I take it I shouldn't wear heels?"

I smile. "Unless you want your heels to sink into the grass, I'd stick with something a little more comfortable."

She sighs. "Well, thank God you called. I would've shown up in heels and a yellow shirt looking like a damn fool. I don't even know why I'm going to this! Dan said it would be fun, but so far I'm only stressed."

"Dan?" She's never mentioned a Dan.

"Dr. Stevens," she corrects. "He's the one who said some of the staff would be tailgating today. And the one who invited me out last Friday."

"Right." I didn't know *Dan* was the one inviting her. I just assumed she had made friends with her colleagues, her *female* colleagues. Sounds like this Dan guy really wants to hang out with her.

"So, how long do you think I have to stay before it's appropriate to leave?" she asks.

"Leave whenever you want, Rayna. Don't worry about what anyone else thinks. And call me when you do. I'll come over to your place as soon as you get home."

I originally told her I'd come by after the game, but now I'm feeling a little territorial. I don't like that Dr. Stevens gets to hang out with Rayna in public, not when it's something I can't do. But I'll take her any way I can, though jealousy is starting to roar its ugly head, even if I'm the least jealous guy there is.

"Okay," she says, and I hope she's smiling. "See you later. Have fun, Hayes."

"You too."

Five hours later we're walking through campus on our way to the baseball team's tailgate spot. Most of the party left before us, but Jason, Emily, Kevin, Bony, and me were the last to leave. The pregame tailgate was rowdy as all hell and my attempt to stay somewhat sober quickly went out the window when Kevin made the team compete in shotgun competitions. Being able to shotgun a beer in under three seconds made me the man to beat, and also made me drink way too much in a short span of time. I could feel the alcohol flowing freely through my veins as we passed other tailgate parties.

I notice a familiar perky ass clad in skintight blue jeans and a white top ahead under a blue and white East Valley tent. She's surrounded by other younger adults, assumedly professors, one standing particularly close to her. The guys don't notice her right away, but I sure as hell do. Her back is to us, but as we get closer to their tailgate, Kevin being Kevin, notices her sexy curves and calls out to her.

"Professor James! Looking good!" he shouts.

She turns around, her eyes skating over Kevin before they land on me. Her face flushes and she immediately looks back to Kevin with a soft smile before she turns back to, who I would assume is, Dan. She's holding a drink in her hand, and I can't help but wonder if she's having fun. I want to talk to her, to hang out with her like he's able to do right now. Like Emily can hang out with Jason. I want to show her off to the world and not have to hide her behind closed doors, pretending that I don't see how fucking beautiful she is.

We walk past Rayna's tailgate and continue toward the field, meeting up with the rest of the team ten minutes later. My buzz is gone though. After seeing her, all I want is to be with her. I pull out my phone, hoping to see a call, a text, anything from her, but my screen is blank. She must be having fun. She isn't ready to leave.

I fill up a red solo cup with beer from the nearest keg and chug. It'll be easier to think about her hanging out with Dan if I'm drunk.

Fuck, what is wrong with me?

Hours pass, and I still haven't gotten a call from Rayna. The game is about to start, and the rest of my team is either heading into the stadium or going to one of the bars off campus to watch. I call myself an Uber instead and take it to Rayna's place.

I call her cell from the Uber to let her know I'm on my way to her condo, but the call goes directly to voicemail. A few minutes later, I'm walking into Rayna's empty condo and finding no sign of her. I look around the expensive living space and wonder what the hell I'm doing, showing up to her place without her even knowing. This girl is driving me crazy. I would never do something like this, just show up unannounced. What if she shows up here with Dan, expecting me to be at the game still?

Fuck.

It's too late now. I'm here. And if I wasn't here, here is still the only place I'd want to be.

I jump in Rayna's walk-in shower, turning on the water so that it rains over my drunken body. Afterwards, I slip on a pair of sweats I left the other night. I settle on the couch with a tequila and vodka mix on the rocks from her bar cart, curious if the two could actually taste good together, but also just because it reminds me of her. But it doesn't. It's damn awful, yet I keep drinking.

An hour later, I hear the lock click as someone scans the keycard, the door opening a moment later. Rayna saunters in, in a relaxed and easy way, before she turns around and jumps, startled from my unexpected presence. I immediately get off the couch, searching her eyes for something that shows she's okay with my being here.

"Hayes," she says softly.

"Rayna."

"My phone died."

"I know. I tried calling when I was on my way here."

"How long have you been waiting?" she asks as she drops her purse on the island.

I look at my watch. "About an hour."

"I'm sorry. I tried not to leave early. I didn't want to make you leave your friends."

"I wanted to leave my friends," I say. "I wanted to be with you, Rayna."

A small smile spreads across her face. Her hair is pulled back into a long ponytail, the way she normally wears it for class. It's beautiful, showing off every feature of her face: her delicate nose, her high cheekbones, those enchanting turquoise eyes, and of course, my favorite, her pouty and kissable lips.

"Did you have fun?" she asks as she walks over to me.

I nod. "Did you?"

She shrugs. "I didn't know people were that crazy about football. It's like a different world. Is that how your baseball games are?"

I chuckle. "Not as big here, but when it comes to the majors, yes."

"Wow. I've got a lot to learn."

I smile. She didn't have to say it out loud for me to know what she means. She wants to be there for the games. And I want her there for them, for every last one of them.

"I've been wanting to kiss you since the second I left this morning."

"Then kiss me," she urges.

And I do. I bring her body to mine until she's enclosed in my arms, her small frame melting into me. Her lips are the most perfect fucking lips I've ever had the privilege of kissing.

After a few moments, she pulls away, and I'm instantly left wanting more. "Hayes, what the hell were you drinking?" she asks, a sour expression on her face as she presses a finger to her lips.

I grin, grabbing my glass off the coffee table and bringing it to her. "Try for yourself."

She takes the glass hesitantly, placing her lips on the rim and taking a small sip. Her nose instantly scrunches as she chokes back the vile substance. "Ew, Hayes. You can't like that. What is it?"

I laugh, unable to hide the hilarity behind this moment. "Why, Rayna, it's a tequila-vodka, of course. I thought it was your favorite."

She breaks out in laughter that takes over her entire body and makes her head fall back. "Why are you drinking that?" she asks as she tries to gain back her breath.

"It reminds me of you."

"I hope I'm not that revolting."

I wrap my arms around her again, taking the glass and setting it to the side. "Far from it, baby. Far from it."

Chapter Sixteen

Rayna

The next few weeks fly by quickly and soon it is already time for midterms. My classes have had two exams so far, the second having had a much better grade point average than the first. Even Hayes improved on the second exam, despite his reluctance to join my office hours.

My students seem happy to have me as their teacher, especially for a class they dreaded taking for so long. I never doubted my abilities to teach, but the positive and constructive feedback is always welcome.

Dan introduced me to a few more professors in our building at the tailgate, and I've been spending my lunch and coffee breaks with them, though that time is rare. I'm usually with a student while stuffing my face simultaneously. I've taken a liking to Andrea Reynolds, the chemistry professor and Dr. Nick who teaches Physics. His real name is Nick Caoimhe, pronounced CWA-MEE, but no one ever gets it right, so he sticks to Dr. Nick.

Dan, Andrea, Nick, and I are the youngest professors in our department, so it only makes sense that we all became friends. The older professors have been welcoming to me thus far but are nitpicky when it comes to sticking to the old system and the way things used to be. Much like Dr. Arnold not wanting to give students office hours, the rest of the professors have their way of doing things that the four of us don't agree with.

I finally met Hayes's baseball coach last week while running through campus, passing their stadium as their practice was just letting out. I eyed a sweaty Hayes with his bag slung over his shoulder, throwing a wink my way. I introduced myself to his coach first, taking the opportunity to thank him for requiring his players to take my course. He was pleased to meet me and said that despite the terrible rumors about my class, the boys actually seem to be enjoying themselves this year. It's the first time in his twenty years of coaching that he's ever had a player talk highly of Sports Nutrition, and that was all I needed to go home with a smile plastered across my face.

Hayes and I have fallen into a comfortable routine. He stays with me most nights, though we have to limit it because his roommates have been asking too many questions. The nights that he stays at his place, I want nothing more than to be able to be there with him, to talk to his friends as his friends and not as other students of mine, to be in his world like he's beginning to be part of mine. He spends most of his weekends with me, though he sometimes heads out with his baseball team. I wish I could go out with him on those nights too. We've talked about me just showing up and it being a "coincidence" like it had been before, but there's no way either of us can be in that sort of situation and pretend like the other doesn't exist. So, I fill my free time with my new colleagues. I've met Dan, Andrea, and Nick out for dinner or drinks on more than one occasion.

My students will take their midterms this upcoming Thursday. Tomorrow's lecture is saved for an optional review class for any students who have questions on the material from the first half of the semester. I encouraged them to write down any and all questions they might have for me and bring them to class tomorrow. If we don't get to them, I'd be sure to answer the remaining in an email sent out to the entire class. Again, the older professors think I'm doing too much for my students, but

I don't believe in feeding them to the wolves. I'll help them in any way I can, though it is still their responsibility to retain and understand the material.

It's the middle of October, and the campus is filled with beautiful autumn color trees losing their leaves. The temperature today is a seemingly perfect sixty degrees, my favorite running weather. After a long day of meeting with students and preparing the midterm, then fitting in a short run, I'm finally on my way home. When I arrive, I spot Hayes's old truck in the parking garage and instantly smile from ear to ear, knowing he's already here. He came straight from practice.

I hurry up the stairs, excited to see him for the first time today. When I walk into the condo, I hear footsteps in my bedroom. Sauntering into my room, I see a very sexy and naked Hayes walking from the bathroom to the closet with a huge grin on his face. His muscular shape is covered in water droplets from his hair, clearly fresh out of the shower. I can smell the vanilla-cucumber body wash he insists on using because it reminds him of me.

I set my purse and keys on the dresser, eager to see him.

"Hi there, Professor James," he says.

"Hello, Hayes Murphy."

"Let me get dressed."

"Don't bother."

He has my clothes off in under ten seconds and the next thing I know I'm exploring his body, memorizing every muscular curve while he thrusts himself inside of me. We lay in bed together afterwards, wrapped in each other's arms.

"How was your day?" he asks softly, his fingertips tracing the length of my arm.

My cheek is pressed against his chest. "Busy. Are you coming to my class tomorrow?"

"I wouldn't miss it."

"How do you feel about the midterms?"

"Honestly, pretty good. After tomorrow's review and then studying a bit Wednesday, I should be good to go."

"I'll probably be home late on Wednesday. You don't have to come over."

He kisses the crown of my head. "Just call me when you leave campus. I'll be studying after work and can either finish up with my own private lessons or just head over to sleep with my teacher," he jokes.

"That sounds so bad."

"Nah. It sounds *great*. Every guy's wet dream."

I slap his chest. "Shut up."

He holds me tighter. "I'm only kidding, baby."

"I got something in my email today about a conference in Washington DC I have to attend next month," I say. It's part of the Higher Education Conferences of America requirement that all higher education teachers have to attend. There are three held annually each year, though East Valley professors are required to attend the one in DC. The other HECA conferences are held on the west coast. "It's during Thanksgiving break."

"That's shitty," he says. "What if you want to go home to your family?"

"It's the Sunday to Wednesday before Thanksgiving, so I can fly out Wednesday night and be home for Thanksgiving in Chicago Thursday."

"Well, that's good," he says, though I sense a bit of hesitation on his part.

"What does your family do for Thanksgiving?" I ask.

"Usually Mom cooks, but it's just her, my dad, and me. I don't have a big family or any aunts or cousins. Neither of them have siblings."

I smile. "That sounds perfect."

"Yeah. What about you?"

"Same. It'll just be Dad, Sam, and me. Though sometimes Dad invites guys from his firm who have family out of state they're not able to visit because of work."

"Who cooks?"

"Me."

100

He smiles. "Perfect. We should have our own Thanksgiving Sunday when we get back then. But I'm warning you, I can't cook for shit. Only waffle toast."

I laugh. "I'd like that."

Tuesday morning I'm walking into my lecture hall for the first round of review with my students when I see Dan waiting for me near the lectern, coffee in hand.

"You weren't in your office, so I figured I would stick around and wait for you to get back." He hands me the coffee.

"You're like my caffeine savior. Thank you. I'm going to need about thirty more cups of this to get me through the rest of this week."

He laughs as the first couple students start to trickle in. He steps a few inches closer to me so as not to have to talk loudly over the heavy footfalls and mumbling of students taking their seats. "Have any plans for after midterms? This Saturday in particular?" he asks.

I think for a moment. Hayes said he and the baseball team were going out to lunch with their coach for his birthday after an added morning practice. We didn't talk about potential plans once lunch was over. I shake my head. "I don't think so."

"Great. I'd like to cash in on that rain check."

I laugh. "Haven't we cashed that in a few times now?"

"Not officially."

"Okay, what did you have in mind?"

He takes another step closer, touching my elbow as he leans in toward my ear. "Dinner. I'll pick you up at seven?" he whispers.

I've never spent time with Dan alone, and right now, I'm pretty sure that's what he's insinuating. I feel my cheeks redden at his closeness and the fact that he's basically asking me on a date in front of my students.

Shit.

My students.

I quickly turn my head toward the theater style seating, my eyes immediately drawn to Hayes. He's standing on the steps, fists clenched, his eyes locked on Dan. I look back down to see Dan still holding me close to his body. I pull my arm away and take a step back. "Let's talk about this later. My class is about to start."

Dan nods, walking out.

The heat of Hayes's stare is so strong I can feel it from here.

Chapter Seventeen

Hayes

This must be Dan.

Dr. Stevens.

Whoever the fuck he is, the way he's standing so close to her makes my fists clench until my knuckles turn white. But there's nothing I can do. I can't tell him to stop touching her. I can't tell him that she's mine. All I can do is stand here, my two feet planted on the steps, and stare at them as my blood boils inside my veins.

Rayna's head turns a moment later and our eyes lock. The next second, she's pulling her arm away, whispering something to Dan before he exits the lecture hall.

"Murphy!" Jason calls out from his seat, breaking me from my trans.

I look over to where he's seated and the seat next to him noticeably empty where I should have sat my ass down minutes ago.

"What the hell are you doing?" he asks.

My head turns back to Rayna as she gets the projector ready near the lectern, about to start class. Her eyes flash to mine again in warning.

"Nothing," I mumble before I scoot into my seat.

Jason turns his head and looks toward Rayna before returning his gaze to me. "You okay?" he whispers.

"Yeah."

Rayna starts the optional review session, the last class before our midterm on Thursday. I don't hear anything she says over the next fifty minutes as she's answering question after question. I silently shame myself for being stuck in my head because now I'm going to have to review all this shit later by myself. But all I can think about is the way he touched her, and I can't believe how enraged it has me. Rayna's talked about the friends she's made here. She hangs out with them frequently, as I hang out with mine too. We can't see each other in public, not in Timbers at least, and it's important to me that she has friends. But now I feel an overwhelming urge to put this Dan guy in his place and tell him to fuck off. It's not like Rayna can tell him she's taken. What is she supposed to do, tell him she's dating one of her students?

This isn't the first time our little arrangement has left me unsettled. It's been months of private conversations, countless intimate moments together. I wouldn't give up my time with her for anything. But how much longer can I be okay with this? How much longer do I have to go through my day seeing her and acting as though she's nothing more to me than Professor James? How many more times can I watch as other men hit on her, having no idea that she's already taken?

I walk out of class in a hurry, my eyes never meeting Rayna's, though I can feel hers watching me. My phone rings a few minutes later as I'm walking back home with Kevin and Jason.

"Yeah?" I answer.

"Hayes," she says softly.

I slow down my steps until Kevin and Jason are ahead of me. "Hi."

"I don't know why he did that."

"I do."

"It's not like that. We're only friends."

"Yeah. But I can assure you he's interested in being a hell of a lot more."

She sighs. "I didn't know. He's never touched me like that before. I promise."

I sight. "This is getting hard for me."

"What does that mean?"

"It means I don't want to keep you a fucking secret anymore."

"We already talked about this, Hayes."

"Yeah."

"Come on," she urges. "It's not going to happen again. And it won't be like this forever."

"Look, I just got home and I have a lot of studying to do. I'll talk to you later."

A few long moments of silence pass before she answers. "Are you still coming over tonight?"

I hesitate for a moment. "Yeah, if you want me to."

"I do."

"Okay."

"See you later, Hayes."

"Bye." I hang up as I'm walking into the house.

Jason's already inside, standing in the kitchen waiting for me. "What happened earlier, Murphy?" he asks.

"I don't know what you're talking about."

"Don't play dumb with me, dude. I'm not an idiot. What's going on between you and Professor James?"

My eyes shoot to him. *Fuck.* "What do you mean?"

"I saw the way you were looking at her. You froze in place when that guy was touching her. What the hell was that about?"

"It was nothing."

"Hayes," he says, and I know he's not going to take my shit answers anymore. "I know you better than anyone. Tell me what the fuck is going on."

I sigh. "Where's Kevin?"

He shrugs. "I don't know. He grabbed his keys the second we got home and left."

At least Kevin's not here to overhear this. No one else needs to know about Rayna. "Rayna...uh...Professor James is the woman I've been seeing the last couple of months."

"I figured as much," he says, not feigning the least bit of surprise.

"Then what the fuck are you asking for?"

"You wanted to beat the shit out of that guy today, didn't you?"

"Yeah, so?"

"So, you two are serious?"

I like to think we are. We're as serious as two people can be who can't be seen in public together and only spend time together in one condo. "I guess."

"And you're keeping it a secret because..."

"Because she's my fucking professor," I finish for him.

"Right." He brushes his fingers through his hair. "When did this start?"

"I met her the night of the championship shots. Found out the next day that she was our new professor."

"Damn."

"Yeah."

"So that's why you had such a piss poor attitude the beginning of the semester?"

I shrug.

"Can she get in trouble?" he asks. "You know, for dating a student?"

"I don't know. She's more afraid for her reputation. Afraid it might look bad."

"It *does* look bad."

"Shut the hell up. We're both consenting adults. She just happens to also be my teacher."

"Must piss you off something fierce when Kevin talks his shit about her."

I scoff. "You have no idea."

"So, what are you gonna do?"

"What *can* I do? She doesn't want anyone to know. I just have to trust that nothing is going to happen between her and Dan."

"Dan?"

"Dr. Stevens or some shit. I don't know. The asshole that was touching her today."

"She live in that fancy condo I picked you up in that one day?"

I nod.

"When are you going to see her again?"

"Tonight."

"Then I suggest you two figure out your shit before you get kicked off the team for beating the fuck out of that professor."

Chapter Eighteen

Rayna

I avoid Dan the rest of the day. I don't know why he touched me like that. Or why he had to come so close to me, especially in front of my students. I've never given him the impression that we were more than friends. Not once. Then, of course, Hayes had to be standing there to witness the whole thing. I knew he was upset. Or mad. It was written all over his face. The way his fists clenched made me fear for Dan's safety. It wouldn't be good for those two to be in a room together again, not after what Hayes saw.

I drive off campus earlier than I had originally planned, more than ready to see Hayes. I give him a call at a quarter to six to let him know that I'm heading home. He doesn't answer, so I wait a few minutes before calling again. He finally answers after a few rings.

"Hello?"

"Hi. I'm on my way home."

I hear shuffling in the background. "I'll be right over."

"Okay." I hesitate for a few minutes. He was pissed when we spoke on the phone earlier. "Is everything okay?"

"I don't know. I'll see you soon."

He hangs up.

Great.

A short while later, I'm in my condo changing into comfy clothes when I hear Hayes walk in. I don't know what mood he's going to be in, or what to expect, so I stay in my room and wait for him to find me. It doesn't take long before he's walking into my bedroom and taking a seat on the bed. I stare at him from my closet, now comfortably dressed in leggings and one of his sweatshirts he left here that is three sizes too big.

"Come here," he says softly, patting the bed beside him.

I amble over to him and take a seat.

He wraps his arm around me and pulls me closer to him. "What are we doing, Rayna?" he whispers into my hair.

I shut my eyes because I already don't like where this conversation is heading. "What do you mean?"

"I wanted to beat the shit out of that professor."

"I know."

"I'd get kicked off the team if I did that. Hell, I'd probably get expelled."

I nod.

"The funny thing is that wouldn't have stopped me."

I hear what he's saying behind his words. His baseball team. His education. Two important things in his life, but I'm more important. In Hayes's eyes, he would choose me.

"Nothing is going on with Dan, Hayes."

"Does he know that?"

"He will," I assure him.

"Jason knows about you," he says out of nowhere.

I pull away and look in his eyes. They look tired. "Oh." I don't know what else to say.

"Yeah."

"Why'd you tell him?" I ask.

He shrugs. "He figured it out. And honestly, Rayna, I didn't want to keep it a secret. It doesn't feel right anymore."

"What doesn't feel right?"

"Hiding. I'm not ashamed to be with you. Are you ashamed of being with me? Because that's what this is starting to feel like."

"I'm not ashamed of you, Hayes. You know why I've wanted to keep this between us from the start. You knew what this job meant to me. You knew going into this that we'd need to stay quiet until you graduated. Why has that suddenly changed for you?"

"Because I'm tired of listening to guys talk about your ass and not being able to shut them up. Because I don't ever want to watch another guy put his hands on you without me being able to stop them. And because I care about you a hell of a lot more than I care about my reputation, or my education, or even my fucking future, Rayna." He rests his elbows on his knees, burying his face in his hands. "I care about you more than I ever expected to," he mumbles into his palms.

The realization hits. *He's falling in love with me.*

I rest my hand on his back, feeling his tense muscles underneath. "I care about you too," I say softly.

"Not enough."

"What is that supposed to mean?"

He stands up abruptly. "I'm falling in love with you, Rayna. I don't give a fuck what anyone else says about us. But *you* do. *You* want to keep this a secret, keep *us* a secret. Next year I'm going to be traveling all around the country, playing ball in a different city every other night. Right now, we're in the same city. Right now, I want to be able to take you out to dinner. I want you to meet my fucking parents. I want to meet the guy who raised you. I want to hold your hand in public. I want you to be cheering for me in the stands at every damn game even though you don't have the slightest clue about baseball. I want to be able to fall in love with you completely, Rayna. I never thought I could feel like this. But I do. And I don't care if you think less of me for it, but I want all those things, and I fucking want them with you."

My heart pounds in my chest as Hayes wears his so visibly on his sleeve.

"How do I do this, Rayna? How can I do this?"

"I don't know," I answer honestly. Because I don't. He doesn't need to hear about how much I care for him, or how I'm falling in love with him too. He needs to hear that I'm okay with whatever fall out comes from making our relationship public. But I'm not ready for that. I'm not ready to risk my reputation, my job. I know it's not illegal to date my student, though it is extremely frowned upon. It was a competitive interview process to get this position. They don't have to keep me next year. Hell, they don't have to keep me next semester. What will happen if people find out about us now, after I've only been working here for three months? Will I be fired? Or asked to resign? I'm not sure I'm prepared to find out.

He grips the back of his neck with his fingers intertwined. He looks lost. Scared.

"Please don't do this," I whisper.

"Do what, Rayna? Break your heart? Because right now, you're the one breaking mine."

"I want to be with you, Hayes."

"Not enough."

"Yes, enough. You can't blame me for fearing for my job. You dating your professor isn't going to stop you from getting drafted into the MLB. I could lose my job. And then what will I do? Follow you around the damn country like a lost puppy?"

He shakes his head. "Wow. Okay."

I sigh. "That's not what I meant."

"Then what did you mean, Rayna? You don't want to be with someone who has to travel for their career? You wouldn't be willing to make that kind of sacrifice for me?"

"How can we possibly be arguing about something that hasn't even happened?"

"Because it *will* happen, Rayna. It will happen if you choose me. This is my life. This is what my family needs. They gave up everything so that I'd have this opportunity. I don't know who I'll play ball for, but the odds are against me that I would stay in Michigan. And then what? You wouldn't apply to schools elsewhere? You are hell bent on staying at East Valley?!"

"Because I already gave up my dreams for my damn ex-husband, Hayes. God forbid I do something for me!"

"I want *everything* for you, Rayna. I want you to have the career. I want you to have the life you always wanted, but I'm sorry that I'm being selfish by wanting that life to be with me. We'll never work if you can't even consider working somewhere else."

"That's not something I need to consider right now, Hayes. It's only been a few months," I argue.

"Then you can call me when it's something you can consider." He walks into the hallway, away from me, away from this conversation.

"Stop!" I yell, following behind him.

He stops and turns around, waits for me to speak. His shoulders are slouched. He looks defeated.

"Please don't leave."

"Why? What are we even doing here? We don't stand a chance."

My eyes cloud with tears because I know he's speaking the truth. We don't stand a damn chance unless I'm willing to put my life on hold to cater to someone else's needs, like I did for my ex-husband. And that worked out so well for me the first time.

I break down into full blown tears. It's the first time he's seen me cry. Hell, it's the first time I have cried in a long time. I collapse to my knees as tears fall into my palms. Moments later, Hayes is crouching in front of me. Holding me. Comforting me. Soothing me. He's a better person than I am. This is my fault. He wants to go all in, and I'm the one keeping us in this constant standstill. Keeping him a secret.

"I'm sorry," I cry out into his chest, my tears soaking through his shirt though he doesn't seem to care.

He sits with me in the middle of my hallway, continuing to show me what kind of man he is. He's the kind of man I want to be with. The kind of man I *should* risk it all for. What the hell is holding me back?

"You are the most beautiful, incredible woman I have ever met, Rayna," he whispers into my hair. "I'm sorry I can't be the person to give you the world." He places a soft kiss on my forehead before he lets me go.

Chapter Nineteen

Hayes

Empty. That's how I feel. Like I've emptied out everything I have, my motivation, my happiness, everything that makes me, me. Now I'm just a shallow version of myself walking through life in this shell of nothing.

The last time I felt like this was when my parents had to take out a second mortgage on the house to help pay for baseball. Why did leaving Rayna make me feel the same way as my parents' financial troubles? How the fuck should I know? All I do know is that I'm continuing with my life without the same passion I once had, because honestly, I feel like I have nothing left. I worked my double shift yesterday to keep my mind off things, then had a few beers with Kevin afterward. Now I'm walking with my roommates to Rayna's class for our midterms. I think I'll do fine. Not as well as I would if I wasn't so distracted by ending things with Rayna, but I'll pass. I'm not worried.

My palms begin to sweat as we get closer to Chestnut Hall. I admitted to Rayna that I was falling in love with her. I've never admitted that to another woman in my life. I've never felt this way for anyone but her. Not that it matters now, because whatever we had wasn't important enough to Rayna. *I* wasn't important enough to Rayna. I've felt empty since walking out of her condo Tuesday night. I've felt empty every fucking moment since.

We enter the building with a few minutes to spare before our midterms are set to start. My palms haven't stopped sweating, and I feel my heart begin to beat more rapidly. I don't want to see her. The last time I saw her, the last time I touched her, I was holding her in my arms as she cried because she knew I wasn't enough for her. *I* knew I wasn't enough for her. Nothing hurts quite as bad as realizing, despite your best fucking efforts, that you're not enough.

Kevin enters the lecture hall first. I don't even realize it, but I'm stopped a few steps away from the door. I see Jason leaning against the wall waiting for me. He doesn't say anything, just stands there, waiting, like he knows this is hard for me.

I didn't have to tell him what happened. He could see it on my face the second I got home Tuesday night. He knows me better than anyone. I've never cared about my relationships ending. I've never cared about a single human more than I care about Rayna. Now I have to walk into this fucking lecture hall and take a midterm while the love of my goddamn life watches. I don't want to be in the same room as her. I don't even want to look at her, too afraid I might finally lose it for the first time since we ended things.

I feel pathetic.

I feel lost.

I feel so fucking empty.

Class is about to start. I know I have to go in. I take one last deep breath before I get ready to face her.

I walk into the auditorium, Jason only a step behind me. We have to pick up our midterms from Rayna before we take our seats. There is a small line of students waiting to be handed their tests, only four people between Rayna and me.

Three.

Two.

One.

Zero.

I stand face to face with her. My pulse dances inside my chest, adrenaline pumping through my veins like it does before I pitch a baseball game. Our gaze meets as her almond-shaped eyes look through me like they can see I'm no longer Hayes Murphy but a carbon copy of Hayes Murphy, empty on the inside, though completely the same on the outside.

She hands me my midterm.

I take it from her, her fingers accidentally brushing against my hand as I take the stapled papers.

"Good luck, Hayes," she says softly.

Taking my test, I don't acknowledge her. I leave, finding my seat near Kevin.

The next fifty minutes feel like the longest minutes of my existence. It takes me the entire class period to finish my midterm, but not because I don't know the material. Surprisingly, I found the test itself pretty straightforward. It took me the entire fifty minutes because my mind kept switching to thoughts of Rayna. The way she felt when I held her in my arms as she cried, the way her pouty lips felt as they kissed mine, the smell of her. Every small detail I could recall about her seemed to pop into my thoughts at the most inopportune times. I could feel the heat of her gaze on me sporadically as she looked up from her spot at the front of the lecture hall.

I stand up and hand her my midterm without a word before finally exiting the suffocating feel of that room. My eyes don't meet hers. I pretend she's not even there.

Jason's waiting for me outside the building. "How was it?" he asks.

"Not bad."

"I meant being in there with Professor James."

I look around to see if anyone can overhear him, but we're alone outside. Kevin's probably already at home. He finished his midterm in thirty minutes, surprisingly. I finally reply, "I felt like I was suffocating. It was distracting."

"That why it took you so long?"

"Yeah."

"It'll get easier. And we're already halfway through the semester. Come December, we'll be out of her class."

"Will it though? Get easier?"

He pats me on the back in a brotherly display of affection. "Have to believe it will."

"I told her I was falling in love with her," I admit.

"Damn."

"Figures this shit would happen with someone I can't be with."

"And remind me why that is again?"

"She doesn't want anyone finding out. Wants to keep us a secret because of her job."

"And you don't want to keep it quiet anymore?"

"There's nothing to keep quiet about anymore, but no. I didn't. I want a real relationship with her. I want everything with her, but she doesn't. She doesn't want to risk her job or her reputation."

"Can you blame her?"

"Yes, I can blame her! If this was the real fucking thing, then nothing should be standing in our way. She should choose me like I want to choose her!" I basically yell. She's gotten under my skin. I can't remember the last time I yelled at my best friend.

"Come on, Hayes. You can't say that you'd choose her over your career in the majors."

"That's different."

"How?"

"My parents gave up everything for me to play ball. I'll be able to set them up for life with just my first-year rookie contract. I'll be able to set her up for life eventually too."

"I don't think the money matters to her, bro."

I shake my head. "No, you're right. It doesn't matter at all. She's got plenty of it."

"So, what's the real issue here?" he asks.

117

"I don't know where I'll end up. I could get drafted to a team across the country. I could literally end up anywhere, but she has no intentions of leaving East Valley. Ever. This is her dream job."

"Just like playing in the MLB is yours."

"Yeah."

"What's wrong with you both being passionate about your careers?"

"Nothing. I love that she loves her job. She's damn good at it too, or I would've failed that fucking midterm back there. But how could there ever be a future for us? How can we spend the next year behind the four walls of her condo, then potentially live across the country from each other the next? I don't want to hide her anymore, dude. I want to show her off, be with her as much as I can while I can. I want to kick Kevin in the nuts for talking about her ass the way he does. And I want all the other guys who think it's okay to hit on her in front of me to back the fuck off."

"You don't see this lasting past this year?"

"I want it to, but I don't see how it can. I can't be what she wants. I can't stay put in Michigan, not unless by some miracle I get drafted to the Tigers."

Jason sighs. "I guess this wouldn't be a good time to tell you Emily and I are dating?"

I look over at him, and he flinches like I'm going to hit him. I shake my head. "I'm happy for you, man. You're both good people. You deserve each other."

"You deserve someone like that too."

"I had someone like that. I just let her go."

Chapter Twenty

Rayna

Friday morning, I'm back in my office at seven o'clock sharp. I got home late last night and realized it was because I was stalling, the need to avoid my condo evident. I avoided it on Wednesday too, staying late at work with the excuse of prepping for midterms Thursday. My condo is filled with every memory of Hayes. Every moment we've had together, intimate or not, has been spent in my condo. And that damn bar. I won't be going there anytime soon.

When he walked up to me at the start of class yesterday to grab his midterm, he stared at me with a blank expression, almost as if he didn't recognize me. It felt like I was nothing to him. He stayed the entire fifty minutes taking his midterm, and I feared that us ending things affected his test. I grabbed his out of the pile immediately after class, needing to face the fallout if I caused one of my students to fail. Luckily, he didn't do half bad. He finished with a B minus, though he missed questions I know we reviewed on Tuesday. Had the incident with Dan not happened, he probably would have known those answers. Had we not ended our relationship this week, he probably would have aced the exam. He didn't fail, but I still feel like I failed him.

About an hour into grading another stack of midterms, a soft knock sounds at my door.

"Come in."

Dan walks in, closing the door behind him. I haven't seen him since Tuesday, when he asked me to dinner and stood closer than what's appropriate. "Hey," he says.

"Hey."

"Have a second? I was hoping we could talk."

"Sure," I say. "Have a seat."

He does, and there are a few moments of awkward silence before he speaks again. "I'm really sorry about the other day. I didn't mean to make you uncomfortable or pressure you into going out with me. I talked with Nick and Andrea, and the three of us are actually going to grab dinner tomorrow before the premier of the new *Fast and Furious* movie and were hoping you might want to join us. If you'd want to, of course."

I'm relieved he's no longer pushing the subject of him and I potentially going on a date. I've gone out with these new friends of mine before and have always felt extremely comfortable and welcome. Besides, who else do I have? They're the only friends I've made here. I don't want to burn any bridges, especially after how kind Dan has been since we met.

"That sounds like a lot of fun. Do I need to watch *Fast and Furious* one through thirty to make sure I understand the plot?" I joke.

He laughs. "Nah, no prep is needed. I think you'll enjoy *Fast and Furious* thirty-one without doing any homework on the franchise."

I smile, thankful there's no awkwardness between us. I need friends now more than ever, and I'm grateful to have the distraction. No longer spending the day with Hayes, as I had every other Saturday over the last few months, I would have found some excuse to come to work if Dan hadn't asked me to hang out with our friends. Anything to avoid that damn condo.

"Thanks for inviting me, Dan. I'm excited. Sounds like it will be a fun night."

He smiles wide as he stands. "Can I pick you up or did you want to meet at the restaurant?"

"I'd love a ride, if you don't mind. I think I'll be having a few glasses of wine with my dinner. It's been that kind of week. What time should I be ready?"

"Andrea made the reservations at San Julio's for six. How's five-thirty sound?"

"Sounds perfect. Thanks again."

"Sure. See you tomorrow. And don't work so late today. It's Friday. I'm sure you have somewhere better to be."

I try to keep my smile, but it unintentionally wavers as he leaves my office. I wish I had somewhere better to be tonight, but unfortunately, work is the only place I have right now. My condo is strictly off limits unless I'm going there to shower or sleep. I hope I get over this quickly.

Chapter Twenty-One

Hayes

My game is off at practice, and everyone knows it. I can't hit the ball for shit. I'm not throwing any strikes. Three of the freshmen hit homeruns off me during our scrimmage. It's the shittiest practice I've had since I started playing for East Valley three years ago. It may have something to do with the terrible hangover I've been milking since Thursday night. I might've felt better for this practice if I hadn't decided to binge drink Friday too.

There's another party tonight at one of the football players' houses. I shouldn't go, but I know the last thing I'm going to do tonight is sit at home by myself, sulking. The drinking helps get Rayna off my mind. Sort of.

I jump in the shower when I get home. Kevin is hosting a pregame at our place before we head over to the party. I can't wait to get a few beers in me so I can forget about that shitty practice. The warm water trickles down my back as I wash my hair, wishing I was in Rayna's shower. I miss the smell of her body wash. I miss knowing that by the time I get out of the shower, she'll be home. She'd reach for the towel wrapped around my waist, dropping it to the floor, her clothes soon following. *Damn.* It feels like it's been forever since I've been inside of her.

My dick reacts to the thought of her. Her slender body, perky ass, perfectly round breasts, the heat of her gaze when I was inside of her.

Fuck.

I start to stroke myself in the shower. It's been so long since I've had to jerk off. I can't even get myself off without thinking about the woman I have been falling in love with. It's a weird form of torture, not being able to physically have her, yet thoughts of having her the only way I'm capable of any pleasure.

I picture her lips as they cover my length, the warmth of her breath as she takes all of me in. I have to put my free hand on the shower wall to steady myself. I pick up the pace as I imagine her head moving forward and backward, sucking me off. I hardly ever came in her mouth, not because she didn't want me to but because I'd rather come inside of her. Usually at this point, when I knew I was getting close, I'd gently pull her by her hair until she knew I'd had enough. Her mouth would fall to mine, and I'd sink into her heat.

"Fuck," I moan.

My hand strokes my dick as I imagine I'm inside Rayna, fucking her in the shower, on the bed, on the couch, anywhere I can have her. Two seconds later, I'm shooting my load. I feel pleasure for all of ten seconds as I come, followed quickly by an overwhelming sadness.

I can't do that again. Why the hell would I do that to myself in the first place? I've been trying to get her off my mind all week. Now I'm imagining fucking her just so I can get myself off? It only makes me miss her more. I don't want to pretend my hand is Rayna. I want the real thing.

I rinse off and get out of the shower as fast as I can, wanting to forget this ever happened. I change into a pair of jeans and a sweatshirt before I head downstairs and grab a few beers out of the fridge.

There are already a few guys from the team here. I notice Bony sitting on the couch, playing Jason in a game of Madden. I join them, handing them each a beer.

"Thanks, man," Bony says. He sets his controller down as Jason's team picks their next play, and pops open the tab.

"Where's Kevin?" I ask.

"Went to pick up a few girls," Jason says.

"Emily coming?" I ask.

Jason eyes me. "Yeah. That cool?"

"Of course. She's your girl. She's always welcome."

"Right," he says, almost as if he forgot.

I drink my beer quickly, and already I'm standing to grab another. I open the fridge just as Kevin opens the front door, walking in with two girls hanging off either side of him and another noticeably avoiding giving Kevin any affection. I like her best already.

"What's up man?" Kevin asks. "You in a better mood yet?"

I ignore his jab and toss him a beer.

"What would you ladies like to drink?" Kevin asks.

The two girls hanging on his arms giggle and whisper in his ears. His eyes get big and the next thing I know he's heading up the stairs, the two of them clinging to him like lint on a sweater.

The third chick they showed up with lingers in the kitchen awkwardly.

"Do you want something to drink?" I ask. "Like an actual beverage?"

"Beer is fine, if you don't mind."

I toss her a beer before I walk back to the couch where Bony's team is kicking Jason's ass. The girl lingers in the kitchen. There are a few other people lingering throughout the house for the pregame, but it seems like she doesn't know anyone besides the two girls who disappeared with Kevin. She doesn't know what to do and it makes me feel bad for her.

"Want to join us?" I offer.

She turns her head to meet my gaze from where I sit on the couch, then shrugs. "Sure." She takes a seat on the couch next to me since it's the only seat available.

"What's your name?" I ask, trying to be polite and make conversation. If she doesn't know anyone, I can at least introduce her to Bony, Jason, and myself so she knows three more people here.

"Bexley," she says.

"Haven't heard a name like that before."

She rolls her eyes. She probably hears that all the time.

I try to recover. "Nice to meet you, Bexley. I'm Hayes, that's Bony and Jason."

"Bony?" she asks.

"Tony," Bony says.

"Dudes a stick. We call him Bony," I explain.

She laughs, smiling for the first time since she walked into our house.

"How do you know Kevin?" I ask.

"I don't." Just as I suspected. "My two roommates are sisters, and *they* know Kevin."

"Damn, *sisters*?" Jason asks. "Kevin must be in heaven up there. That's like a dream for him."

I ignore Jason's comment, though he's right. But I'm not going to sit here and talk to Bexley about what her roommates are likely doing with Kevin right now.

Bexley finishes her beer just as I do, and I stand to get us another. I sit back down next to her as she pops open the tab, mumbling thanks.

"You guys going to the party tonight?" I ask her.

She nods.

"Should be a good time."

"Should be," she agrees.

An hour later and a few more beers deep, we're walking over to the party a few blocks from the house. Bexley stays with me, her roommates still hanging all over Kevin. Apparently, they're looking for another go at it tonight because they can't take their hands off him.

"Are they always like this?" I ask, nodding my head in their direction.

"I think they're just into football players. Or whatever sport it is you guys play."

I laugh. "Baseball."

"Right, sorry."

I realize that Bexley is another girl who doesn't give a fuck about who I am. That must be why it's been so easy to talk with her this whole night. At first, I just felt bad for her, but keeping conversation with her has been easy. It just flows. I look at Bexley for the first time tonight. *Really* look at her. She's blonde, with high cheek bones and a cute heart-shaped mouth. She's in great shape, and I can tell she spends a decent amount of time at the gym. She has long, slender legs, though the muscle is evident. I don't know how I hadn't noticed her breasts before, but her top exposes a nice amount of cleavage. She's a beautiful girl. Much prettier than her two roommates, if I'm being honest.

Once we get to the party, Bexley and I head straight for the keg in the backyard. Jason disappears somewhere with Emily, while Bony tries to get in on the action with Kevin and the sisters.

Hours later, I know I've had too much to drink. I want nothing more than for this day to be over. This week to be over. I'll text Kevin and Jason to let them know I'm heading out. I don't feel like looking for them through this crowd of people. I don't know if it's rude if I leave without Bexley or not. She hasn't left my side all night, but not in a clingy sort of way. Just in a way that tells me she doesn't normally go to parties, nor is she extremely social. I guess I make her feel comfortable. And again, she's easy to talk to and has served for a nice distraction from Rayna.

Until now. Damn it.

"Hey, I think I'm gonna head home," I tell Bexley.

"Oh, alright. I'll go find Tina and Nicki."

"I don't think you're going to find them anytime soon. This place is filled with people. Besides, they'll probably end up going back to my place with Kevin. Do you want to just walk back with me? You can crash on the couch if you want."

She thinks for a moment before accepting my offer. We walk together the couple of blocks back to my house. Once inside, I grab a few blankets out of the closet and throw them on the couch for her. The clothes she's wearing look tight, and she probably doesn't want to sleep in them. Maybe I should offer her clothes. Rayna was always so excited to get out of her jeans at the end of the night.

Fuck. I did it again.

"Did you want to borrow some clothes? To sleep in?" I offer.

She smiles awkwardly. "Yeah, actually. If you don't mind?"

"Not at all. Come upstairs. I'll grab something of mine."

She follows me up the stairs and to my bedroom. I open one of my drawers and pull out a pair of sweatpants before moving to my closet and grabbing one of my several East Valley T-shirts. She's standing near my bed when I hand her the clothes.

"Here you go. They'll probably be big, but these pants have a draw string so you can tighten them to keep them up."

"Thanks," she says softly, staring at me with a look in her eyes that I can't quite figure out. Though it becomes apparent what she's thinking once her gaze flickers to my lips.

It's so quick, I almost don't know if I imagined it. I know I could kiss her right now if I wanted to. She's standing in my bedroom, not making any movement for the door. I'm ninety-nine percent sure kissing her is exactly what she wants me to do. Normally, she'd be exactly the kind of girl I would've ended up sleeping with at the end of the night. Maybe even dating. She's been cool as hell to hang out with. But unfortunately for me, the thought of kissing anyone who isn't Rayna doesn't feel right.

"Bexley," I whisper. "I can't kiss you. I'm sorry. I just got out of something pretty serious and it's just too soon."

She nods but doesn't look pissed or even upset. "You're a good guy, Hayes. I know you could tell I was uncomfortable today. Thank you for making this night bearable for me."

I smile. "It was my pleasure."

"Goodnight," she says as she walks out of my bedroom.

"Goodnight, Bexley."

If only Rayna thought being a good guy was enough.

Chapter Twenty-Two

Rayna

Dan picks me up at half past five. We drive in his sports car to the restaurant Andrea and Nick are meeting us at, riding in a comfortable silence. It's the best I've felt all week, though if I'm being honest, I'm not feeling all that great at all. I feel like I have a hole in my heart the size of a baseball.

No matter how much I miss him, I know that this is for the best. It hasn't even been a week. Nothing has changed. I haven't changed my mind. I can't risk my career, my reputation. I can't keep giving up things I love and making sacrifices for other people. I did that enough with my ex-husband, and he did nothing to deserve it. I won't make that same mistake again.

We pull into the restaurant's parking lot. Dan and I walk in together, quickly spotting Andrea and Nick waiting for us at the table.

Andrea stands immediately, her arms flying out beckoning for a hug. "Rayna! I haven't seen you all week. How did midterms go?"

I offer a friendly hug. "Good. Glad they're over."

Nick stands next and gives me a one-armed hug, then offers Dan his hand.

We take our seats just as the waiter arrives to take our drink order. Dan orders us both a glass of wine, and I smile, knowing full well that I told him I'd be needing a couple of glasses after the week I'd had.

I drink four glasses in total before we leave to head for the movie theater. Dan only drinks one glass, being the responsible one for the night, chauffeuring my ass around. When we get to the theater, there's a small bar in the lobby and I order another glass of wine.

I take a seat between Andrea and Dan just as the previews begin in the dark theater. I've never seen a single *Fast and Furious* movie, so I know I'm going to be lost as hell. But that's fine, because my only purpose in being here is to get drunk and be anywhere but my condo.

Two hours later, and the credits are rolling. I try to stand, having sufficiently drank enough to leave my small body unstable. Dan reaches his arm out to steady me. I laugh and wave it off like I'm fine. I'm not. I hardly ate at dinner, my appetite poor while my thirst never quite felt quenched.

We say our goodbyes in the parking lot before Dan drives me back to my condo. Again, we ride in a comfortable silence, broken only when he pulls into my building's lot.

"I'm glad you came tonight, Rayna. I had a lot of fun."

I smile. "Me too. I needed that. Thanks for inviting me out."

"Always."

I get out of the car and make my way up to my condo, insisting I don't need Dan's help. It takes a little longer than normal, but eventually I make it to my door. A sinking feeling overwhelms my core as I walk into the dark, lonely space. I head straight for the bar cart, pouring myself another glass of wine in hopes that it will put me to sleep. Unfortunately, it doesn't, and soon I've polished off an entire bottle of red.

I stupidly scroll through my phone until I land on his contact information. I stare at it for what feels like an hour but was probably all of three seconds before I hit the call button. It rings several times before it goes to voicemail.

"Hey, this is Hayes. Leave a message."

He didn't answer.

Like an idiot, I call again.

"Hey, this is Hayes. Leave a message."

I don't leave a message. Instead, I toss my phone across the room and stomp to bed. It was a mistake anyway. Better that he didn't answer because I probably would have begged him to come over. What good would that have done?

I crawl into my oversized empty bed and cry myself to sleep on the side Hayes used to sleep on.

Chapter Twenty-Three

Two missed calls.

I got home sometime after midnight last night and fell asleep as soon as Bexley left my room. Rayna called in the middle of the night. Twice.

My first instinct is to call back right away. Maybe something was wrong? My second instinct is to pretend like it never happened. Why did she call? Did I even want to know? Does she regret calling? So many questions I can't really answer unless I speak to Rayna. But I can't. I can't face her. Not yet.

I roll out of bed and am not the least bit surprised when I feel the raging headache, like someone is taking a jackhammer to the back of my eyeballs. This has to be some sort of new record for me. I'm looking at day four of being hungover.

I brush my teeth and take a piss before heading downstairs. Bexley is still sleeping peacefully on the couch. I'm actually really glad I met her. Last night probably would've been damn miserable without her company.

Jason joins me in the kitchen a few minutes later, followed by a half-naked Emily. It's nothing I haven't seen before, but the sight takes me by surprise. She's wearing one of Jason's T-shirts that is way too big on her, so it basically covers everything. But there's no denying that she's not wearing any pants.

"Morning," I mumble as I bring a cup of freshly brewed coffee to my lips.

Jason nods. He looks like shit.

"Morning!" Emily says in an overly excited manner.

Jason takes out two mugs and pours Emily a cup of coffee before he pours his own. "What time did you get home last night?" he asks me.

"A little after midnight."

He nods toward the couch where Bexley is sound asleep. "She left with you?"

"Yeah."

His eyebrows shoot up in questioning.

"It wasn't like that," I state.

Jason shrugs as if he couldn't care either way.

It could've been like that. I could've slept with her. Could've had her naked in my bed right now. I have no doubt she's someone I could be interested in. But I feel the same way as I did last night. I know she's not Rayna. She will never be Rayna. No one will ever be Rayna, and I think that's my problem. I wonder how long it'll be before I won't care anymore. Will it be when I'm finally playing in the MLB? My status as a ballplayer is only going to grow once I play professionally. I know I'm going to have women throwing themselves at me, hoping I will set them up for life with fancy cars and trips. It's going to get worse, and I'm honestly not looking forward to it. Kevin thinks I'm nuts. Or gay. I know I'm not the latter, though the former is questionable. What guy wouldn't want girls throwing themselves at him? They say the best way to forget someone is to be inside someone else. But something tells me no matter who I'm with, they'll never make me feel the way Rayna does. Or did. Basically, I'm fucked.

I hear Bexley moan on the couch. She drank just as much as I did, so she's probably feeling like shit. I don't even know if her two roommates came back with Kevin or not. Once I fell asleep, I was out like a light. I didn't hear anything coming from Kevin's room. Hell, I hadn't even heard Rayna's phone calls.

I pour another cup of coffee and grab some Advil before I walk it over to Bexley. I pop two in my mouth once I've handed over her personal hangover cure.

"Thanks," she mumbles.

I take a seat on the couch next to her, pulling part of her blanket over my shoulders. I never sleep in shirts, and I hadn't bothered to put one on before coming downstairs. This house is cold as fuck.

"How are you feeling?" I ask.

"Like shit."

"Me too."

"Are Tina and Nicki here?"

I shrug. "Don't know. I passed out. Didn't hear anyone get home last night."

"I heard them," she says, rolling her eyes. "You're lucky."

My stomach grumbles, and despite the coffee, my headache seems to only be getting worse. I turn to find Jason and Emily curled up leaning against the kitchen counter. "You guys wanna grab breakfast?"

"Sure," Jason answers.

I look to Bexley. "How about you? You hungry?"

She nods. "I could eat."

The four of us pile into my shitty truck twenty minutes later and drive a few miles to the nearest Denny's. We get a table for four and order enough food to feed an army. We all look like shit, and there's no denying the other customers in this place are hungover as well. This is a college town after all. I'm sure the waitstaff is used to it.

Bexley orders a tower of pancakes. When they arrive, her eyes light up like she just won the lotto.

"Holy shit," I mumble, eyeing the ten fluffy pancakes piled on top of each other. "You gonna be able to eat all that?"

She smiles. "Is that a challenge?"

Emily and Jason laugh. "There's no way," Jason challenges.

Bexley looks like she's up for the task because she starts digging in and devouring the pancakes like her life depends on it. I settle for greasy hash browns and eggs with a side of crispy bacon. And more coffee.

Bexley is about halfway through her stack of pancakes when something catches my eye. I watch as a woman wearing an oversized sweatshirt walks up to the countertop near the kitchen and takes a seat at one of the bar stools. A coffee is quickly placed in front of her a few seconds after she sits. I recognize the sweatshirt because it's like the one I have with East Valley Baseball written across the front. I can't tell if I recognize the woman because she has the hood pulled over her head.

Bexley only has a quarter of the pancakes left but looks like she's starting to give up. Her motions are slower and the way she chews looks painful.

"You're going to make yourself sick," I say.

She nods. "You're right. I can't do it. You guys win."

Jason laughs but gives her a standing ovation anyway. This attracts the attention of other customers as they look around to see what the commotion is about. Bexley sinks into her seat in embarrassment, and I give Jason a look telling him to sit the fuck down. Our silent communication works because he takes a seat, but not before I make eyes with the woman underneath the hood sitting at the counter. Like everyone else, she turned to see why someone might be clapping in the middle of Denny's at nine in the morning. My heart sinks when I realize it's Rayna, wearing *my* East Valley Baseball sweatshirt.

I don't know what I'm thinking, but I abruptly stand, mumbling something about going to the bathroom before I hightail it out of here. Rayna's eyes are locked on me the entire time as I walk throughout the busy diner.

There's no one else in the bathroom when I walk in. I have no idea what I'm doing in here because I don't have to piss, but this is the second time now I've made a run for the bathroom after seeing her out in public. It's like it's the only place I can go to think when I just need a minute to calm down.

I hadn't expected to see her outside of the classroom. It feels wrong to be in the same room as her right now. I jerked off to thoughts of her yesterday. I turned down sleeping with a cool chick for her last night. It hasn't even been a week and it's clear I'm not over her. I told her I was falling in love with her, so how could I be? I feel like the biggest goddamn pussy in America right now because the second I see her, I fucking run and hide. I can't even face her.

A few minutes pass before I build up the nerve to walk out of the restroom. When I do, my eyes immediately go to the empty seat she had been sitting in. She's gone. I feel a sense of relief coupled with disappointment. When I sit back down at the table, Jason's giving me a weird look. I don't know if he saw Rayna, but he definitely knows something is up with me.

She called me twice last night, then showed up to Denny's wearing my sweatshirt, hiding what I'm assuming is a hangover underneath that hood. Is that all her calls were? A drunken mistake? It's exactly what I was afraid of. I don't want to be Rayna's drunken mistake. I don't ever want her to think of me as a mistake, but that's how I feel right now. Like everything her and I have been through since August has been a mistake. How could I have been falling in love with someone who has to act like I don't exist outside the confinements of her condo?

I sit at the table in silence until the server brings our check. Jason covers the tab, even though I offer. He just waves me off like it's a ridiculous assumption that he wouldn't just pick it up.

The group thanks him before we head back to my truck. I've only mumbled a few words since spotting Rayna. I know they can tell something is wrong with me, Jason especially. But he doesn't dare question me until we're back home. Bexley leaves with her roommates, and I don't know where Emily is, but she's not with Jason when he walks into my room, shutting the door behind him.

"What happened at the diner?" he asks, taking a seat at my desk.

I'm sprawled out on my bed, my hands covering my face as I try and fail to forget all thoughts of Rayna. She consumes my mind. And now Jason wants to talk about her, so not thinking of her isn't an option right now. "Rayna was there."

"Shit."

"She was wearing my baseball hoodie. She showed up alone. Sat at the counter."

"Did you go talk to her? Is that why you went to the bathroom?"

"No. I hid in the bathroom like a fucking coward."

"Oh."

"She was gone when I came back out."

Jason leans forward in the chair, his elbows resting on his knees while he presses his hands together. "What happened with Bexley last night?" he asks.

"Nothing. She slept downstairs."

"Did you want something to happen?"

"No."

"Why?"

"She's not Rayna."

"Bro, no one's going to be Rayna. No one except Rayna."

"Exactly. That's why I'm fucked."

"Just talk to her again. You haven't been yourself since you two ended things."

"She called me twice last night, but I was already passed out. Do you think I should call her back? See what she wanted?"

"Is that what you want to do?"

"I don't know."

"I think you need to talk to a chick. Want me to get Emily in here?"

"No."

He nods.

"You two seem happy," I say.

"Yeah. We're happy."

"Good. Now get out of my room. I'm going back to sleep."

He stands and walks out, leaving me to feel more alone than I've ever felt in my entire life.

Chapter Twenty-Four

Rayna

He looked as white as a ghost the second he spotted me in the diner. Then he rushed to the restroom, much like our encounter at Off Base. The difference, I didn't follow. I didn't run into him in the hallway outside the restroom. We didn't leave together. I left alone. I threw a couple bills on the counter for my coffee before I made a run for it. Worst part? I'm wearing his damn sweatshirt. Couple that with the fact that I drunk dialed him last night *twice*. He'd had to have seen the missed calls by now. He didn't call back, didn't text to see what I wanted. Nothing. Silence.

Damn it.

I drive around aimlessly, wanting to be anywhere but at home right now. I've been to that Denny's a few times since I've moved here. There's something about diner coffee and the smell of greasy bacon that appeals to me. It reminds me of Sunday mornings when my mom used to have breakfast ready for Sam and me before we even woke up.

I eventually make it back to my condo after my poor attempt to avoid it. Apparently, it's the safest place for me to be so that I don't risk running into Hayes again. I scan the key card to open my door just as my phone starts to ring in my pocket. I pull it out and look on the screen.

Hayes.

He's calling me.

Shit.

I hesitate for three seconds before answering the phone with shaky hands. "Hello?"

Silence meets me. I know he's there, I can hear his breathing, but he doesn't speak.

"Hayes?" I whisper.

"Rayna," his gruff voice echoes.

I don't know what to say. I called last night because I was drunk. I wanted to see him.

"Are you okay?" he asks.

"Yeah. I'm okay," I lie, because no part of me is okay right now.

"You called me last night."

"I know. I'm sorry."

"Why?" He sounds nervous, as if he's afraid the only reason I called was because I was drunk. It was the middle of the night, so it's safe for him to assume that's why I called. And he'd be right. Though, the alcohol only gave me the courage to do what I've wanted to do all week.

"I wanted to see you," I answer honestly.

"At two in the morning?"

"I'm sorry. It was inappropriate. I shouldn't have called, especially not in the middle of the night."

He sighs. "Do you still want to see me? You left the diner. It didn't seem like you wanted to see me then."

"I drank too much last night, Hayes. I shouldn't have called." I don't know why I said that. I should be saying, *Yes, I still want to see you.*

"Alright."

It's silent on both ends of the line, neither of us knowing what to say next.

"Yes," I finally say.

"Yes?"

"Yes. Yes, I still want to see you."

"Has something changed for you, Rayna?"

"What do you mean?" I ask.

"Has something changed for you? Or am I going to come over, continue to fall in love with you, only to still be kept a secret? For everything to be exactly how it was before?"

My eyes fill with tears, and I press my hand to my mouth to muffle my cries. "No," I whisper.

I'm met again with silence. Then, "Goodbye, Rayna."

He hangs up and I sob, collapsing in front of my door in a pathetic puddle of nothing.

The following Tuesday, the lecture hall fills up just before the start of class. I notice the hitch in my breathing the second Hayes walks into the room. I always notice when he walks in. He sits in his usual seat next to Jason and Kevin.

The easiest way for me to distribute the midterms to the class is by calling out their names one by one. When I call out Hayes's name, he stands and walks down the steps toward me, seemingly looking unaffected by the closeness we are about to encounter. Me, on the other hand, my legs feel like they're about to give out.

I hand him his midterm.

He takes it without muttering a word, not even making eye contact.

I spend the rest of the lecture reviewing each of the questions from the exam.

When the class leaves, Hayes once again does not look my way. One second, he's in my lecture hall. The next, he's not.

Once he's gone, I can finally breathe again.

The following Thursday, he walks in a few minutes late. The rest of the class is seated, and I've already begun my lecture when all eyes move to Hayes as the door creaks open. He walks in and takes his usual seat, ignoring the stares. He pulls out his notebook and laptop, and I continue on with my lecture. It's as though he doesn't notice me. It's as if I'm not even there.

Chapter Twenty-Five

Hayes

The weeks go by slowly. I go to class. I go to practice. I go to work. I go to parties. I stop drinking excessively during the week, though Saturdays are fair game since Coach has always designated Sundays as a mandatory day of rest.

I continue to ignore Rayna's existence. It's just easier that way. Easier than looking into those damn turquoise eyes and falling under their spell. If I wanted to sleep with her again, I know I could. She called because she wanted to see me in the middle of the night. What other reason could there be other than a late-night booty call? She said nothing changed for her, so what would be the point of putting myself through that?

Bexley hangs out with us a few more times, mostly at parties. I can tell she's starting to develop a crush on me, or whatever it is girls call it these days. Maybe she just wants to fuck, I don't know. I know I'm still broken over Rayna though, because I haven't even entertained the idea.

Before I met Rayna, Bexley would've been exactly the kind of girl I'd want to be with. She's actually a lot like Emily. But nothing with Bexley would ever be long-term, so again, what's the point? Jason argues that I should just sleep with her already so I can fuck Rayna out of my mind. He doesn't get it though. I can't. The only way I can get off anymore is doing exactly what I did in the shower the night before that party. Rayna's the only one who does it for me. I'd have to imagine that Bexley was Rayna to even get hard, and Bexley doesn't deserve that. I'm living in my own personal hell, having to fuck my hand to thoughts of my professor who would willingly sleep with me but wants nothing more. Sounds like a dream to anyone else. Not to me.

It's almost Thanksgiving. It's been one month since Rayna and I last spoke. I still see her every Tuesday and Thursday morning in her lecture hall. I don't go to office hours. I avoid Denny's. I avoid Off Base. I even avoid driving the road that leads to her condo. I'm fucking pathetic.

It's why I'm excited to head home this weekend for Thanksgiving break. Coach scheduled a few practices right after the holiday, giving us a nice break before our season kicks into full gear. After Thanksgiving, things begin to pick up. There's a small break again for Christmas and the New Year, but after that our season truly begins. Preseason practice is six days a week, some days consisting of weight training after batting practice. The off-season is when things are more laxed, but preseason really gets us into the mindset to start off spring ball on the right track.

The team is looking good this year, and I've been working with the new pitcher a lot. He's going to be my relief pitcher to prepare him for next year when he'll be leading the team. He's showing a lot of potential.

I try to ignore the twinge of jealously and rage I feel when I walk into Sports Nutrition this morning and see her speaking with Dan. It's the first time I've seen him in over a month, after I watched him put his hands on Rayna and stand way too fucking close. Thankfully, he's keeping a respectful distance this time. Normally I make it a point to not let Rayna know I've noticed her. I don't make eye contact. I look in any direction but hers, though I've *always* noticed her. I *always* see her. But I don't pretend today. I want her to know that I see him. That I see *them*. More importantly, I want her to know that I still want to be the one standing next to her in public. The one to ward off other guys when they hit on her. I don't know if that's what is happening right now, but anyone can see the twinkle in his eyes as he stares at her. That guy is enthralled with Rayna, and justifiably so. I've never met a woman who was not only as beautiful as her, but as smart as her. Compassionate. Kind. Loving. She's fucking everything I want and can't have.

I take a seat next to Jason, my eyes still locked on Rayna and Dan. She laughs at something he says, and I feel the knots in my stomach tighten. I haven't heard that laugh in a long time. Dan smiles, mesmerized by Rayna. I'd do anything to be him right now.

He walks out a minute later and Rayna turns, her eyes immediately drawn to my seat. To me. She freezes, her smile dropping. I haven't looked at her in over a month, and she knows it. She also knows that I just saw Dan. That I still don't like the way he looks at her. Can she see that I still care? That I want to be the one to look at her like that? I want to be everything for her, if she'd just give me the fucking chance.

Her shoulders drop as she turns quickly and rushes into her office. Class is supposed to start any minute, and it's not like Rayna to start late. It's also not like her to disappear into her office with an auditorium full of students, though that's exactly what she does. And it's not like me to stand up and follow her into her office, but that's what I do.

Jason calls out for me. I ignore him. The auditorium is filled with chatter, no one else noticing me as I'm making my way to Professor James's office. I don't knock on her door. I open it and shut it behind me before she can object to my being here.

I find her staring out the window behind her desk, her hands crossed over her chest. She doesn't turn around. I think she already knows it's me.

"Why are you in here, Hayes?" she mumbles, confirming my thoughts. I can tell she's crying.

It's taking the entire weight of the world to hold me back right now, to keep me from wrapping her petite frame in my arms the way I want to. "Are you okay?"

This makes her turn around. "Do I look okay?" she asks. Her eyes are bloodshot and puffy, her nose red from her rubbing it. Even her pouty lips seem poutier, sadder.

"You look beautiful," I answer softly. Because she does. Always.

"You should go back out there. I'll be out in a minute to start class."

"Are you okay?" I ask again.

"No, Hayes. No. I'm not."

"Can we talk after class?"

"I'm flying to Chicago this afternoon. We're having an early Thanksgiving since I'll be in DC next week."

"I thought you said you would be home in time for Thanksgiving?"

"The conference ends at five Wednesday night and there weren't any available flights to Chicago until Thursday morning. Figured it would be better to spend a long weekend there than to rush and miss half of Thanksgiving."

"So, you're going to spend Thanksgiving Day alone?"

She shakes her head. "Not entirely. I'll still be in DC with the other professors until our flight back to Timbers."

"Right." I nod. "Dan will keep you company."

"It's not like that, Hayes. I already told you."

"It's like that for him. How can you not see that?"

"Just leave it alone. I'm not your problem anymore."

"That's not by choice, baby."

A soft knock sounds on the door.

Rayna quickly wipes at her eyes before whoever is knocking enters.

Jason peeks his head inside.

"What are you doing?" I ask.

"Professor James," Jason says, looking at Rayna and ignoring me. "I'm sorry to interrupt. Class was supposed to start a few minutes ago. I know your *reputation* is important to you, and I don't think you want to start the rumor mills going that class started late because you were busy doing something you shouldn't be with my friend here." He finally looks to me.

"Thank you, Jason. We were just finishing up. I'll be out there in a second."

She turns her back to me, and I take that as my signal to leave. I follow Jason up the steps to our seats.

Rayna walks out a few minutes later, apologizing that she had to take care of a few questions a student had, that student evidently being me. No one can probably tell she's been crying. She continues with the entire lecture as if nothing ever happened, as if she wasn't just looking at me like I had intentionally ripped her heart out and fed it to the wolves. But I can tell. She hasn't been herself in a long time. Not as happy, as bubbly. It's like she's a shell too. We're both walking around as empty versions of ourselves, incapable of being full without one another.

That's when I realize we're done falling. We've already landed. I'm in love with her. And she's in love with me too.

Chapter Twenty-Six

Rayna

I board my flight set to land at ORD at five-thirty. Sam is picking me up from terminal three before we drive the forty-five minutes to my dad's house in Chicago, though it'll more than likely be over an hour with the rush hour traffic. He lives in a modern three-story building overlooking Lake Michigan in one of Chicago's wealthier neighborhoods, Lincoln Park. It was renovated from a two-flat apartment with a basement to a single-family home. I'm excited to spend a few days there. I haven't been since I left for Michigan, and after the day I've had today, I could really use the break.

I take my seat in first class, the conversation between Hayes and I playing on repeat in my head. He called me right after class, but I didn't have it in me to answer. Emotionally, I just couldn't handle it. I needed time. Time to relax. Time to think. Time away from Timbers and East Valley and him.

When I saw him looking at me in class for the first time in over a month, I broke out in a cold sweat. His face was almost emotionless, though his eyes told a different story. He noticed Dan. He wanted *me* to know he noticed Dan. To know that it still bothered him what he saw between us. Dan hasn't asked me on anymore dates, hasn't hinted at wanting to be anything more than just friends. I think he respects the boundaries I've put in place. But I couldn't keep my emotions in check when our eyes met. I ran for my office, knowing he'd follow. I don't know how I knew — I just did. And sure enough, he had. His presence was overwhelming, and I knew instantly that it was him who had walked in. If his friend Jason hadn't walked in when he did, I don't know where that conversation would have led. It's better that I don't. I just need to focus on myself and my family this weekend. To be thankful for what I do have, even if that doesn't include Hayes.

I doze off during the short flight. When I find Sam waiting outside of baggage claim, I wave to him, a big smile spreading across my face. Sam's my older brother. He had more time with Mom than I did, and I think he's always felt especially sorry that I lost my mom at such a young age. Him and my dad sometimes treat me like a fragile piece of china that may crack at any moment. I know they do it out of love, but it's another one of the reasons I needed to get out of Chicago. To prove that I can stand on my own two feet.

Sam smiles, getting out of the car to wrap his arms around me in one of his giant hugs. Sam is tall, towering over my small frame by at least a foot. He used to play basketball but stopped after he graduated from Northwestern.

"How's my baby sis?" he asks as he takes my luggage, hauling it into the trunk of his Lexus.

I smile. "Good. I've missed you."

"Not as much as we've missed you. I can't wait to hear all about your little town in Michigan."

An hour later, we're pulling up to my dad's house. Sam moved out shortly after Mom passed away and has lived in the same high-rise apartment complex downtown for the last decade. He parks on the street, grabs my luggage out of the trunk, and carries it up the few steps to the front porch. We walk in using Sam's key. The house is quiet, and at first, I think my dad isn't home until I hear shuffling upstairs followed by his heavy footsteps as he makes his way down the tall flight of stairs.

"There's my baby girl," he says, eyes gleaming.

"Hi, Dad," I say, though it's muffled with the way he squeezes my body against his chest.

My dad is a big burley guy, still quite handsome even in his fifties. My mom was the most beautiful woman I'd ever seen. Dad always says that her beauty is unmatched. Together, they were a couple that turned heads. This is the longest I've gone without seeing my dad. Without seeing Sam. They're the only family I've got, and part of me feels guilty for leaving them the way I did.

After the initial greetings and small talk, we take a seat on the couch in the living room, Sam disappearing for a second before returning with two glasses of red wine and a beer for Dad.

"Tell me all about this job you left me for," Dad says with a smile on his face, though I know his words are coupled with sadness.

"I love it," I answer honestly. "My students seem to have taken a liking to me as well. At the midterm, I only had one student who was on the verge of failing and I worked with him closely to get his grade back up. He did well on his last exam, so he shouldn't have a problem passing the class now."

"It's important to you that all your students pass," my dad acknowledges.

"Of course, it is."

"I wish my professors were more like that. They would have happily handed me a failing grade," Sam mumbles.

I laugh. "Oh, please. You were incapable of receiving anything below an A plus. You're an overachiever, just like Dad."

"Don't act like my little girl isn't just as big an over achiever now," my dad says.

"I'm not. I didn't get straight As."

"That's not a prerequisite to being an over achiever, honey."

"Dad, you and Sam are like two peas in a pod. You both work too hard, too much."

"And you aren't like us, Rayna? You don't work too hard? Too much? Because I seem to remember a lot of late-night phone calls from you over the last few months and you telling me you had just gotten home. Something about making your office hours *flexible*."

"That's not the same as working into all hours of the night, Dad. I just try to make myself available to my students. So, I can help them. If they want to succeed, then why not do what I can to help?"

My dad laughs. "Rayna, that's all I try to do every day. Help my clients succeed. They want to win their cases. They need me to do that, and I do what I can to help. I give them what time I have. You're more like me than you'd like to admit. Your mother always knew that about you and your brother. She joked that she was merely just an incubator. That she had just made miniature versions of me."

My face turns solemn with the mention of Mom. She's not someone we talk about often. I know it still upsets him to think of her and what we used to have. "I always thought I was more like Mom," I admit.

"You look just like your mother did at your age," he says. "She gave me the most beautiful little girl in the world. But your ambition? Your drive? That's all me, sweetie."

"Mom used to complain that you worked too much."

He nods. "She did. I didn't work nearly as much as I do now. She always came first. As do you and Sam. That's why I'm here and not at the office right now. I don't plan on going back in until you hop on that flight out of here. Your mother would strangle me if she saw me putting work before the people I love most."

I know he's only joking because Mom obviously isn't here anymore to strangle him, but the thought still brings a smile to my face. "I miss her," I whisper.

Dad brings his arm around me and pulls me in. "I miss her too, Rayna. Everyday."

"I wish I could talk to her. Just one more time."

"It would never be enough. I could have spent every single day of my life with your mom, and it still wouldn't be enough."

Sam sits across from us silently.

"Come here," I say, motioning him to sit next to me. He does, and I wrap my free arm around him. I'm sandwiched between my dad and Sam, two of the people I love most in this world.

I realize that taking my dream job and moving to another state doesn't mean I put work before the people I love most, it just means I was following my dreams. But if Dad or Sam ever asked me to move back home, I would in an instant. There are other jobs out there. Other schools I can teach at. There's so much possibility and endless opportunities that it's foolish of me to assume I'll be teaching at East Valley for the rest of my life. I've put my career first recently, not opening myself up to the opportunity of more change. I don't want to settle. I don't want to dictate my entire life on my desire to teach at my dream school. There could be other dream schools.

My dad doesn't even realize it, but he's said exactly what I've needed to hear all along. Likely what Mom would have told me if she were here. I've pushed Hayes away because of a job. I turned away the possibility of a happier life, a loving relationship, all because of where I wanted to earn my paycheck for the time being.

Suddenly, I can't wait to get back to Timbers. I fight back the urge to call Hayes and tell him that I'm in love with him. That I want everything with him, the dates, the baseball games, the rolling around in the sheets with him at all hours of the night. I want to tell him to hell with my reputation, my job. If I lost my job because of my relationship with him, then I could find another. I want to tell him that I don't care if he plays baseball for a team in another country, I want to be there too so long as he's there. I want to choose him just as he keeps choosing me. I want to put him first. Our happiness, our *love*.

I had no idea just how badly I needed this trip, time with the people I love most to realize what I already knew. That my life isn't complete. There's one person missing.

After a much-needed holiday break and an early Thanksgiving dinner with my dad and Sam, I am boarding my flight from ORD to DCA. Washington DC this time of year is likely as cold as it is in Chicago, though not as cold as Michigan. The news is reporting a snowstorm, expecting over ten inches to accumulate over the next three days in Timbers. Growing up in Chicago, I'm used to snowstorms. Though, this one is supposed to be accompanied by high wind gusts and power outages. If you don't have a gas heater, they're suggesting you seek shelter that does.

The storm isn't something I need to worry about, seeing as I am on a direct flight to the capital and most of Timbers is emptied out for Thanksgiving break. Hopefully the news issued their warning to residents early enough so they could seek out accommodations.

I haven't spoken to Hayes since last Thursday in my office. I was tempted more than once over the last few days to call him, but I refrained because I really want this to be an in-person conversation. I know I love him, and the realization that I am putting my career first hit me like a ton of bricks. What would my mom say? She'd be so disappointed in me for choosing a job over the person I love. She taught me better than that, and she made sure my dad put us first always, no matter how important his job was. And he always has. Now it is my turn to show Hayes just how much he means to me.

The flight to DC is short, a little over two hours before I am landing on the icy tarmac of DCA. Most of my coworkers flew out of Detroit. Dan said his flight was set to land thirty minutes before mine, so he offered to wait for me so we could take a shuttle to the hotel together.

Once the plane completes its taxi into the gate, I reach into the overhead bin to grab my carry-on luggage. I packed everything I might need for my week away from Timbers into a tiny suitcase. I find Dan waiting right outside my gate. He isn't with Andrea or Nick, and I wonder if they are using the restroom or if they went ahead and got their own shuttle to the hotel.

I smile at Dan as I approach, rolling my suitcase behind me with my purse slung over my shoulder. "Hi."

"Hey. Have a good flight?" he asks.

I nod. "Not bad."

He reaches for my suitcase. "Here, let me."

I allow him to take my luggage. He pulls it behind him, his own in a leather duffle bag slung over his shoulder.

"Where are Andrea and Nick?" I ask as we make our way through the terminals and into baggage claim to call a shuttle.

"They were on an earlier flight. They landed this morning."

I frown. "Oh. I thought Andrea said you guys were all flying together?"

"I switched my flight to a later one. I had some things I needed to take care of. Besides, it all worked out. Now we're able to take the shuttle to the hotel together."

I nod.

Dan calls the hotel to let them know we've landed. Twenty minutes later, the hotel shuttle arrives, picking up Dan and I along with a young couple and their two kids.

It's a short ride to the hotel, and soon we are checking into our rooms. Dan's room is on the same floor as mine, as are Andrea and Nick's. The hotel we are staying in has twenty-six floors, so I wonder if this was a request made on our account.

Dan and I ride the elevator up to the fourteenth floor.

"Andrea said her room is 1402. Nick is 1427," Dan says.

I look at my keycard. "I'm in 1414."

Nick smiles. "I'm 1415. Looks like we're neighbors."

The elevator chimes before the doors open. Dan is still rolling my suitcase for me, stopping in front of my room. I scan the key card and open the door. He rolls my suitcase in, setting it on the luggage rack.

"Thanks," I say.

"Did you want to grab dinner with us in an hour? Andrea made reservations at the restaurant."

"Sure. I'll meet you down there."

He smiles. "Okay. See you soon." He exits, shutting my door behind him.

I plop onto the bed. My room is modern, with a flat screen TV and a queen-size bed with numerous throw pillows on top. There's a small table with two chairs and a long dresser if I choose to not live out of my suitcase. Most of what I brought for this trip will need to be hung in the closet though, once it's been ironed.

It's been hard to keep Hayes from my thoughts ever since the realization of what I've done struck on Thursday. Three nights later, it's still all I can think about. I know it'll still be another week until I can see him. I don't know when he was planning on going home for Thanksgiving, but I do know I won't be back before he leaves and that he is supposed to come back next Sunday. We were going to have our own Thanksgiving together. I wonder if he's thought about that. I know I have.

An hour later, I'm dressed in one of my black business dresses. This is a business trip after all, so it's important to look professional whenever I leave my hotel room. You never know what introductions might be made outside the four walls of my room.

I spot Dan waiting for me near the elevator doors in the lobby.

"You look nice," he says.

"Thanks."

We walk together into the restaurant. Andrea and Nick are sitting at the bar, both sipping on martinis.

Andrea eyes me first, immediately standing with a big grin on her face as we approach. "You made it!" she shouts. I can tell she isn't on her first drink. "It's about time. Good thing Dan switched his flight so you wouldn't be alone the entire trip here, but he almost got stuck from that snowstorm. They're delaying all flights in and out of Detroit until at least Wednesday."

"Really?"

She nods. "How was Chicago?"

"Relaxing. And much needed. How long have you guys been here?"

Nick takes over the conversation. "Probably longer than necessary, but someone was ready to drink the second our flight took off from DTW."

"Oh, please. Today is the only day we don't have anything work related on the agenda. Sunday fun day!"

Dan laughs before taking a seat on the barstool next to Nick. The only open seat is the one on the other side of Dan, so I take it.

"What are you drinking?" Dan asks me.

I glance at the drink menu, then eye Andrea. "I think I'll have what she's having."

Dan chuckles. "Okay." He looks to the bartender. "Two of whatever she's on."

"They said our table will be ready in a few minutes," Nick says. He looks over Dan's shoulder at me and smiles. "You look nice, Rayna."

I notice Dan's shoulders stiffen but do my best to ignore it. "Thanks."

The bartender brings my drink, and I unexpectedly finish it in three gulps.

"Damn," Dan says. "Must've been thirsty."

I eye the bartender. "I'll take another."

"That's my girl," Andrea says. "Dan, switch seats with me." Andrea stands up, not giving Dan much of a choice.

Reluctant, he gets up and switches seats.

The bartender brings me another martini, and Andrea and I clink glasses in cheers.

"So," she does her best attempt to whisper. "What's going on there?"

"Where?"

She nudges her head back. "Oh, come on. Everyone knows he's had his eye on you since the second you started working at East Valley."

"Dan?" I ask.

She nods.

"Nothing's going on there. He asked me to go to dinner once a while ago, but it didn't happen. We're just friends."

"I don't think *he* wants to be just friends."

"It's not like that."

"Well, what about Nick then? He's sexy."

"Andrea!"

Nick laughs behind her. "I can hear you. You think I'm sexy?"

Andrea waves him off. "Please. I think everyone is sexy when I'm drinking. You too, Dan. You're a good-looking bunch. Remind me why you're both single?"

Nick counters Andrea, "Why are *you two* still single?"

"Who says I'm single?" Andrea says.

"Let me take you out, without these two." Nick nudges his head in mine and Dan's direction.

"Hell no."

"Why not?"

"Because you both eye Rayna like she's the last woman on this earth. Neither of you are very sly about it, if you ask me. Besides, you're not my type." She pauses for a moment. "Rayna is," she says matter-of-factly.

My face reddens. Why is she doing this? Why is she calling them out? And Andrea is gay? I had no idea. So, I'm about to eat dinner with three people who all want to see me naked? Fun.

I wave down the bartender. "I need two tequila shots please."

Nick laughs. "Relax, Rayna. You're hot. But I don't have puppy dog eyes for you, unlike someone over here."

Dan has stayed quiet up until this point. "I'm going to see if our table is ready." He stands and walks to the hostess kiosk at the same time my shots arrive.

I down them one after another.

"Rayna," Andrea whispers. "Did I freak you out?"

"Nope. Just stressed me out a little."

"Sorry. Vodka tends to make me speak what's on my mind."

I smile. "It's okay. And you're beautiful, Andrea. But you know you're not my type, right?"

She laughs. "Yes. Unlike you, my gaydar works just fine."

"How come you never told me?"

She shrugs. "What's there to tell? Sometimes it freaks girls out. I didn't want to make you uncomfortable."

"That doesn't make me uncomfortable." I eye Dan as he talks to the hostess and then Nick. "But you guys are my only friends in Timbers. I don't want anything to be weird."

"Don't worry, Rayna. Dan has done a good job so far of accepting that you're just friends. It doesn't have to change now, not if you don't want it to."

"I don't."

Dan returns to the bar. "Our table is ready."

"Finally," Nick mutters.

Nick and Andrea start walking to the hostess kiosk.

Dan lingers behind as I take out a few bills for the shots. "Sorry about that," he says quietly.

I shake my head. "Don't worry about it."

I take a few steps forward until I'm in front of Dan. I feel him press his hand to the small of my back as he leads me toward the table where Andrea and Nick are now sitting. I try not to tense under his touch, but it's hard not to after everything that's just been said.

We take a seat at the four-person booth. Dan slides into the seat next to me, our thighs brushing. I order another martini because I suddenly feel like there's no way to get through the rest of this dinner without being drunk.

After another three martinis and a few bites of the appetizers we ordered to share, I am sufficiently wasted and ready to crawl into my bed. Problem is, I can hardly keep myself upright. The room spins around me, and I can feel myself slumped over, leaning on someone's shoulder, presumably Dan since he's the one who sat next to me. It's definitely time for me to go to bed. Dan helps me out of the booth. My legs feel like Jell-O beneath me as I stand. Dan hooks his arm around my waist, and the only reason I'm standing is because he's holding all my weight up. I hope we don't walk by anyone important. This would not be a good impression at my first HECA conference.

He somehow gets me into the elevator. All my body weight is pressed against him. His back is pushed against the elevator walls while my back is flush with his chest, leaning on him because if I don't, I'll fall. I'm drunk, but I can still recognize the feel of him hardening against my backside. If I wasn't full of so much alcohol, I'd probably be mortified. But right now, all I can think of is getting into my room. Into my bed. And I can't do that without Dan right now.

The elevator takes an eternity to reach the fourteenth floor. Once it stops, I thank the high heavens for allowing us to take that ride without any other guests. I'm already embarrassed for how much I drank, but I'm even more embarrassed that Dan having to hold me is turning him on and there's not a damn thing I can do to stop it from happening. I don't even think I could form words if I tried. If I speak, I'm not sure it would be coherent.

I cling to Dan as we walk toward my room.

"Where's your keycard, Rayna?" he asks.

I try to talk, but something like *hurse* comes out of my mouth. I know he understands that as purse because he reaches inside and pulls out my keycard.

The door opens, and I almost collapse from the amount of effort it took to get from the restaurant to my room. Dan stops me from faceplanting and picks me up, carrying me like a child as my head rests against his chest.

"Thanks," I murmur as he sets me down on the bed.

He pulls back the covers, tucking me in underneath them. He disappears for a moment before returning with some water. "Here. Drink some water, Rayna."

I lift my head, my arms apparently immobile as Dan lifts the cup to my mouth. I take a few sips before my head crashes back down to the pillow. "Sorry," I say. At least that's what I think I say.

My words must be more decipherable than I thought because he quiets me and tells me there's nothing to be sorry for. His fingers brush gently down my long, dark hair. He moves a few pieces out of my face. I don't have the energy to tell him to stop. I'm not sure I want to because it feels good and is helping me to relax. When his hand cups my cheek, I lean into his warm touch. I'm on the verge of falling asleep when I suddenly feel his lips brush against mine. It's a quick kiss, but there's no denying it happened. When my eyes suddenly fly open, Dan backs off.

"I'm sorry," he says, his hands in the air. "I'm so sorry."

My lip's part to say something, anything, but words don't come out.

Dan walks out of my room before I have the chance to form whatever sentence I was trying to say.

I lay in bed, feeling every bit as drunk yet somehow a little more sober from what just happened. I could see the guilt written on his face. Whatever drove him to do that, he instantly regretted it.

A soft knock sounds on my door a second later. I know it's probably Dan wanting to apologize for kissing me. It takes every ounce of strength I have to get out of bed. I cling to the walls and make my way slowly to the door. I pass a mirror on my way, getting a look at myself. What I see is not pretty. My hair is a frizzy mess from laying on the pillow, my lipstick has rubbed off, and my eyes look as red and bloodshot as they did the last time I smoked pot in high school. It's safe to say I look like shit. Good news? Dan's already seen me like this and it doesn't matter what I look like for the inevitable apology.

But when I open the door, it's not Dan I see.

Chapter Twenty-Seven

Hayes

I knew she was landing in DC today, I just didn't know when. She had told me all about this trip last month when she first heard about it, so I knew small details that I didn't think were important until now, like which hotel she would be staying at. Her trip to Chicago was news to me, and after leaving her office Thursday, I knew the first chance I would have to see her short of showing up at her dad's house would be when she arrived in DC. Her conference starts tomorrow, and she's here until Thanksgiving. I couldn't stand the thought of not seeing her for ten days after leaving things the way we did last Thursday. So, here I am. I drove eight hours straight today, having no idea what time her flight from Chicago would land. I checked into my room a few hours ago. The receptionist wouldn't give me her hotel room number, so I waited in the lobby hoping like hell I would run into her. After several days and an eight-hour drive, waiting a few more hours to see her shouldn't be a big deal.

I only had to sit in the lobby for a little over an hour before I see her. Unfortunately, I don't like what I see. Dan has his arm wrapped around her waist, holding her up and walking her to the elevator. I watch them get on, then watch as the digital numbers above the elevator door indicate which floor they are on. It stops on floor fourteen.

I hop on the next elevator and ride it to the fourteenth floor. When I get off, there is no one in the hallway. I impatiently pace the floor, trying to listen for Rayna's voice in one of the rooms. Dan steps out of a room moments later before walking across the hall, into another room. He doesn't notice me as I hide around the corner. Rayna isn't with him, so I can only assume the room he just left is hers.

I hurry to what is hopefully Rayna's room. Room 1414. I hesitate, then knock because I honestly am not sure what I just witnessed. I knock softly, feeling like I am going to piss my pants from nerves. What will she say when she sees me? Will she be happy? Mad? Why was Dan in her room in the first place? Thoughts of him holding Rayna in the lobby makes my fists clench.

Rayna opens the door a few minutes later, and immediately, I know she is drunk. Her eyes are blood shot and her hair is a mess, but she somehow still manages to take my breath away. Her mouth parts as if to say something, but words don't escape her. She has one hand on the wall, the other on the door, holding herself up.

"Can I come in?" I ask.

Her mouth remains parted as her head bobs up and down. She tries to take a step back, her hand still holding the door open, but she loses her footing and almost collapses. I quickly reach out, grasping her by her waist to keep her upright.

"How much did you have to drink, Rayna?"

She doesn't answer, but she doesn't need to. The answer is clearly too much. I hold her up and guide her back to her bed. She plops down ungracefully. I take a seat next to her. Obviously, tonight isn't going to be the night I can talk to her. I have no idea how long her conference is each day, but this is going to have to wait until she's sober.

"Lay down, Rayna. I'll call you tomorrow, and we can talk."

She grabs my wrist quickly when I go to pull back the blankets to cover her. "No. Stay."

I nod once. "Do you want me to get you some more comfortable clothes?" She's wearing a tight black dress that is probably the least comfortable thing to sleep in.

She moves her head up and down, mumbling a yes.

I find her suitcase on the luggage rack and shuffle through, smiling when I eye one of my T-shirts. I grab it and toss it onto the bed.

"I'm going to unzip your dress, okay?"

Her head bobs again.

I reach behind her and unzip the dress until it's loose enough to pull over her head. Her arms shoot up, and I maneuver the dress over her until she's left in nothing but her bra and panties. Knowing Rayna like I do, I know she would never want to sleep in her bra. I reach behind her again to unclasp it before grabbing the T-shirt and slipping it over her. I take her discarded clothes and lay them on top of her suitcase.

When I return to the bed, Rayna is sprawled out across it, half beneath the blankets. I reach for the comforter and pull it over her body. I feel like I need to leave, to let her sleep it off, but the only words she's managed to say out loud were those asking me to stay. I pull up a chair next to her bed. She reaches her hand out to me, her eyes heavy lidded and full of sleep. I hold onto her hand, gliding my fingers up and down her smooth forearm with my free hand. She falls asleep almost immediately.

An hour goes by. I look at the clock, seeing it's nearly eleven PM. I haven't eaten a thing since I stopped at a random rest stop on the drive here and ordered a burger. I call for room service, ordering something for Rayna as well so it can hopefully help soak up some of the alcohol.

I notice her stir when I finish reading off my credit card to the front desk. When I hang up, her eyes are open. She looks more alert, though her eyes are still red. She's probably already developed a killer headache.

I point to a glass of water sitting by her bed. "Drink some water. Do you have any Advil?" I ask.

She picks up the water glass and puts it to her lips. "Purse," she mumbles after taking a drink.

I find her purse and dig through it until I have the Advil, then pour two into my hand and slip them into her palm.

She takes them immediately, followed by more sips of water. "I thought I was dreaming. What are you doing here?" she asks.

"I came to see you."

"I see that. Why, Hayes?"

I take a deep breath. I guess I'm doing this now. "I love you, Rayna. I'm not just falling in love with you. I am *in* love with you, and I have been for a while. I can't keep pretending like you don't exist. I don't want to live in a world where you don't exist."

She's quiet for a few seconds, staring at me like she can't believe the words that just came out of my mouth.

"I love you too," she finally says.

"What?"

She smiles. "I love you too, Hayes."

I smile, the biggest, cheesiest grin I can manage before I take her face in my hands and pull her in for a kiss. I'm careful not to make her move too suddenly, as I'm sure her head is pounding. But she can't tell me she loves me and expect me to not want to kiss her.

I nuzzle my face into her neck and continue to kiss her, and she giggles and squirms beneath me.

"Say it again," I urge her.

"I love you."

I continue to kiss her, my dick growing hard beneath my jeans. I ignore it, because there will be plenty of time for that later when she's feeling better. But right now, all I want to do is hold her, touch her, be here with her. I scoot myself next to her, wrapping my arm around her until my head is resting on the same pillow as hers. "Why did you drink so much, Rayna?"

"I was having a bad night."

163

Before I can ask about it, there's a knock at the door. "I ordered us room service. You should probably eat something."

She nods as I get off the bed and walk to the door. When I open it, it's not room service that's standing there. It's fucking Dan.

"What do you want?" I hiss.

He looks taken back by my presence, as he should. There are probably a million and one things running through his mind right now, like *Who is this guy? Why is he in Rayna's room? How did he get in Rayna's room?* But then I see the recognition in his eyes, and I know exactly what questions he's thinking now. *Why is there a student in Rayna's room? Why is Hayes Murphy in Rayna's room? How did Hayes Murphy get into Rayna's room?*

"Is...uh...I came to check on Rayna. Is she okay?"

"She's drunk."

"I know." He sighs, running his fingers through his hair. "Hayes, right?"

I nod.

"I need to talk to her."

"I'm sure she'll come talk to you if and when she feels like it."

"Rayna?" he calls over my shoulder.

I roll my eyes as I hear her shuffling to get out of bed. She appears, wearing only my T-shirt and Dan's eyes bulge.

"Um...sorry. Rayna, can you just come talk to me when you get a chance?"

When she realizes what she's wearing, coupled with the fact that Dan just caught me, her student, in her hotel room, her face reddens. Her hands fly to her mouth, and her eyebrows raise as she dashes to the door, just as Dan is turning around to head back to his room.

"Dan, wait! It's not what it looks like!"

He vanishes behind his door across the hall.

Rayna turns to look at me, fear stricken. "Oh my God."

"It's okay, Rayna."

"I'm not wearing pants!"

"Nothing happened."

164

"He doesn't know that!"

"It's okay. Everything is fine. You didn't do anything wrong."

She takes a deep breath. "Hayes, I have one of my students in my hotel room with me right now. I'm not wearing any pants. And we may not have had sex just now, but we have in the past so that's just a moot point. Things *have* happened." She paces back and forth in front of her bed. "It's fine." I think she's talking to herself now. "I already accepted this. People were bound to find out, I was just hoping it would be on my terms." She waves her arms toward the door and looks at me. "Not like this. Shit. He kissed me, Hayes! He kissed me before you showed up."

"He *what*?" I asked, enraged.

"It wasn't like that...or, I don't know. Maybe it was. He apologized. I couldn't even say anything because I was on the verge of passing out. Speaking of, I feel like I could again. I'm still drunk, and this is all too much. Can you hand me my water?" She takes a seat at the end of the bed.

"I shouldn't have answered the door. I'm sorry. I thought it was room service."

She shakes her head. "Stop. It's not your fault. It's fine. He's not going to say anything."

"And what if he does, Rayna?" Is she going to let me go again? She can't keep changing her mind about us. She's either all in or she's not.

"Then we'll deal with it."

"Yeah?"

She smiles. "Yeah."

"What made you change your mind?"

"I was talking to my dad the other day about my mom and how she would drill it into his head that family comes first, *not* work. My dad is a workaholic, but he never made any of us feel like we were second fiddle. It's only a job. And there are hundreds more just like it. I'm sorry it took me so long to figure that out. But I love you, and I don't care where you end up playing next year. If you want me there, I'll be there. Even if you play in Alaska. But I imagine it's pretty cold there, and sometimes it's dark all the time. Is there a chance you could play in Alaska?"

I laugh and kneel in front of where she sits, taking her face in my hands. I pull back a strand of her hair and tuck it behind her ear. Her eyes gaze into mine, and I'm momentarily put back to the first time I saw them at Off Base. Their unique turquoise coloring, teal and green specs meshed into one beautiful color.

"There's no MLB team in Alaska," I say softly. "But if there was, you'd look adorable in a parka."

She grins. "I just want to be with you. I'm tired of hiding. I'm tired of keeping our worlds separate."

"So, you're going to be okay if you can't teach at East Valley?"

She nods. "I'll be just fine."

"I love you so much, Rayna."

"I love you too."

Chapter Twenty-Eight

Rayna

After the initial shock of Dan kissing me, Hayes showing up and telling me that he loves me, and Dan finding Hayes in my room, I begin to relax with a naked Hayes in bed next to me. Our room service arrived an hour ago, and after we filled up our stomachs, we took a shower together just like we used to. My head is still pounding, but I feel more content right now than I have in a long time. I've missed the feel of his body next to mine. I've missed the way he touches me and kisses me. He makes me feel beautiful and *loved*.

I look up to Hayes, his eyebrows furrowed ever so slightly. I can tell something's on his mind, even though he's trying hard not to think about whatever it is. "What are you thinking about?"

"What?"

I gently rub between his eyes. "You're all tense here. Something's up. What's wrong?"

"You can tell, huh?"

"Of course, I can."

He squeezes his arm around me, bringing me a little closer. "I'm trying not to run across the hall and beat the shit out of Dan for kissing you."

I let my head fall back down to his chest. "That's not necessary. I don't look at him like that."

"But he looks at you like that, Rayna. I've told you that from the start."

"Yes, well that was when he thought I was single. I'm pretty sure he figured out what was going on here."

"Good."

"Promise me, Hayes. Promise me you won't go hitting professors who look at me the wrong way. You can't get kicked off the team."

"I don't know if I can promise that."

"Hayes! Promise me! It's not worth it. And I can't come watch you play if you're not on the team."

"You're going to come watch?"

I grin. "Duh. Isn't that what you want?"

"Yes."

"Then I'll be at all your home games. And if I'm fired, then I'll come to the away ones too."

"You're not going to be fired."

"That's still to be determined right now."

"What time does your conference start tomorrow?"

I look at the clock and sigh. It's so late already. Or early, depending on which way you look at it. "Eight sharp. Should be done around six."

"Is it okay if I check out of my room tomorrow and stay in yours?"

"Yeah, of course. But how long are you staying? I feel bad I won't even be around most of the time."

He shrugs. "I've always wanted to see DC. I'll do some sightseeing during the day, and we can head out Wednesday night after you're finished."

"My flight is Thursday morning, though."

"About that..." He looks nervous.

"What is it?"

"I was hoping you'd drive back to Michigan with me. My parent's place is on the way to Timbers."

"You want me to meet your parents?"

"If you want to meet them, yes."

"What will they think when they find out I'm your professor?"

"They'll see how happy and in love their son is, and they'll be happy too. Don't worry, baby. They're going to love you just as much as I do."

"Okay. If you're sure."

He kisses the top of my head. "I've never been more sure of anything in my entire life."

I walk into the lobby the next morning at a quarter to eight with coffee in my hand. Hayes got up early and picked us up Starbucks. I spot Andrea and Nick outside of the conference room, both looking hungover as shit. I'm sure I don't look much better.

"Good morning," I say.

Nick smiles. "Good morning, Rayna. How are we feeling on this lovely morning?"

Andrea elbows him. "Give her a break. The girl needed a few drinks." She wraps her arm around me and whispers, "Seriously, though. How are you alive right now?"

"I'm good, you guys. I could be better. But I swear, I'm alright."

"It's going to be a long day," Nick says.

"Don't remind us," Andrea says.

"Have you guys seen Dan?" I ask.

Andrea raises her eyebrows. "Nope. Have *you* seen Dan?" she asks.

"Not since last night."

Just then Dan walks off the elevator. His eyes find me immediately and he quickly averts his gaze. "Morning," he says as he approaches.

Nick gives him a head nod followed by Andrea's chirpy good morning.

"Hey, can we talk?" I ask Dan quietly, away from Nick and Andrea's prying ears.

He looks at his watch. "Sure. I was going to grab a donut." He nods toward the breakfast table that's been set up for us. "Want to walk over with me?"

"Sure."

We walk in silence to the other end of the lobby.

Dan grabs a plate and slowly eyes the various pastries. "I'm sorry, Rayna. I shouldn't have kissed you," he finally says.

"No. You shouldn't have. But I also shouldn't have been that drunk in the first place. Thank you for bringing me to my room."

He doesn't acknowledge my thanks. We both know the real pressing issue here is that one of my students is currently in my hotel room.

"Dan, I'm going to tell you this, hoping that you'll respect me enough to let it come out on my own terms. I met Hayes Murphy *before* I started working at East Valley. I had no idea he was a student there, let alone *my* student. I tried to break it off the second I found out. Obviously, you can see that didn't last. I was afraid it would look bad or that I might get fired. But I'm willing to accept whatever happens to me because I can't just stop loving someone. So, I'm sorry you had to find out this way, but I would appreciate it if you could keep this between you and me until I have a chance to talk to administration about it."

"You've been with this guy since we met?" he asks.

I nod. "Basically, yes."

"I never stood a chance."

I give him a sympathetic smile. "You were my first friend here, Dan. You have no idea how much that means to me. I don't want to stop being friends just because there isn't something romantic between us."

He lets out a deep exhale. "You're beautiful, Rayna. And I don't just mean on the outside. He's a lucky guy, and I hope he treats you the way you deserve."

I smile, this time a real genuine smile. "He treats me like I can walk on water."

That gets a smirk out of Dan. "No one will hear about this from me."

"Thank you."

I get back into my room a little after six and find Hayes sprawled out on the bed shirtless, looking all the more attractive by the day.

He smiles up at me. "How was it?" he asks.

"Long. My ass hurts from sitting so much."

"You wanna go for a run?"

I shake my head. "Nah. I'm feeling lazy."

He smirks. "You want me to massage your ass?"

I pick up a pillow and throw it at his head. "What did you do today?"

"Walked around mostly. Saw the Capitol Building and the White House."

"How historical of you."

"I'm going to the Lincoln Memorial tomorrow and maybe to see the Smithsonian Museum."

"I didn't take you for a history buff, Mr. Future MLB Star," I tease.

"My mom would kill me if she found out I was in DC and didn't see all the major sites."

"Well, in that case, make sure you tour the Library of Congress."

"I wouldn't dare skip out on the *Library of Congress*."

I laugh. "You have no idea what that is, do you?"

"It's a library, Rayna. Duh."

"It's the world's *largest* library!"

"Still a library."

I find another pillow and throw it at his head.

He laughs, then sits up and places his hands on my waist. "Come here," he says, pulling me closer to him until I'm standing between his legs, our gaze at eye level because of our significant height difference. "Did you talk to Dan?" he asks, his voice taking on a gentler tone.

"I did."

"And?"

"I told him that I can't stop loving you just because you're my student, and that I'll deal with the fall out. But I would appreciate if administration can find out on my terms."

"What did he say?"

"That you better treat me right."

He smiles. "I can do that."

His lips brush against mine in a soft, delicate kiss. "I've been wanting to do that all day," he whispers against my lips.

"Then why'd you stop already?"

His eyes glaze over before his lips find mine again, this time in a more powerful, needy kiss. It doesn't take long before he has my gray two-piece pant suit on the floor. I'm completely naked before he even bothers to take off his pants.

I'm still standing between his legs as he sits in front of me on the bed. He pulls his mouth away from mine for a moment and looks at me, all of me. He starts with my eyes before he works his way down, roaming over my breasts, his eyes finally falling to my legs.

"Do you even know how beautiful you are, Rayna?"

I don't know what to say so I just look down.

His fingers move to my chin to lift my gaze back up to his. "I love you so much. But not because of your body. I love you, Rayna. Because you're *you*."

"I love you too." I cup his face in my palms. "And it's definitely *not* because you're going to be rich for hitting a baseball far."

Hayes laughs, his head falling to my stomach. "Rayna, I'm a pitcher! I'm going to be rich because I can throw one hell of a fastball."

"I knew that. I swear."

He kisses my stomach. "Mmhmm."

Chapter Twenty-Nine

Hayes

I call my mom Tuesday morning after Rayna leaves for her conference.

"Hello?"

"Hi, Mom."

"Hi, love. Are you on your way home yet?"

"About that. I won't be coming home today. I'm actually going to be getting in a little after midnight on Thanksgiving Day. I'm bringing my girlfriend with, and we're in DC for a conference for her job until tomorrow night."

"What? You're in DC? And what girlfriend? Is this the same girl Jason was mentioning a few months ago that had you wrapped around her finger?"

"Yes, Washington DC. And what do you mean? When did you talk to Jason?"

"Oh, Hayes, you're not the best at calling, you know. I talk to Jason every once in a while. He mentioned that there was a girl occupying your time. So, who is she?"

I smile. "Her name is Rayna."

"Pretty name. So, she'll be staying with us for Thanksgiving?"

"Yes."

"What about her family?"

"They had an early Thanksgiving last weekend since she had the conference this week. Her dad and brother live in Chicago."

"Well, we can't wait to meet her."

There's silence on the other end for a second before she speaks again.

"This must be pretty serious, Hayes." There's concern etched in her voice. "Have you talked to her about your future and how important it is to you? And you're sure she's with you for the right reasons?"

"Yes, Mom. She knows everything. And she's more than supportive. Money isn't important to her. She's got plenty of it, anyway, believe me."

"You sound happy."

"I'm very happy, Mom. You're going to love her, I promise."

"Okay, love. Thanks for calling. See you in a few days."

"Love you."

"Love you too."

I hang up, then I get dressed and take a taxi to the Library of Congress. After a guided tour, I find a small calendar in the gift shop with pictures of the library and buy it for Rayna's office at East Valley before heading out to the streets of DC. I linger around, stopping for roasted peanuts from a street vendor and taking a walk around the park. I head back to the hotel so I can change and go for a run before Rayna gets back. Changing into my running pants and long sleeve Nike shirt before lacing up my gym shoes, I run for a few miles, still trying to get some form of exercise in since we don't have practice all week.

I hop in the shower as soon as I get back. Rayna should be getting back any minute, and I can't help but feel excitement knowing that I'm about to see her. Will it always be like this with her? Will I always feel like a little boy that has the biggest crush on the pretty girl?

I still can't believe Rayna feels the same way about me. I never would have guessed that our one-night stand all those months ago would've ended up turning into this. I've never brought a girl home to meet my parents. I've had a few long-term relationships, but they were never as serious as this one feels. Rayna is *it* for me. She is the real deal, everything I could ever imagine wanting in a woman. I'll give her the world for as long as she allows me to.

I step out of the shower, listening for her with building anticipation. I dry off, leaving the towel on the hook and not bothering to put on any clothes. A few minutes later, I hear the key card scan on the other side of the door before it opens. I hide in the bathroom, making sure she's alone before I step out and greet her with my bare ass out.

"Hayes?" she calls out as she looks around the room for me, the door closing behind her.

"Yeah?" I ask, walking by her, toward the bed, stark naked.

I turn around in time to see her eyebrows raise, her smirk prominent. She's wearing a tight pink dress today with tan heels and is looking fucking sexy as all hell. My dick immediately responds to the sight of her, and I know she notices because her cheeks turn a rosy color that perfectly complement her dress.

"You look...comfortable."

"You don't. Can I help?"

She laughs, setting her purse down on the table. "Yes, please get this thing off me. I'm suffocating."

"Gladly."

I saunter toward her, pulling her into my arms as I kiss her. My hands reach behind her in search for the zipper, eventually finding it on her right side. I unzip the dress as she pulls her arms out of it, the cloth falling to the floor in a puddle of pink. She's still wearing her bra and panties, though I discard those almost as quickly. I pick her up and she wraps her legs around me, my length pressed between her legs. I can feel her as her hips thrust into me, seeking the friction she so desperately needs.

176

I walk over to the window, opening the curtains that look over our nation's capital. I press her back against the window as I continue kissing her, my mouth moving from her lips to her neck.

"Hayes," she says breathless.

I grunt into her neck, letting her know that I hear her.

"People can see."

There are no other high-rise buildings around us, and we are pretty high off the ground. But if someone was intentionally looking to this window from the street, they would probably get a pretty good view of Rayna's ass. Either way, it's dark out and the view into our room is easier with the lights on. I reach for the lamp in the corner and shut it off, leaving Rayna and I in total darkness, the only light coming in from the streets below.

"Not anymore," I whisper into her ear at the same time I slide my length inside of her.

She moans and presses into my thrust.

It doesn't take long before I'm coming inside of her at the same time she yells out my name in her own climax. Rayna's never been quiet during sex, which has never been a problem because we haven't had sex outside of her condo until this trip. I wonder if there are any faculty members in the rooms next door. Or if Rayna's screaming is loud enough that Dan could hear it if he was out in the hallway. Either way, I don't give a fuck. The more she cries out, the harder I come.

My hands cling to her ass as I set her down on the bed before getting a towel from the bathroom to clean her up. When I return, her cheeks are still flushed and her breathing is labored.

"You okay?" I ask, smirking.

"That was intense."

"You may have a future as an exhibitionist," I tease.

She rolls her eyes. "Shut up."

I laugh. "How was the conference today?"

"Long. Boring. How about you?"

"Toured that library."

"*That* library? Hayes, it's the *Library of Congress*!"

I kiss her forehead. "I know. I'm only playing. I toured the *Library of Congress* and got you something for your office."

She perks up. "You did?"

I grab the bag off the table and hand it to her. "It's not a big deal. You just haven't shut up about the library, so I thought you might want something to remember it by."

She takes the calendar out of the bag and starts flipping through, studying each of the pictures. "This is perfect for my desk. Thank you, Hayes. That was thoughtful of you."

I shrug. "No big deal."

She frowns.

"What's wrong?" I ask.

"I might not have an office to put this in anymore. At least I already converted my spare bedroom into a study. I don't have a calendar in there."

I sigh. "Rayna, you're going to still have an office. You're not going to lose your job. We know this isn't illegal. I'm a consenting adult. You're a consenting adult. You're not using your authority over me in any way, and I'm not getting treated differently than any other student." I pause. "Except for outside of the classroom. Then I'm definitely treated differently, if you know what I mean." I wink.

She shakes her head as she laughs. "I can assure you, any special treatment you get outside of the classroom is for you and only you."

"Good." I smile. "That's the way I like it."

"How else do you like it?" she challenges.

I scoop her up by her waist and flip her over until she's on her stomach. She's been naked this entire time, so it doesn't take long for me to be ready for her again. I pull her waist toward me, sending her ass shooting up into the air as she balances on all fours.

"Your ass..." I admire it for a moment. "You have the sexiest ass."

I bend down and run my tongue along her divide before sliding my length back inside of her. I've never had the desire to fuck someone in the ass before, but if Rayna's ever game, then I would happily slide my dick into hers. For now, I take pleasure in the view as I thrust in and out of her again. She seems to like it from behind because her moans grow louder and soon she's putting a hand between her legs, rubbing herself as I continue to thrust. The sight of her pleasuring herself is enough to send me into another mind-blowing orgasm. We come at the same time, her crying out my name as I push myself into her.

"Fuck," I grunt.

Rayna collapses onto her stomach, her ass falling to the side. I can see her shoulders rising and falling quickly as she tries to catch her breath. I pick up the towel from a few minutes ago to clean her again before leaving it in the dirty towel bin in the bathroom.

I return to the bed, pulling Rayna with me under the covers until her body relaxes against me. "You are something else, baby."

"What's that supposed to mean?"

"You know that saying, lady in the streets, freak in the sheets? That's you. *Fuck*. It's hot."

She buries her head into my chest, likely embarrassed. I let her hide as I run my fingers through her long hair.

"Is it as good for you as it is for me?" I ask.

Her head tilts up to look at me. "What? Sex?"

I nod.

"Yes, Hayes. I don't think good quite describes it though."

I smile. "Was it like that with your ex-husband?" I regret the question as soon as it leaves my lips. Why the hell would I want to hear about my girlfriend fucking her ex-husband?

"No," she says sternly. "This is different. We are different. Nothing is the same. This is so much better. And I love you so much more than I could have ever possibly loved Corey."

She never mentioned his name before, but now I want to beat the living shit out of this Corey guy for ever hurting someone like Rayna. "I've never felt this way about anyone, Rayna. This is it for me. You're *it* for me. Does that scare you?"

"A little. But not in the ways you might think."

"I want to marry you," I admit.

Her eyes widen as they study my expression, searching for truth. But the truth is, I couldn't be more serious. I'll never find someone like Rayna again. And I don't ever want to. I want to make her the happiest woman on earth because she makes me the happiest man on earth.

"You're serious," she whispers.

I kiss the crease in her eyebrows where her worry shows. "I'm serious. But don't worry, I'm not asking you to marry me right now." I kiss the tip of her nose and then her lips before I continue. "I'll ask your dad for your hand. I'll find the perfect ring. I want to give you everything, Rayna. You already have all of me, but I want you to have the rest too. The world."

She lays her head back down on my chest. "Nothing would make me happier than being your wife."

I smile a big-tooth, cheesy smile that only Rayna can bring out in me. I smile because I know this is forever. I smile because Rayna's going to give me the chance to give her the world.

Chapter Thirty

Rayna

The snowstorm in Timbers hasn't let up yet. The news is reporting another three inches of snow before nightfall. The conference ended a little early today due to the inclement weather that is making its way across the US. I didn't have any problems canceling my flights, especially with the inevitable cancelation of many flights out of DCA and into any midwestern state anyway.

Hayes and I have been on the road for three hours now. He said it took him eight hours to drive to DC on Sunday, but with the weather and expected traffic delays, our ETA to his hometown of Springport, Michigan just keeps getting pushed farther and farther back. We're just outside of Pittsburgh with another six hours left.

"Do you think your mom would be upset with us if we ended up getting a hotel room for the night?"

Hayes shakes his head. "No. She'd rather us be safe and get there in one piece."

"Okay." I look out the window at the snow-fallen landscape. "This is my fault. If I didn't have this conference, you wouldn't be late to your family's Thanksgiving."

He grabs my hand and brings it to his lips, kissing my knuckles one by one. "No, baby. This was my decision. My parents are just going to be happy to see us."

"Do they know yet? Who I am?"

He shakes his head. "They know you're my girlfriend, but I thought the rest might be a better in-person conversation."

"What do you think they're going to say when they find out I'm your professor?"

"They're going to love you, Rayna. Stop worrying."

But that's all I've done since we hit the road. Are they going to think less of me because I'm Hayes's teacher? Would they rather me be his age, still in college, and trying to figure out what the hell I want to do with my life? A small part of me hopes they'll admire that my life is already figured out. That I have enough money to support myself and that I in no way am after Hayes for his future millions. But a bigger part hopes they can just see how much I love their son and how much he loves me. I don't want either of our careers to play a factor in our relationship anymore. I love Hayes because he's Hayes, not because he's going to play professional baseball. And I know he loves me because I'm me, not because he's trying to live out some fantasy of fucking his teacher.

"Babe…"

I turn to face him.

He squeezes my hand gently. "I love you. They're going to love you. Stop worrying."

"I love you too."

Another hour goes by and then traffic starts to slow down. It's pitch-black outside, and we're driving on an expressway with little light. It's difficult to see the cars ahead of us with the snow falling so heavy and the darkness that stretches on for miles. The only indication that traffic has slowed are the glimmers of red taillights up ahead.

Hayes slows the car down as we approach, eventually coming to a complete stop. "This can't be good," he mumbles under his breath.

We don't move for twenty minutes before Hayes unbuckles his seatbelt and moves to get out of the truck.

"Where are you going?" I ask.

"I'm going to see what's going on. Maybe someone needs help changing a flat."

"I'm going with you."

"No, Rayna. Stay in the car. It's dark out. I'll stay on the shoulder. Just give me a few minutes to check it out."

I nod as he gets out of the truck, disappearing into the darkness. My phone has no service, offering little distraction as I wait. The few minutes turn into ten, then twenty. After a half hour goes by, I shut off the truck and get out. The only light allowing me to see as I stand on the shoulder of the expressway comes from my phone. It's bitterly cold, and I'm suddenly upset with myself for not getting out sooner. Hayes is going to freeze out here without a heavier jacket.

I start walking down the road. Several other passengers have stepped out of their vehicles, trying to get a look ahead to see what's going on. I keep walking, finding no signs of Hayes anywhere.

I can feel myself panicking the farther down the road I get, still not spotting him. I eventually see headlights in a ditch. The closer I get, the better I'm able to see the overturned car on the side of the road. Another banged up car is blocking the single lane highway. There aren't any police or ambulance lights around, though by the looks of both of these cars, there should be.

I finally spot Hayes in the ditch. It looks like he's holding someone. I rush down to see what's going on and if there's any way I can help.

"Rayna, I told you to stay in the car!" His teeth chatter and his hands look like they're on the verge of developing frostbite.

I pull the gloves off my hands and hand them to him. "Put these on. Give me her."

He hands me the little girl in his arms. She has a small gash on her head. It doesn't look deep enough to need stiches, but nonetheless, it looks painful.

"Hi, what's your name?" I ask the little girl now in my arms.

"Gracie."

"Hi, Gracie. You look cold. Let's see if we can find you a blanket."

I walk back toward the street, knocking on windows to see if anyone has a blanket in their car. A nice gentleman in a black truck pulls out a wool blanket from his back seat and hands it to me through the window.

I smile. "Thank you."

I go back to the scene of the accident after I wrap Gracie in the blanket to warm her up, finding Hayes near the overturned car in the ditch.

"What's going on?"

"Her dad is still stuck in the car. We were able to get her out of the back seat, but the door up here is jammed."

"Has anyone called 911?"

"No reception out here."

Shit. I look around, back to the car on the road that's badly beat. "What about that car? Everyone okay in there?"

He nods. "Seems to be. Her dad is okay too, just stuck. He's going to freeze to death if he has to stay out here all night."

The car that's on the road is blocking the entire expressway in both directions. There are headlights facing us for miles going either way.

"I'm going to see if I can turn the truck around and drive to the nearest town. Maybe I'll get a cell signal." I look to Gracie. "I'm going to take her with me if her dad is okay with it."

Hayes nods.

I duck down until I'm able to see Gracie's dad. There are other gracious people pulling at the car, trying to free the man.

"Hi there. My name is Rayna. My boyfriend Hayes is one of the guys who's been trying to help you get out. If it's okay with you, I was going to take Gracie with me into our car to warm her up. I'm going to drive down the road to see if I can get a better signal in town. Would that be alright with you?"

The man nods, the desperation on his face evident. "I love you, Gracie. You stay with this nice woman, okay? They're going to get me out of here soon."

"Love you too, daddy," Gracie says.

Hayes puts his arm around me and kisses the top of my head. "Be careful."

I take the blanket off Gracie and hand it to Hayes. "I'll try to hurry. Put this on her dad to keep him warm."

Hayes nods and takes the blanket, bending down to cover up the man inside the car. I hurry back to the truck, putting Gracie in the passenger seat and buckling her up. It takes me several four-point turns, but I'm eventually able to get the car out of the line of traffic and turned around to drive in the opposite direction.

I frequently check my cell service as we drive. I get off at the first exit, noticing my phone now has two bars.

"You okay, Gracie?" I ask. "You warming up?"

She nods as I dial 911.

"911, what's your emergency?"

"There's an overturned vehicle off I-79, just past exit 46."

"Is anyone hurt?"

"There's a man stuck inside the car that's stuck in the ditch. A few cuts and bruises on the other passengers, but they all seem to be okay."

"We just dispatched to your location."

"Please tell them to hurry. I don't know how long it's been, but there's no reception out there and the man in the car is going to freeze to death if they don't get him out of there soon."

"Ambulance, fire, and police are on their way, ma'am."

"Thank you." I hang up and look to Gracie. "People are on their way to help your dad."

She only nods. Her eyes are glossy, and I can tell she's scared and probably still cold.

I turn around and begin to drive back to the scene of the accident, passing all the cars that are backed up as I drive on the wrong side of the road.

"How old are you, Gracie?"

"Four."

"Do you have any brothers or sisters?"

Gracie shakes her head.

I can see blue and red lights up ahead, so I know we're getting close to the accident site. I'm also silently thanking the 911 operator for dispatching them so quickly.

"Look, Gracie! They're already here to help your dad!"

I stop the truck as close to the accident site as I can get, then jump out, grabbing Gracie. The firefighters are using the jaws of life to get the door out. Moments later, someone is helping Gracie's dad out of the truck. There is blood dripping from his forehead, but he doesn't seem to care. He's looking around frantically, likely for his daughter.

I rush over, and he eyes us immediately. The wool blanket is wrapped around him, but his outstretched arms reach for Gracie anyway.

"I'm so sorry, Gracie. I'm so glad you're okay," the man says.

"I'm okay, Daddy," I hear her muffled voice say into his shoulder.

He looks to me, his arms wrapped around his little girl tightly. "Thank you, Rayna. Thank you so much."

I smile and nod as the paramedic's usher Gracie and her dad toward the ambulance to get a better look at them. I look around for Hayes, but he finds me first, his arms wrapping around me from behind as his cold nose nuzzles into my neck.

"Hayes, you're freezing."

"I know. Let's get in the truck."

We walk over to his truck that is still sitting on the wrong side of the road, blocking oncoming traffic. We're going to have to move now that the tow truck has arrived.

"I'll drive," I say. "You warm up." I climb into the driver's side, blasting the heat to help Hayes bring his body temperature back up. "What do you want to do?" I ask. "There was a hotel near that exit I drove to. It's probably not smart to drive anymore in this. The roads aren't plowed and it's already hard to see."

186

"You're right. Let's get a room. I'll call my parents when we get there to let them know what happened."

I turn the truck around again and drive until we reach exit 46. I pull into a hotel just off the expressway. Hayes calls his parents from the truck while I run inside to get us a room. When I return, he already has our luggage out. We walk back to the hotel, finding our room on the second floor.

"What did your parents say?" I ask.

"Mom was worried. She was a little mad I was driving on the roads like that to begin with."

I frown. "I hope they're better in the morning."

"They will be," he assures me.

We get into our room, and Hayes discards our luggage near the window.

"I need a hot shower to warm up," he says. "Join me?"

"You go ahead. I wasn't out there as long as you were. I'm warm."

Hayes frowns as he walks toward where I stand. He cups my cheek with one hand. "You okay?"

I nod. "I'm fine."

"Baby, what's wrong?"

I shake my head. "Nothing. I was worried about you. Then I was worried about Gracie and her dad. It was just an emotional night."

He kisses my forehead and then brings me in closer to his chest and wraps both of his arms around me.

"I'm okay. Gracie's okay. Her dad's okay. Everyone's okay, thanks to you," he whispers.

"I shouldn't have let you leave me in the car. I should have gone with you so that I could've left to call 911 right away. Why didn't anyone think of that?"

"Baby, it's not your fault. I shouldn't have insisted you stay in the truck. I told you I'd be right back, and I wasn't. I'm sorry. And honestly? I don't know. I was so concerned with keeping Gracie warm and trying to get her dad out that I didn't even think to tell someone to drive away. I guess no one did. Not everyone reacts the same under pressure. You did exactly what we all needed you to do. You saved that man today, Rayna."

I sigh. "I'm glad he's okay."

Hayes kisses the crown of my head again. "Everyone's okay."

He pulls back, his hands gripping my shoulders as he looks me in the eyes. "I didn't think it was possible for me to love you more, but seeing you tonight with Gracie..." He shakes his head. "The way you took care of her, the way you held her, the way you comforted her. I love you so much right now it hurts."

I smile as a single tear runs down my cheek. His words mean a lot. Not only because the man I love is telling me how much he loves me, but because he's acknowledging the way I cared for that little girl. It's the same way my mom cared for me. "Corey and I tried to have kids," I confess. "We tried for a year, but I never got pregnant. I thought it was my fault, that maybe something was wrong with me. But when I went to see a fertility specialist, they said that my egg count was above average and I was definitely fertile. Then that raised questions to Corey's fertility." The tears are harder to hold back and now they're falling faster than I'm able to wipe them away.

Hayes picks me up and carries me to the bed. He takes a seat, keeping me wrapped in his arms as I cry into his chest.

"Corey was infertile. It was going to be impossible for us to have kids. He was upset for obvious reasons, but I loved him and I married him, so I thought we'd be able to work through it. There was no rush to have kids, and there were other options for us. He started cheating on me shortly after we found out that he'd never be the biological dad to our kids. He shut me out, started looking for attention elsewhere. And he definitely found it. Anyway, for a while I didn't think I'd ever be able to have kids, then when I found out that it was possible for me to, I was so happy it hurt. But Corey was hurting for different reasons, the same reasons I had been hurting the entire year prior. What he did was unforgiveable, and that's why I left him. But for a while there, I gave up on that dream of ever having children of my own."

Hayes holds me tighter as he listens to everything I have to say. I've never told anyone about our infertility problems, not even my dad or Sam. Everyone knew Corey cheated on me, but they didn't know how badly he was hurting that ultimately led him to cheat. It was hard to blame him for what he did, but he should have turned to me when things got bad. For better or worse. That was our "for worse," and we didn't make it through. For that reason, I knew our marriage was over.

"You're going to make an amazing mother one day, Rayna. No matter how it happens, you will be one. I just know it."

His words bring a soft smile to my face.

I pull back and kiss his jaw, the soft stubble grazing my lips. "I didn't think I could love you more either. But I do. Every day, I love you more."

Chapter Thirty-One

Hayes

We get to my parent's house around noon on Thanksgiving Day. Rayna has been quiet for the last hour, and I know it's because she's a ball of nerves. I wish there was something I could say to make her relax, but no matter how many times I tell her that my parents are going to love her, she continues to be paranoid.

I park in the driveway outside of the split-level house I grew up in and turn to Rayna, grabbing her hand. "You ready?"

She takes a deep breath. "Yup."

I reach over for her with my other hand, grabbing the back of her head and pulling her toward me. I kiss her pouty lips, the ones that I've become so accustomed to, yet still fill me with desire every time I kiss them.

"I love you, baby. And so will they. Okay?"

She nods.

I get out of my truck, walk around the hood, and help Rayna out. She insisted we stop and get flowers for my mom on the way, so one hand is holding the bouquet of yellow daisy's while the other grips my hand for dear life.

"Relax," I whisper. "It's going to be fine."

I walk in through the front door, holding it open for Rayna as she walks in before shutting the cold winter air out behind us.

"Hayes, is that you?" I hear my mom call from the kitchen. A moment later, she meets us in the small foyer. "Thank God you two made it here in one piece. Your dad and I were so worried."

I wrap my arms around my mom's small frame. "Hi, Mom."

"Hi, love."

My dad joins us near the front door, and I release my mom and give my dad a one-armed handshake and hug.

"Mom. Dad." I place my hand on the small of Rayna's back. "This is Rayna."

My mom smiles the biggest smile her small mouth is capable of. It's bright enough to light up the entire room.

I instantly feel Rayna's body relax under my touch.

"Rayna, it is such a pleasure to meet you." My mom pulls her in for a hug.

My dad soon follows. "Welcome, Rayna," he says with one of his signature smirks. I know what he's thinking. Rayna is a looker, much like my mom. I already know they're going to love her as much as I do once they get to know her.

"Thank you so much for having me. These are for you." She hands my mom the daisy's. "And I'm so sorry about getting here late. That snowstorm was something else."

My mom waves her hand. "Don't worry. We still have a few hours before the turkey will be done anyway. In the meantime, there are appetizers in the kitchen." Mom turns to me. "Hayes, why don't you show her around. You can put your bags in your bedroom. I need to find a vase to put these in. They're so beautiful. Thank you, Rayna."

Rayna smiles, and I nod as I pick up our bags. I show her around, ending in my bedroom that looks exactly like it did when I left for college. There are baseball trophies lining every shelf, signed baseball posters, and a few pictures hanging up of me with friends from my childhood.

"You have a lovely home," Rayna says as she glances at all the trophies before moving on to the pictures. "This is Jason, right?" she asks, holding up a picture of us in sixth grade.

"Yeah. His family lives down the road. We grew up together. Always played ball together too."

"I'm excited to get to know him outside of being his teacher. He seems like a good friend."

I smile. "What'd you think of my parents?"

She cocks her head to the side like she can't believe I'd ask that. "Hayes. Are you worried I wouldn't like them? They're your parents. I love them already. They both seem great."

I pull her into my arms. "Just like they love you already. See? Nothing to worry about."

"Until they find out what I do for a living."

I shake my head. "That won't matter. You'll see."

We sit for dinner at five o'clock. My mom has definitely outdone herself this year, likely because there's a fourth guest with us for the first time in my entire life. There's a golden-brown turkey carved, Mom's homemade mashed potatoes and gravy, green bean casserole, sweet potato casserole, and rolls she made from scratch.

"Everything smells amazing, Laurie," Rayna says.

My parents insisted she call them by their first names, Laurie and Asher, instead of Mr. and Mrs. Murphy.

It's cute how nervous Rayna has been, but she's finally starting to feel more comfortable.

"Wait 'til you take your first bite," Dad says.

We fill our plates. Rayna especially takes to Mom's sweet potato casserole, and Mom's eyes light up when she goes for seconds.

After dinner, Rayna and I try to clear the table and wash the dishes, but Mom shoos us away. We relax on the couch in the living room, watching football with my dad. Once Mom finishes with the dishes, she offers Rayna a glass of wine, which she graciously accepts. Dad and I settle for beers as we sit with our overfull stomachs and enjoy each other's company.

Dad turns down the volume on the TV when Mom takes her seat in the living room with us. Now comes the time for questions. I know my mom is going to want to know all about how we met.

I squeeze Rayna's tense shoulder. She knows what's coming too. The sooner we can get this over with, the sooner she can permanently relax.

"Now that I have some time to unwind, I want to hear all about how you two met," my mom says, just as I predicted. The excitement in her tone can't go unnoticed. Neither can the sparkle in her eyes as she looks from me to Rayna.

I start talking, because I know Rayna is nervous for where this conversation is going to go. "I was out with the team doing our annual championship shots."

My mom rolls her eyes.

"Rayna was about to start a new job. She'd just moved to Timbers this year from Chicago and was really nervous for her first day. So, she ended up at the same bar as us. The second she walked in, I couldn't take my eyes off her. I knew had to go up and talk to her. I mean, look at her."

My mom and dad both laugh.

Rayna shakes her head and laughs quietly to herself.

I pull her in closer to me, kissing the crown of her head.

"That's sweet," Mom says.

Dad continues to sip his beer. I'm sure he knows exactly how the rest of that night went, but it says a lot that all these months later, she's still with me. That she's *here*, with my family. They already know I'm in love with her. I wouldn't have brought her here otherwise.

"What do you do, Rayna?" Dad asks.

And here we go.

Rayna takes a deep breath. "I'm a teacher. Well, college professor, actually."

Dad's eyebrows shoot up. "I see. What is it that you teach?"

"Sports Nutrition," Rayna answers.

My dad's brow furrows as he puts two and two together. "That the class Coach makes you boys take?"

I nod. "That's the one. Rayna took over for Dr. Arnold who used to teach it. He retired. She does a much better job than he ever did."

My mom chimes in now. "So, you're Hayes's professor?"

Rayna's cheeks redden as she nods. "I didn't know he was a student when we met. We actually broke it off for a while because of it."

"How old are you?" Mom asks.

"Twenty-seven."

Dad gets another big cheesy grin on his face as he takes a sip of his beer.

"Is there…um…any rules against this?" Mom asks.

This time I answer for Rayna. "No. And like she said, we didn't know she was going to be my professor. Besides, it's only for another month. But there are no laws against it. I'm not a minor. It's only a few years difference, and it just happens to be a weird coincidence that the woman I met at the bar ended up being one of my professors."

My mom nods her head in understanding. "You look worried, dear," she says to Rayna.

If it's possible for Rayna's cheeks to redden more, they do. A deep shade of crimson takes over, likely a combination of nerves and the wine.

"I love Hayes very, very much. Your opinion of me matters to me, a lot. I don't want either of you to think I make a habit of getting together with my students, because I don't. I've been teaching for the last three years, and I can assure you this has never happened. Had we not met prior to him becoming my student, things would never have gotten to this point. Like I said, we…*I* broke things off because I was afraid of losing my job. But if there's anything my family has taught me, it's that it's only a job and there will be more. I love your son more than I can even put into words. You have raised the best man I've ever known. My life is better because he's in it, and I hope that

194

you can accept me, because if you do, I promise to love him for the rest of my life."

Mom stands up and reaches her arms out for Rayna. Rayna stands just as my mom pulls her into her small body. My mom looks to me from over Rayna's shoulder, giving me a wink before pulling away to look Rayna in the eyes.

"Everything happened exactly how it was supposed to happen," Mom says.

Rayna's shoulder relax as I watch her wipe a tear from her eye.

I smile because the two women I love most on this earth are accepting one another.

Dad gives me his nod of approval before he stands to get us another beer.

Rayna sits back down beside me, and I pull her in close, kissing her cheek before moving my mouth closer to her ear.

"Told you," I whisper.

Chapter Thirty-Two

Rayna

The Monday morning after a holiday weekend is always a drag. Hayes and I were on a high, the pressure of meeting his parents behind us. The weekend couldn't have gone better.

Monday night we spend the night wrapped in each other. He kisses my forehead, then my nose. "You're so beautiful, baby," he whispers.

I smile because Hayes calling me beautiful will never get old. He looks at me with such infatuation and awe. I've never felt more beautiful in my life.

He continues to kiss my neck, then my chest. His fingers swirl in tiny circles over my stomach. "When are you going to talk to administration?" he asks.

It's something I've been thinking about. When is the best time to let your boss know that you're seeing one of your students? Would it be better to wait until he's no longer in my class, or does that risk them finding out a different way? There are only three weeks left in the semester. Four more lectures and one final stand between Hayes as *my* student and Hayes as just *a* student.

"I don't know. Do you think it might be better if I wait until the semester is over?"

"Do *you* think that would be better?"

"It might risk them finding out another way."

"Dan?"

I shake my head. "No. Not Dan."

"Then how?"

His tongue circles my nipple and it instantly pebbles. I tilt my head back and look at the ceiling as he sends a tingle directly between my legs.

"Someone might see us."

He sucks on my nipple before biting gently with his teeth.

I gasp.

"Someone might see us doing this?"

"No. Someone might see us together in public."

His head pops up in that moment, his lips red and puffy from kissing. "Does that mean you're letting me take you on a date?"

I grin. "That means I'm letting you take me on a date."

His lips crash into mine then, his tongue instantly filling my mouth. He slides his length effortlessly inside of me. A few minutes later, our skin glistens from sweat, our breathing heavy as we recover.

"I think you should talk to them yourself," he says afterward. "Rather than risk someone else telling them."

I nod. "You're right. I will."

He tucks a strand of hair behind my ear. "I love you. No matter what happens. I love you."

"I know you do."

The following morning, Hayes walks into my lecture hall with Jason and Kevin, as they always do just before my class is set to start. Hayes shoots me a wink as he turns to walk up the steps toward their usual seats. I instantly feel a fluttering in my core.

Someone from the HR department walks into the auditorium just as I'm about to start class. "Professor James, may I speak with you in your office for a moment?" she asks.

I nod. "Sure."

I follow the woman into my office, shutting the door behind me. I feel the heat as it rises on the back of my neck, causing me to instantly sweat.

The woman holds out her hand. "I'm Dr. Keating. I'm the head of HR. I spoke with Dr. Zaneuiga. He asked me to speak with you directly about scheduling a meeting for your semester review."

Dr. Zaneuiga is the head of the College of Science and technically my boss. "Of course. I can make just about anything work. Tuesdays and Thursdays are my only lecture days."

Dr. Keating smiles. "Wonderful. I'll plan something for tomorrow then. Likely in the morning. I'll email you with the details." She walks toward the door. "I don't want to keep you. It was a pleasure meeting you, Professor James." Then she exits my office.

I walk out, trailing behind the woman who just nearly gave me a heart attack. My first inclination was that she wanted to discuss Hayes. Thankfully, that wasn't the case.

Hayes gives me a questioning look when I walk back into the lecture hall and take my usual stance behind the podium. I give him a slight head shake, and he sits back and relaxes in his seat. It was clear that he suspected the same.

After the lecture, my cell phone rings. It's Hayes.

"Hi," I answer after the first ring.

"What did she want?"

"To schedule a meeting with Dr. Zaneuiga, the head of my department. It's for my end of semester review."

"Oh," he says relieved.

"I thought the same thing at first. That she was coming to discuss my potential relations with a student."

"With a student," he mimics.

"With Hayes Murphy."

I can hear the smile in his voice as he responds, "And what is it that you might discuss about your potential relations with Hayes Murphy, Professor James?"

I laugh. "I cannot confirm nor deny any speculations."

"Oh, I can confirm. As a matter of fact, I'll be confirming them in a couple of hours."

Hayes asked me to come to his house tonight, despite having not talked to administration yet. Jason's already known about us, and he told Kevin yesterday. Kevin's reaction was exactly as I suspected. Hayes said he asked a bunch of questions he refused to answer, then gave him a pat on the back. He's not going to say anything, and for that, I agreed to come over.

"I'll see you in a few hours," I tell him.

"See you in a few hours. I love you, baby."

"I love you too."

Hayes greets me outside his off-campus home before I get out of my car. The smile plastered across his face has me giddy like a schoolgirl.

"Hi," I say as I step out of my little red car.

"Hi," he says as he pulls me in, kissing me on the lips.

He grabs my hand and leads me in the side door, entering through the kitchen. Jason's sitting on the couch with Kevin, playing some sort of video game. They both turn around, first gazing at me before moving to Hayes, then back to me.

"Hi...uh...Professor James," Jason says.

Kevin smiles as he blatantly checks me out from head to toe. I changed before I came over, into jeans and an off the shoulder sweater. My knee-high boots clink against the tile floor as I walk deeper into the kitchen, toward the living room where they sit.

"You can call me Rayna," I say.

"Rayna, you look smokin'," Kevin says.

Jason rolls his eyes. "Dude."

"Now I can beat your ass without feeling bad. Lay off," Hayes says.

Kevin laughs. He's purposely causing trouble, I can see it in his eyes, though I know he means no harm.

Jason stands up from his seat on the couch and makes his way over to me. He wraps his arms around me in a friendly hug and whispers in my ear, "I'm glad you finally came around, Rayna." When he pulls away, he's smiling.

Hayes gives him a questioning look before shrugging it off.

"Oh, dude! Guess who I ran into last night at Off Base," Kevin says.

I can't tell if he's talking to Jason or Hayes, but they both simultaneously ask, "Who?"

"Natalie. That bartender. She tried to come home with me, but I ended up going to some other chick's house."

"So that's why you didn't come home until this morning," Jason says. "I had the house to myself. Can't say I hated it."

Hayes laughs. "Guess she got over your ass quickly, Jason."

Jason shrugs. "Bet you she's still not over *your* ass."

I give Hayes a questioning look. This is the first time I'm hearing about a girl named Natalie.

"She's just another girl who is only interested in me for my baseball status," Hayes says, feigning little interest in the topic.

I wonder how many other girls there are who are after Hayes for his *baseball status*.

"She was all over me after her shift," Kevin says. "At first, I liked it, but then it just got to be too much. She's a stage five clinger, dude. What did you ever see in her?" he asks Jason.

Jason shakes his head, "I obviously wasn't thinking."

Hayes chuckles. "Oh, you were thinking alright. Just with the wrong head."

"Alright, alright. I don't need my professor knowing about my sex life."

He's right. Is this as weird for them as it is for me?

Hayes wraps his arm around me. "She's just Rayna when we're here. My *girlfriend*." He kisses me on the top of my head. "Which means don't come in my room." He leads me up the stairs, yelling out behind him, "Seriously, don't bother me unless the house is burning down!"

Chapter Thirty-Three

Hayes

I lay in my bed naked with Rayna. It feels damn good to have her here with me. It didn't take me long at all to get her clothes off. Shortly after I brought her upstairs, I shut and locked my door, pushed her up against it, and had a difficult time keeping my hands off her. She didn't seem to mind though. She kissed me with more fervor than she has in the past, maybe because this thing between us finally feels real, like it's not a ticking time bomb set to detonate any moment. She's giving me a real chance.

"We might have to use our inside voices next time we do this here," I tease.

Rayna's eyes widen, and she brings her hand quickly to her mouth. "Was I loud? Oh my God, could they hear me? Why didn't you say something?"

I laugh, kissing the tip of her nose. "I quite enjoy when you yell my name out as you're coming. Why in the world would I want to stop you?"

She playfully slaps my chest. "I do not need my students to hear what I sound like when I have an orgasm, Hayes!"

"They're not your students when you're here. And I'm only messing with you. You weren't *that* loud." I am only kidding with her, but if they were upstairs at all in the last thirty minutes, then they could definitely hear something. Rayna is not quiet, and I enjoy that more than I'm willing to admit to her.

Her cheeks blush and it only makes her cuter. "You're adorable, you know that?"

She shakes her head in disbelief. "Adorable and *loud*, apparently."

I kiss her one last time before I get up, pulling on a pair of sweats. "Hungry?"

She nods. "Starving."

"Let's go downstairs and see what there is to eat."

Rayna dresses and follows me back downstairs. Her cheeks are still flushed, her hair a bit of a sexy mess, and her lips look like they have been thoroughly kissed. If the guys didn't hear us, they sure as hell can tell by looking at us what just happened. Not that I give a shit.

I can see the look in Kevin's eyes that he's holding back from saying something. His smirk after he checks out Rayna is apparent. His gaze meets mine, and he shoots me a wink. I shake my head, laughing to myself. Kevin thinks I'm living some teenage boy fantasy, which, I guess I am. But I don't see Rayna as a professor I'm sleeping with. If anything, her profession has only hindered our relationship. We're both able to accept it for what it is now, but being away from her was the exact opposite of a fantasy, and it was all because she is my professor.

"You guys hungry?" I ask as I descend the last step.

"Just ordered a pizza," Jason yells from the couch.

"Awesome."

I lead Rayna over to the couch. She snuggles up next to me, still wearing her jeans but now instead of a sweater she's looking sexy as hell in one of my baseball T-shirts.

Jason's watching sports highlights on ESPN. Rayna pretends to watch, though I know she doesn't have the slightest clue about any of the teams being discussed.

Ten minutes later, the doorbell rings with our pizza. Kevin answers it and sets the pizza on the table. We all grab a few slices and sit back down on the couch. It's nothing special, sitting here watching ESPN and eating pizza with my roommates, but having Rayna here makes it better. She fits in perfectly, as I knew she would. She's the coolest fucking girl I've ever met.

I lean into her, nuzzling my lips into her neck as I leave a few soft kisses there before trailing to her ear. "I love you," I whisper.

She smiles before turning to kiss me on the lips. "I love you," she whispers back.

I'm only able to work my morning shift at the Auto Repair now that practice is six days a week. By the time six o'clock rolls around, my body is exhausted and I can't wait to see Rayna.

I drive my old truck to the familiar lot, park my car, and grab my duffle bag full of clothes I plan to leave here. By the time I walk into her apartment, the aroma of spices that I started smelling the second I got off the elevator finally makes sense. I find Rayna in her kitchen, mixing something in a pot as something else sizzles in a pan.

I walk up behind her, placing both hands on her waist before kissing her neck and pressing myself into her back. "Smells amazing, babe."

She smiles and tilts her head back to kiss me on the lips. "I got home early today. And we're celebrating, so I decided to cook my mom's favorite. Chicken Carbonara."

"What are we celebrating?"

Rayna sets down the spoon she was using to mix the sauce and turns around. She's grinning so big, the smile reaches her eyes. "I told Dr. Zaneuiga everything during my semester review. He appreciated my honesty and said our relationship in no way impacts my job. He actually met his wife when he was a teacher here thirty years ago and *she* was a student."

"You're shitting me. That's amazing, Rayna! See!" I hug her, twirling her around in a circle in the kitchen, her legs lifting off the ground. "I'm so proud of you. And I love you. So damn much."

I set her down, her eyes twinkling as she looks up at me. "Even if it hadn't gone well, I would have chosen you. I will always choose you."

I kiss her, hard. Her mouth instantly parts for me, making way for my tongue. I'm in desperate need of a shower, but right now I don't care. All that matters right now is this moment, the moment I've been waiting months for. Rayna is all I want, all I'll ever need. If my future in the MLB was to be taken away tomorrow, I can't say that I wouldn't be okay. I would be. Everything I've ever wanted I've found in Rayna. Now there isn't a single thing holding us back. Not the unknown of her career, not the uncertainty if this is something we can make last. I have no doubts. Absolutely none. I'm so madly and deeply in love with this woman, something I never thought would be possible with anyone.

"Fuck, Rayna. Will the food be okay? I only need five minutes," I ask breathless.

She's already begun unbuckling my belt, tugging down at the elastic band of my baseball pants. Once the pants are at my ankles, I reach for Rayna's pajama shorts. I quickly remove them before I lift her onto the island. We don't bother with the rest of our clothes. I slide myself inside of her, feeling how wet she already is.

"Fuck," I hiss.

Rayna grips the back of my head, slightly tugging at my hair. It might hurt if it didn't feel so good. It doesn't take long before she is crying out as she comes, my end quickly approaching behind hers.

Afterward, her body slumps against mine. I hold her, stroking her hair as she rests her head against my chest.

"Everything, Rayna," I whisper. "I'm going to give you everything."

She lifts her head, her beautiful turquoise eyes hazy. "You," she says. "I only want you."

Chapter Thirty-Four

Rayna

The following week, I'm sitting in my office, waiting for a student who requested to meet with me today. She's interested in taking my course next semester and has some questions. I call Hayes, knowing I have a few minutes to spare.

"Hi, baby," he answers.

"Hi there," I say. I'm smiling so big just with the sound of his voice. I can't remember smiling this much, ever. Hayes makes me so damn happy.

"How's your day been?"

"Relatively slow. I have a meeting with a student here in a few minutes, but that's about all today."

"I'm sure your office hours will pick back up once we start our review tomorrow for the final."

"Definitely," I say. "I've had a few emails about scheduling office hours this weekend. I'm trying to enjoy how slow it is right now."

"I guess I'll have to schedule office hours so I can see my girlfriend then."

I laugh. "I guess you will."

"We have a practice scrimmage against Michigan State tonight. It's in the dome, so it won't be cold. You should come watch."

"My first opportunity to watch my sexy boyfriend pitch? I wouldn't miss it. What time?"

Hayes chuckles. "Starts at five-thirty."

I look at my watch. "Perfect. I'll head over after this meeting." I pause for a moment. "Hayes, this is something people come to watch, right? I'm not going to be the only one in the stands?"

He laughs again. "Yes, Rayna. People come to watch. A lot of people. You won't be alone."

I smile. "I can't wait."

"I'll see you at your place after the game. I love you."

"I love you. Good luck."

"Thanks."

The knock sounds shortly after I get off the phone with Hayes.

"Come in!"

The door opens slowly. A young blonde pops her head inside my office. "Hi, Professor James. I'm here for our meeting."

"Yes, come on in. Natalie, right?"

"Yes. Natalie Calloway."

I hold out my hand. "It's a pleasure to meet you, Natalie. Take a seat."

I close the door behind her. She sits in one of the two chairs facing my desk as she fidgets with her bag. I take my usual seat behind my desk. She's glancing around the room, her focus everywhere but on me.

I clear my throat to gain her attention. "So, Natalie, you had questions? You said in your email you're interested in taking my class next semester, so how can I help ease your mind?"

Her focus finally fixates on me. She studies my eyes for a few moments before she speaks. "Yes. I was curious how the class is different from when Dr. Arnold taught it. I attempted the course my freshmen year but dropped it after two weeks. I heard from some of my friends in the class that it's easier now."

"I wouldn't say it's easier," I answer honestly. "The class studies the same subject matter Dr. Arnold covered. My teaching style may differ from his, and I also have pretty generous office hours. In order to succeed in this class, it's important to understand the material from the start. Without having a basic understanding of the day-one concepts, it's difficult to move on. You're always needing to build and expand your knowledge with me. So, I make sure all of my students are on track before they even try to learn more. That's where the office hours come in handy. I'm always willing to meet with you outside of class, to go over exams or answer any lingering questions."

"That's…generous."

"I won't let anyone fail if they put in the work."

"I see."

"Does that answer your question? I have no doubt that you'd succeed if you're wanting to try to retake this course."

"Yes. It answers my question."

For some reason, I feel uncomfortable. "Is that all? Or do you have more concerns?"

She hesitates for a moment before speaking. "Hayes Murphy," she says.

My brows furrow as I look into her deep brown eyes. When she first walked in, she had a hard time looking at me. Now, her eyes bore into mine, not even blinking.

"What about him?" I ask.

Last week my boss had basically said there was nothing wrong with my relationship with Hayes, that he met his wife while she was a student, and while there were no rules against what we are doing, it's important to refrain from any type of PDA on school property. I assured him that sort of thing would never happen and has never happened in the past. I knew it was only a matter of time before word got out about my relationship with Hayes, but I didn't think it would travel this quickly. We had only been out in public together once so far, and it was last Saturday for dinner.

"You're dating him." She doesn't ask it as a question. She says it as a statement.

"I am."

She tilts her head to the side, her eyes still focused intently on mine. Honestly, they're making me feel a bit uneasy. "Why?" she asks.

Her question catches me off guard. How do I answer that? Should I even answer that? "Natalie, I'm not sure this is an entirely appropriate conversation to be having. If you don't have anymore questions regarding my class, if you don't mind, I have some work to get done." I move to stand up from my chair so I can walk her out.

"Sit back down," she commands.

"Excuse me?"

"Sit."

"Natalie, I —"

"Sit!" she shouts as she stands to block me from the door. Her hand is tucked into her handbag, her forehead showing tiny beads of sweat beginning to form. She's nervous.

Why is she nervous? "Natalie, what is this about?"

"Why did he choose you?"

"I'm sorry?"

That's when the tears begin and her breathing picks up. In her haste to wipe her eyes, she pulls out the gun that is in her right hand. She wipes away the tears with the back of her hand, moving like she's unaware she's holding a gun.

I feel like I've stopped breathing. I search her eyes for traces of recognition that she brought a gun into my office.

After she wipes at her eyes a few more times, she notices the gun. Her eyes shoot up to mine, searching for something I'm not aware of.

I begin calmly, "Natalie —"

"No!" she cuts me off, pointing the gun directly at me. "No, no, no! Sit back down!"

I do what she says and sit. I eye my cell phone that I set on my desk after I hung up with Hayes. If I could get to my phone, I could call for help. But right now, my main focus is to get this girl calm enough to put her gun down.

"Are you friends with Hayes?" I ask. "Is that why you're wondering about my relationship with him?"

She shakes her head. "No. He hasn't looked my way in months."

"Did you used to be friends?" I ask.

"Not friends. He flirted with me. I thought I'd finally gotten his attention, but he's hardly even acknowledged me since, even when I spent the night at his place and then drove him to class. He acts like I don't exist."

I know that feeling all too well, to feel like Hayes Murphy thinks you don't exist.

"You—" Then it clicks. "Natalie," I whisper.

"What?"

This is *Natalie*.

"You dated Jason?" I ask, the pieces falling together.

She shrugs. "I wouldn't call it dated. We had sex a few times, but that was only because I was trying to get Hayes to notice me again."

"And Kevin?" I ask.

"He wouldn't take me home, no matter how much I flirted. It was infuriating."

"Why are you really here, Natalie? I get the sense you're not interested in taking my class."

"I see Hayes likes them smart. And older. Is that why I never stood a chance?" She looks around the room again, then back at me. This time, she raises the gun until it's aimed directly at my chest. "You ruined everything for me."

"Natalie—"

"Shut up!" she yells. "He finally was flirting with me. He was paying attention to me. He *noticed* me!"

I don't know what to say, so I remain quiet. She had instructed as much, but I still feel like maybe talking would calm her down. Maybe I can reason with her. But I'm speechless. How is this happening? Did Hayes know she was infatuated with him to this extent?

"He was checking me out, I could tell. The night I was serving his team shots. I could see the look in his eyes. He finally fucking noticed me! Then, he just stopped. He acted like I didn't exist again. I've waited years for Hayes to know who I am. He finally did and then you came along. You offered him something he couldn't refuse: a relationship with his teacher! You're his *teacher*!"

My heart beats rapidly, my palms are sweating, and the fear is likely evident on my face. "Please put the gun down."

"He doesn't love you!" she yells. "You're fulfilling some twisted fantasy. He's a guy. You're manipulating him, offering him something he can't refuse. That's what this is, right? You're taking advantage of your power over him. You're his superior."

It's not. But if she believes that, will she let me go? For some reason, I feel like anything I say in this scenario isn't going to sit well with her, so I stay quiet.

"What do you have that I don't?" She scrutinizes me for a moment. "I'm young, youthful. Your body isn't any better than mine." She's quiet for a few seconds as she continues to study me. "Tell me, Professor James, why you?"

"I don't know," I answer honestly.

"Do you love him?"

I nod.

She laughs, a hysterical laugh that brings tears to my eyes.

I feel helpless. I don't know what to do. I don't know what to say. I never thought my relationship with Hayes would put me in danger like this. I worry she's going to go after him next. She's frantic, manic. Her hand is shaking as she points the gun at me.

There are several thoughts that go through my head. Thoughts about Hayes and how much I really do love him. Thoughts about my dad and how excited I am for him to meet Hayes. Thoughts about Sam and how thrilled he's going to be when he realizes my boyfriend is going to be in the MLB. Thoughts about my mom, and how proud she would be of me for choosing love over my career. Then those thoughts turn to sad possibilities. What will happen to Hayes if I die? What will he say? What will he do? Is she going to hurt him too? How will my dad take the news? He barely made it through my mother's death. How is he supposed to deal with the loss of a child? And my brother, will he be able to help Dad through the darkness alone? I don't want to die for many reasons, but most of all, for them.

"Natalie, please—"

The gun sounds off.

There's pain for a moment. It's quick. My face falls to my desk. I stare at my phone, wondering if I can move my hand to call for help now that she's gone. She is gone, I think. Because it's quiet now. The only sound I hear is the sound of my breathing as it becomes more desperate. I gasp for air. More air. It doesn't seem to help. It's getting harder and harder to push the oxygen through my lungs. But there's no pain. I feel no pain.

Chapter Thirty-Five

Hayes

We're warming up for our big scrimmage against Michigan State. In a little under thirty minutes, I'll be throwing the first pitch to start off my final season with East Valley. The atmosphere in the dome is usually electric, but something is off today. I don't know what it is, so I continue to throw to our catcher, Bony.

Coach is discussing something with Michigan State's coach before he hurries frantically into the dugout.

I look around for Jason who is stretching with Kevin nearby. "What's going on?" I ask.

"No idea."

I look back to Coach.

His eyes are anxiously searching the field, never settling on a single spot or person. His frown is evident in his features. When he hangs up, he runs out of the dugout and yells, "Everyone into the locker room. Now!"

The team huddles into the dugout and enters in through the side door that leads to a hallway under the dome's seating and straight into our locker room. Murmurs fill the hallway and escalate the moment we are together inside the familiar room that houses our personal belongings.

"What's going on?" Jason asks.

Coach pinches the space between his eyes before he glances around at the team. "There's been an incident. A shooting."

"A *what*?" I yell.

Coach holds up his hands. "Everyone calm down. It was an isolated incident. The shooter has already been caught, but we are to remain on lock down until the police finish doing a sweep across campus."

"Where was the shooting?" I ask.

He hesitates. "Chestnut Hall."

Rayna.

Jason and Kevin's eyes both meet mine. The shock that I feel throughout my body isn't something I'm familiar with. I move through the crowd of players until I reach my locker. I find my phone and see right away that I have no missed calls or texts from Rayna. She was supposed to be meeting with a student today, so maybe she's safe and barricaded inside her office. Maybe the police already have her and she's okay. Or maybe she's somewhere inside this stadium, finding out the news herself.

I find her number in my contacts and call. The phone rings six times before it goes to voicemail. I try again, still no answer.

Shit.

I find Coach again. "Do you know who was shot? Who the shooter was?"

Coach sighs. "The shooter was a student. A female. One of the staff members was taken in an ambulance to be treated for a gunshot wound."

My face pals. "What staff member? Who?"

Coach studies the worry in my eyes. He's had to have heard about my relationship with Rayna by now, the entire team has. "I'm sorry, son."

He doesn't have to say any more. I'm out of that locker room before anyone can say another word. I run to my truck, tires squealing as I hurry out of the student parking lot.

A police officer stops me at the exit of the lot. "This campus is on lockdown, sir. You're going to have to stay here until we get the all clear."

I wipe my face with my palm. "My girlfriend, Rayna James, she's the one who was shot. I need to get to the hospital. She doesn't have any family here."

The officer's face drops, and I can see the remorse in his eyes. "Park your truck. I can't let you leave on your own. I'll give you a ride to the hospital."

I sigh with relief as I quickly park and jump out of the truck. I sit in the passenger side of the police car, and we drive away, sirens wailing as he swerves in and out of traffic toward the hospital where Rayna is being treated.

I've been on autopilot since I left the locker room, but now there are hundreds of questions running rapid through my head. Why would anyone do this to her? Is she going to be okay? Is she alive still? Who would do this?

When I arrive at the hospital, I rush into the emergency room. The nurse behind the counter watches me as I approach. If she can sense my hysteria, she doesn't let on.

"Rayna James," I say out of breath. "She was just brought in by ambulance for a gunshot wound."

"Are you family of the patient?" she asks.

"I'm her boyfriend. Her family doesn't live here, so I'm the only family she has right now."

She nods her head. "It looks like a Theodore James was called and notified."

"That's her dad. Did he answer? Is he on his way?"

"I don't have that information, sir. I'm sorry." She continues typing and searching something on her computer screen. "Miss James is in surgery right now. You can have a seat in the waiting room, and I'll be sure to let the doctors on her case know that she has a family member here waiting for updates."

"Thank you."

I begin to walk away when the nurse calls out for me. "Sir?"

215

I turn around. "We have some of her personal belongings that were taken with her on the ambulance. Would you like me to get them for you?"

"Yes, please."

"What's your name?"

"Hayes Murphy."

"Alright, Hayes Murphy. I'll be right back."

I take a seat in one of the waiting room chairs. My legs bounce anxiously as I await news. Time seems to move by slower than normal. Only ten minutes go by before the nurse returns with a clear plastic bag of Rayna's belongings. Inside the bag is her phone, car keys, and wallet.

I reach for her phone, debating whether or not I should call her dad or Sam to update them. I haven't met them yet. I'm not even sure Rayna's had a chance to tell them about me. She had plans to introduce us over Christmas break, but that is still three weeks away.

The debate ends quickly in my head as I find her dad's number. I call him from my own cell phone, not wanting him to get his hopes up at seeing Rayna's name flash across the screen.

"Hello?" he answers. His voice is deep, but I can sense the vulnerability, the fear, behind his words.

"Hi, sir. My name is Hayes Murphy. I'm at the hospital where they brought Rayna. I thought you might want an update. Right now, she's in surgery. They didn't give me any other information, but I can call you with updates until you get here if you'd like."

"Are you a nurse?"

"No, sir. I'm...uh...I'm Rayna's boyfriend."

There's silence for a few moments before he speaks again. "Sam and I are on our way, but it's a bit of a drive from Chicago. We should be there in a little over six hours. Updates would be appreciated, Hayes."

"Okay. I'll call you back the second I hear anything."

"Thanks."

When I hang up, I glance around the waiting room. My body feels like it's running on adrenaline that hasn't worn off. The way I'm shaking, the way my heart is beating, the way my breathing is making me feel, I'm just getting more anxious by the minute.

I don't know when Jason and Kevin show up, but one minute I'm alone and the next they're sitting in the chairs next to me. When I've finally registered that it's them, I speak. "When did you guys get here?"

"Five minutes ago. You were staring off into space. Figured you're just in shock. Have you heard anything?" Jason asks.

I shake my head. "No. She's in surgery."

Kevin puts his arm around me and squeezes my shoulder. "She's strong, Hayes. She's going to fight. You know she's going to fight."

I nod. "I know."

After a few minutes, I speak again. "Did you guys hear anything about what happened? How the hell did this happen?"

Jason and Kevin exchange a look that tells me they both know something they aren't sure they want me to know.

"What?" I push. "What don't you want to tell me?"

"Coach said it was a student," Jason starts. "A female student."

"Yes, I know. I heard that part. Do they know who?"

Jason's head falls into his hands.

Kevin takes over for him. "Natalie," he says.

"What?"

"It was Natalie. Natalie shot Rayna."

What the fuck? I'm speechless.

"Another professor heard the gunshot and watched her run out of the auditorium holding a gun."

"How do you know this?" I whisper.

"It's all over Twitter. The police haven't released any official statements, but there were other students in Chestnut Hall when it happened. There were plenty of witnesses that watched Natalie run out with a gun."

"They caught her, right?"

Kevin nods. "Yes. Didn't take long before they arrested her. She was just outside the dome when campus security found her."

"The dome?"

He nods again.

"Why did she do this?"

Jason speaks up. "I told you, dude. She was *obsessed* with you."

"You think she did this because of *me*? *I'm* the reason Rayna was shot? I'm the reason she might fucking *die* today?"

"It's not your fault," Jason says quickly. "There's obviously something wrong with Natalie. She needs help. Now she's going to get it."

"But at what price? She finally gets help, but it'll cost Rayna her *life*?"

She shot Rayna because of me. Then she was heading toward the dome, where we were supposed to be playing a scrimmage game against Michigan State. "She was coming for me next," I say. It wasn't a question. It was a statement. Because that's exactly where she was heading. To me.

"We don't know that for sure," Jason says.

"The hell we don't."

Just then, someone walks out and calls my name. "Hayes Murphy?"

I stand, Jason and Kevin both following behind me. "That's me."

The man walks over to me slowly and holds out his hand. I accept it. "I'm Dr. Porter. Rayna is out of surgery, but she's currently in a medically induced coma. We were able to dislodge the bullet from her chest, but it caused some damage internally as well as some bleeding. She's in the coma to allow her body to rest and heal. She's very lucky. The man who called 911 was able to stop the bleeding in time for the ambulance to get there. If he hadn't done that, we'd be having an entirely different conversation right now."

"So, she's going to be okay?"

"She's not out of the woods yet. If she makes it through the night, that's a good sign."

If *she makes it through the night. There's a chance Rayna won't make it through the night.*

"She's in recovery right now, and we will be bringing her up to a room in the ICU shortly. I'll come get you when she's in there."

"Thank you, Dr. Porter."

He nods before he walks away. That's when I notice the man standing behind him, listening to the entire conversation. He has blood on his hands, on his dress shirt. When my eyes find his, I recognize him immediately.

Dan.

Dan saved her life.

Dan called 911.

Dan saw Natalie running away with a gun.

Dan possibly saved my life.

"Dan," I say.

His gaze meets mine. His eyes look lost, like he's still in shock. I imagine he is. He had to see her like that. I've never been more thankful that Rayna had someone looking out for her.

"You saved her life, Dan."

His bloodshot eyes stare back at me. "There was so much blood," he whispers.

I wipe my eyes, and tears I hadn't even known were there begin to fall onto my jersey. The image of Rayna with a bullet through her chest, blood seeping out everywhere as the life is drained from her is imprinted in my mind. I can't even imagine having seen it in real life.

I walk slowly toward Dan and place a comforting hand on his shoulder. "Thank you."

Chapter Thirty-Six

Hayes

Dr. Porter escorts me into the ICU. The room is cold and white, a complete contrast to the warmth and color throughout the waiting area. My body feels numb. Numb to the internal pain. Numb to the fact Rayna might not make it through the night. Numb that I'm the reason she's lying in this hospital room, wires coming out from beneath her gown, a tube down her throat to help her breathe. I'm just numb.

I stand in the doorway, unsure if I can step over the threshold.

Dr. Porter moves past me and checks a clipboard hanging off Rayna's bed. "Her vitals look good. She's stable right now. Nurses will be monitoring her closely throughout the night. You're welcome to stay if you want."

My eyes are focused on Rayna. Her face is pale. Her hands aren't moving. There's something clipped on her finger that's connected to a machine showing her pulse. It's steady. I can see her heart beating, hear the beeping noise produced every time her heart pumps out blood.

"Thanks."

Dr. Porter walks out of the room before I finally step inside. I slide the glass door closed behind me, leaving Rayna and I in our own private room of beeping and strong bleach scent. I slowly step closer to where she lays. Her eyes are shut, and I can see the rise and fall of her chest. Her perfectly pouty lips are parted for the tube that is helping her breathe. I can't see the gunshot wound. I know it's somewhere on her chest, but the gown and blankets covering her only allow me to see her arms and face.

How close was the bullet from her heart?

I can't imagine a world without Rayna James. My world can't exist without Rayna James.

I pull up one of the chairs in the room so that I'm sitting next to her hospital bed. I reach for her hand. It's eerily cold, yet at the same time warm and comforting.

"Hi, Rayna," I whisper. I don't know if she can hear me, but the fact that she's still breathing, the fact that I can see the beats of her heart telling me she's still alive, is enough for me to think she can.

She's in a coma.

She's not dead.

"I was so worried about you." I stroke my thumb over her smooth skin. "You're going to be okay, Rayna. You're going to be okay. You *have* to be okay. I can't do this without you, and I just got you back, so you have to be okay. For me, baby. For me. You have to be okay."

I cry silent tears as I rest my forehead on her thigh. I grip her hand, never wanting to let go, never wanting to let her out of my sight again.

A half hour passes before I realize I haven't called to update her dad. I find his number that's now saved in my contacts and dial it.

He answers after one ring. "Hayes, is everything okay?"

"I'm in the ICU with her. She's in a medically induced coma. They said she's stable right now, but she's not out of the woods yet. They have her hooked up to machines to help her breathe." I can't stop the tears as I look at her, her beautiful features still beautiful despite the circumstances. She will always be beautiful to me. "She'll be okay. She has to be okay."

I hear heavy breathing on the other end. Then there's silence, followed by a sigh. "I'm glad she has you there with her. We'll see you in a few hours."

"Alright."

"And Hayes?"

"Yeah?"

"Rayna's strong. She doesn't give up easily."

"She is."

I hang up and wipe the newly formed tears, never letting go of her hand. As the hours pass, I doze off a few times, my head resting on Rayna. Nurses come and go frequently, checking her vitals and taking her blood. They said no news is good news in this case. If she makes it through the night unscathed, they'll tapper her off the anesthesia sometime in the next few days.

Several hours later, there's a soft knock on Rayna's glass door. I pick my head up to be greeted with all too familiar eyes. Rayna definitely has her dad's eyes. He's accompanied by her older brother. I stand up immediately, holding my hand out to introduce myself to the love of my life's father.

"Hi, sir. I'm Hayes."

Theodore James looks at my hand before his gaze meets mine. His blue green eyes are blood shot, like he's been crying. I'm sure mine look no different. He doesn't accept my hand. Instead, he wraps his arms around me in a fatherly embrace. It's comforting and exactly what I need, someone to share this pain with, someone who loves her as much as I do and can understand how I feel.

When he lets me go, I turn to Sam. "Hi, Sam. I'm sorry this is how we're meeting."

He pulls me into a similar hug. "Thank you for being here for her. She's lucky to have you."

I stay silent.

After the initial greeting, they both move toward Rayna.

Dr. Porter makes an appearance, knocking once before entering. "You must be Rayna's dad and brother. My nurses have been updating me every hour. Rayna's in stable condition and seems to be recovering how we'd hoped. If everything still looks good by this time tomorrow, we'll be able to wake her up. Right now, we're just hoping to relax her body enough to allow it time to heal."

"Thank you, Dr. Porter," I say.

Theodore and Sam both stand over Rayna, wiping tears of their own.

I take a seat on the two-seater sofa in the corner of the room, allowing them time of their own but also too selfish to leave.

In the morning, Sam offers to run downstairs to get us coffee. No one has slept. Not that anyone could, under the circumstances. We all took turns dozing off in our chairs but were woken up frequently from beeping or nurses coming in to check on Rayna. No one wanted to miss anything.

I returned to my chair next to Rayna a few hours ago and am holding her hand again as Sam returns, offering me one of the three steaming cups of joe.

"Thanks."

He nods.

He takes a seat on the two-seater, Theodore standing and milling about.

Dr. Porter enters a few minutes later smiling. "Good news. She made it through the night. We're hopeful that it can only go up from here. She's gotten through the thick of it, and now it's time to make her as comfortable as possible before she wakes up."

"Is she going to be in pain?" I ask.

"It's possible she may feel uncomfortable. She's getting pain medication through one of those IVs, and we'll up the dosage just before we wake her up so she doesn't come to in excruciating pain. As the pain meds wear off, she will likely start to exhibit signs of pain and that's when we will administer another dose."

"When are you waking her up?" Theodore asks.

"If all is still well tonight, we'll do it then."

Theodore takes a sip of his coffee, pondering something. "How long will it take her to wake up?"

"That all depends on Rayna. Some patients wake up within a matter of hours, others it takes days."

After Dr. Porter answers all our questions, he steps out of the room.

I dismiss myself for the first time since Rayna's family has arrived. I haven't had a chance to call my own parents, so when I step outside and feel the cool crisp air hit my face, I dial my mom's number.

"Hi, love," she answers.

Her soothing voice immediately sends me into a downward spiral. I'm not even sure how I'm going to manage to tell her what's happened.

"Hayes, what's wrong? Did something happen? Are you alright?"

I sniffle, wiping the snot from my nose and trying to get it together so that I can speak. But it's nearly impossible. I'm hysterical. "Mom," I whisper.

"Sweetie, what's going on?"

"It's Rayna."

"What about Rayna, Hayes? What's happened?"

"She's in the hospital. In a coma."

My mom's gasp doesn't go unnoticed. "Is she okay? What happened?"

"She was shot. A student shot her. Yesterday."

I can tell my mom's crying. She's trying hard to mask it, but I know her too well. I can hear it in her voice. "Why would anyone do that?"

The tears fall faster every time I think about why Rayna's here. Every time the guilt becomes too overwhelming for me to bear. "It's my fault, Mom. It's all my fault."

"No, Hayes. Sweetie, no. This is not your fault. Why would you say that?"

"She shot Rayna because of me."

"No. Get that out of your head right now, Hayes Murphy. You did *not* pull that trigger. No matter what led that girl to do what she did, that is on her. *Not* you."

"She might die, Mom."

"She might live, Hayes."

"She has to live. I love her so much it hurts."

"I know, sweetie. I know." She says something to my dad that I can't hear. "Hayes, honey? We're going to drive up to Timbers. We want to be there for you, even if that's from a hotel room. Don't try to fight me on this. We'll be there in a few hours. Is Rayna's family there?"

"Yeah. Her dad and brother."

"Good. Okay, good. I love you, Hayes. I'll call you when we get into town. Stay strong for her."

"I will."

I hang up the phone, wipe my eyes in an attempt to pull myself back together, and walk back inside the hospital. When I get to Rayna's room, her dad and brother are standing in the corner while nurses maneuver around Rayna, uttering words that mean nothing to me.

"What's going on?" I ask, my palms sweating as panic sets in.

"Her heart rate got really low. That machine started beeping loudly and then they all rushed in. They haven't told us anything."

Just then, Dr. Porter hurries in. "What's going on?"

The nurses answer his questions in a rapid-fire session.

Then Dr. Porter brings his attention to us. "She's bradycardic. Her heart rate is returning to normal now. Sometimes this happens. We'll continue to monitor. It's likely this happens in her day-to-day life, especially if she's active. Her heart is strong, as we've already seen throughout the night. Sometimes the heart rate slows. It may be nothing, but like I said, we'll monitor her."

"She is active," I answer immediately. "She runs for miles at a time."

Dr. Porter offers me a soft smile. "Then this may be normal. Our machines are set up to detect any and all changes, so it's likely this isn't as big a deal as it seems."

"Thank you," Theodore says.

I take my seat next to Rayna after the last nurse leaves. I grab her hand, bringing it to my lips before kissing her knuckles.

Theodore and Sam take a seat too. The room is silent for a moment before Theodore speaks up. "Hayes, I have to apologize. Rayna hadn't mentioned that she was seeing anyone. When the hospital called me, my first instinct was to call Sam and get to Timbers as fast as humanly possible. But my second instinct, that was to call Corey. They were together for quite some time, and I thought if something happened to Rayna, that he had a right to know."

"I understand, sir. I'm sure he still cares about Rayna."

"Please, call me Teddy. And yes, he does."

"I love your daughter, Teddy. Very, very much. I know we've only just met and that you don't know me, but I can assure you there isn't anything I wouldn't do for her."

Teddy smiles. "I can see how much you love her. That makes me a very happy man and a proud father."

Over the next few hours, I engage in small talk with Teddy and Sam. In one way or another, I assume they're aware that I'm still in college. After discussing my baseball career and the certainty that I'll be drafted to play in the MLB, I'm not sure how they wouldn't have reached that conclusion. Sam's eyes light up at the possibility of knowing someone in the majors. It isn't brought up how Rayna and I met, or if Rayna is one of my professors, and for that I'm thankful. That's a discussion I want Rayna to be part of.

My mom and dad arrive at a hotel about a mile down the road, assuring me they just want to be nearby in case I need them. Just having them in the same city brings me an unexpected source of comfort.

That night, Dr. Porter informs us that they're going to begin tapering the anesthesia and Rayna will likely wake up, at the earliest, in a few hours.

I never let go of her hand. I wait for any signs that she's waking up. They remove the tube from her throat, and we're all relieved when she's able to breathe on her own. They increase the pain medication. Her vitals are good. The nurses suspect she will wake up any moment.

I wonder what it was like for her in the moments before she was shot. Was she scared? What thoughts raced through her mind? Did she know Natalie had a gun? Did she try to call for help? Then I wonder what I'll say to her the moment she wakes up. Do I apologize? She must know this is my fault. How do I apologize for something like this? How do I keep her safe? Does she know that she's my whole world?

Chapter Thirty-Seven

Rayna

Beep.

Beep.

Beep.

The sound alarms every two seconds like clockwork.

Beep.

Beep.

Beep.

My throat feels swollen, and it's hard to swallow. My mouth is dry, lips are chapped. I can taste blood. My left hand is cold, but my right hand is warm. Something is keeping it warm.

Beep.

Beep.

Beep.

It's dark. My eyes are shut. I try to open them, but they're heavy. Everything is stiff. Can I move? I try to wiggle my toes. It feels like they're moving, but my eyes are shut so I can't see.

Beep.

Beep.

Beep.

I try my fingers next. There's something wrapped around one of my fingers. When I move it, I feel some kind of wire brush against my arm. I try my other hand next. Whatever is keeping it warm is squeezing it tightly and making it difficult for me to wiggle my fingers. I squeeze instead.

"Rayna?"

Beep.

Beep.

Beep.

I squeeze my hand again.

This time, someone squeezes back. "Rayna, can you hear me?"

I squeeze.

"She's squeezing my hand! Nurse!"

I hear several footsteps before the hand grasping mine tries to pull away. I squeeze harder.

The hand stays. "I'm right here, Rayna."

Where is here? Where am I?

Everything comes back to me in that moment. *Natalie. The gun. Reaching for my phone. Did I call 911? She shot me. I must be in the hospital. My chest aches. My throat hurts. My head is in pain. There are so many noises and beeping and people calling out my name.*

Beep. Beep. Beep.

Beep. Beep. Beep.

Beep. Beep. Beep.

"Rayna, calm down. It's okay. They're only trying to help. Calm down, baby."

Beep. Beep. Beep.

Beep. Beep. Beep.

Beep. Beep. Beep.

Am I not calm? I haven't moved. But the beeping is getting infuriatingly louder and more frequent. That must be my heart rate. *Okay, Rayna. Calm down. Breathe in. Breathe out.*

My chest. Deep breaths hurt my chest.

I squeeze the hand again.

"Can you open your eyes?" someone asks.

I try to open them. They're still so heavy. I shake my head instead. *No. I can't open them.*

Someone rubs something cool over my eyes. Something wet. It feels good. So good.

"Try opening them now," another voice says.

I do. I try. They're still heavy, but I manage to open them a sliver before light shines through my eyelids and they're forced shut again.

"It's okay. It'll be easier as the anesthesia wears off."

Beep.

Beep.

Beep.

That's good. My heart rate must be back to normal.

"Are you in any pain?" a deep male voice asks.

I nod. *Yes. My chest. My throat.*

"On a scale of one to ten, how bad is the pain? Ten being the worst. Can you show me on your hands?"

This time the hand disappears from mine quickly. Both of my hands are painstakingly cold now and I miss the warmth the hand provided.

I hold up seven fingers. Two on my right, five on my left.

The hand returns to mine afterward, and I instantly feel more relaxed.

"Does your chest hurt?"

I nod. *That must be where I got shot.*

"Anything else?"

I nod. *Yes. My throat.*

"Can you point to where it hurts?"

I lift my free hand to my throat.

"You were intubated," the deep voice says. "It was to help you breathe while you were in a coma. The irritation will subside shortly."

I was in a coma? How long have I been asleep for? "Hayes?" It comes out as a whisper. And it hurts like hell. I don't recognize my own voice. It's deep and raspy.

The hand squeezes mine. "It's me, Ray. I'm right here."

Hayes. He's here with me. Hayes is here with me. He's okay. I'm okay. And he's here with me. I feel something wet drip down my cheek. At first, I think they're rubbing water on my face again, but then I realize they're tears.

A gentle hand wipes away the tears. "It's okay. You're okay, Rayna. I'm here. Your dad's here. Sam's here. Everyone's here, and you're going to be okay."

Then more tears fall. Tears because I'm so happy that I didn't die. Tears because I'm relieved Natalie didn't get to Hayes. Happiness that my family is here.

The urge to open my eyes is even stronger now. I want to see them. I want to see that they're here with me. They're all I could think about as Natalie was holding that gun on me. I wanted to live. I wanted to live for them. All of them.

Someone wipes away at the tears. Then I feel soft and familiar lips brush against my forehead.

Hayes.

He never lets go of my hand. Not while the doctor talks to them. Not when the nurses poke me to test my blood. Not when they examine my body for any signs of swelling or bleeding. He never lets go.

Beep.

Beep.

Beep.

Chapter Thirty-Eight

Hayes

Rayna falls back to sleep. Her breathing steadies, and I can tell she's more relaxed now. She was fighting herself internally. Battling with how to open her eyes, how to move her muscles, how to make sense of what's happened to her. She struggled to speak, but when my name fell from her lips, I nearly lost it. She's so strong. So damn strong.

Jason drops off a change of clothes for me, and I take a shower in the private bathroom in Rayna's room. They said she'll be transferred to the cardiac floor soon, once she's more responsive and awake. That room likely won't have a private shower, so I take advantage.

A few hours pass when there's a knock on the door.

One of the nurses enters. "Sorry to bother you guys again, but there's someone here to visit Rayna. He claims he's her husband." The nurse eyes me, giving me a sympathetic expression.

Ex-husband, I want to say. But I don't. It's no surprise that he showed up. Teddy admitted to calling him.

Teddy looks to me, then back to the nurse. "Send him up."

The nurse nods and walks away.

Teddy's gaze meets mine again. "I'm sorry, Hayes. He's just worried about her. As we all are."

I nod. "I understand."

Sam shakes his head. I sense that he doesn't care for Corey.

A few minutes later, the nurse escorts a tall, slender man into the room. He has ashy blond hair and at least a days' worth of scruff on his face. He immediately eyes Rayna before noticing me and my hand gripping hers. He looks lost for a moment before he turns to acknowledge Teddy and Sam.

He nods his head by way of greeting. "Teddy. Sam. How is she?"

Teddy answers, "She woke up a few hours ago but wasn't able to open her eyes yet. She said she was in some pain, so they upped her pain meds and it knocked her out again."

"How did this happen?"

"She was shot by a student."

"Why? Why would someone shoot her?"

It is a valid question. It is the same question I asked when I found out. Teddy hadn't asked me many questions, though I suspect he knows I have more information than I am letting on.

I stand up to introduce myself to a man Rayna once loved. "Hi, I'm Hayes." I hold out my hand.

He looks at it for a moment, hesitating before offering his hand. "Corey. How do you know Rayna?"

"She's my girlfriend."

His eyebrows raise, and I can tell he's scrutinizing my appearance. Does it bother him that I'm younger than he is? How does it feel to see Rayna move on to someone else? I don't like knowing that this man has seen Rayna at her most vulnerable, that they've been intimate. She married this man. He held her heart for a long time, which means he must be someone special. I try to remember that she's with me now, that she loves me. But I can't help that small pang of jealousy that he experienced so many firsts with her.

Just then, I hear Rayna moan as she slightly adjusts herself on the hospital bed. It's the most movement she's had since the doctor left.

"Ray, you awake?" I ask from the foot of her bed.

The hand I've been holding reaches out as if seeking mine. I grab it instantly, returning to my seat beside her.

"I'm here," I whisper.

She moans again as her eyes flutter. She's trying to open them.

The rest of the room stays quiet as everyone watches her. I'm too busy looking at Rayna to pay any more attention to Corey. I hate seeing her like this. I can't imagine it's much better for him.

Finally, her eyes open. First, they stare up at the ceiling, focusing on nothing. Then they flicker in my direction, and I see the smallest smile spread over her lips. It's the most beautiful thing I've seen in days.

"Hi," I say softly.

"Hi," she croaks. Her voice is still raspy, a side effect of being intubated, the doctor said. It should return to normal in a few days.

I reach for the water at her bedside and hold the cup to her mouth. "Drink some water. It'll help."

She takes small sips, her eyes on me the entire time. I can't take my gaze away from hers. For a moment there, it feels like it is only her and I in this room.

When I set the water back down, her eyes wander across the room, sweeping across her dad and Sam until they finally land on Corey.

I watch for her reaction.

When her eyes settle on him, they don't waiver. I want her to look back to me. I don't like the way he's looking at her right now, or the way they have this deep connection and words don't need to be spoken out loud, they're just there.

"Hi, Rayna," Corey says softly.

"What are you doing here?" she asks. It's the most words she's said, and they sounded painful coming from her hoarse throat.

"Your dad called me. You were shot, Rayna. Why would I not be here?"

234

"Because we're divorced." She says it so matter-of-factly that it takes Corey a second to pull himself together again.

"I know. You don't need to remind me."

Rayna looks back to me, her eyebrows furrowed.

I squeeze her hand to let her know that it's okay. It's okay that he's here. All that matters is that she is okay.

Teddy stands and walks toward the foot of Rayna's bed. "Hi, sweetheart."

She smiles. "Hi, Dad." She looks over his shoulder at Sam. "Hi, Sam."

Sam walks toward her bed. All four of us are surrounding her, though I'm the only one seated and touching her.

"You had us worried there, sis."

"I'm sorry."

"It's not your fault, Rayna," I interject.

She frowns again as her gaze meets mine. "Natalie," she whispers.

I nod. "I know."

"Natalie?" Corey asks. "Who is Natalie? Is she the one who brought a gun to your office?"

Rayna hesitates for a moment before she speaks. "She's sick."

"No shit," Corey snips.

I squeeze Rayna's hand. "I'm so sorry, Rayna," I whisper so only she can hear.

She shakes her head at me. "Stop. It's not your fault."

Rayna's not able to speak as quietly as I am though, so the second she insinuates that it's not my fault, Corey jumps into attack mode.

"What do you mean it's not his fault? Why would he think it is?" He looks to me. "Why would you think this is your fault?"

Rayna sighs. "Stop it, Corey."

"It's okay," I say. I turn to face Teddy and Sam because they deserve to know why Rayna was shot. I don't give a shit about Corey and what he thinks.

"Natalie is a student at East Valley. She's not one of Rayna's students. She's someone I ran into a few months ago. She ended up going home with one of my roommates that night. He was pretty smitten with her until he realized she was using him to get closer to me. I guess she tried the same thing on my other roommate last week. She must have found out I was dating Rayna and took it to the extreme."

"Wait a minute," Corey says. "How old are you?"

"Twenty-two."

Corey's eyes bulge as his eyebrows raise. He looks around the room and chuckles to himself, shaking his head. "Unbelievable," he whispers under his breath.

I ignore him. "I'm sorry, sir. This is my fault."

Teddy shakes his head and plants one firm hand on my shoulder, squeezing it lightly. "You have nothing to be sorry for. You couldn't know that girl was going to go and do something like this. All that matters is Rayna is okay and that girl is getting the help she needs."

Corey speaks again. "Dude, are you in college still?"

I nod.

"Seriously, Rayna? You divorced me so you could hook up with a student?"

"Please just go, Corey. Thank you for coming, but I'm fine."

"How could you do this to me?"

"Are you kidding me? You *cheated* on me! I divorced you because you were sleeping with someone else!" She coughs, and I offer her more water. She shouldn't be talking so much. I can tell she's in pain.

Corey's cheeks turn a dark shade of red. "Rayna, *please.* I was so worried about you when your dad called. I thought I lost you forever. I'm sorry about everything that happened, but please don't let us really be over. I'm still in love with you."

The fact that he is admitting this in front of her dad, brother, and current boyfriend does not go unnoticed. The guy has balls. Too bad I want to punch him in the face.

"She asked you to leave," I say.

Corey ignores me, his eyes pleading with Rayna.

"I'm sorry," she says. "Please go."

He sighs as his head falls. "I'm really glad you're okay."

"Thanks."

He turns and walks out of the room silently.

Rayna turns to face me, her free hand brushing my cheek. "I'm sorry about that."

I kiss her hand as it runs smoothly across my scruff.

"And this *wasn't* your fault, Hayes. My dad is right. You couldn't have known. Natalie is sick and she needs help."

I nod because she's right, but I still feel like this is my fault. This never would have happened if I hadn't been so adamant on being in a public relationship with her.

Rayna looks to her dad next. "This isn't how I wanted you guys to meet. But, Dad, Sam, this is Hayes. Yes, he's younger than me. Yes, he's a student. Yes, he's *my* student. None of that matters, and I can explain how we met later, but please just know that I have *never* loved someone as much as I love him." Her eyes meet mine again. "I love you."

I smile and kiss her lips for the first time since she was almost taken from me. I don't even care that her dad and brother are here. "I love you so much," I whisper.

Chapter Thirty-Nine

Rayna

I'm released from the hospital a few weeks later and just in time for Christmas. Hayes's parents stayed in town, as did my dad and Sam. We spent Christmas together in my condo, the first of many as one big family.

Hayes and I spend New Year's just the two of us, our families both deciding that it's time for them to return to their lives. I've recovered nicely. While in the hospital, I went through some therapy, but by the time they released me, I was feeling almost back to normal.

Hayes told me Dan was the one who found me in my office. I called him when I was still in the hospital, and he visited twice while I was still admitted. He seemed pretty traumatized but was thankful that I am okay. I'm so appreciative of Dan. If it hadn't been for him, I probably wouldn't be here right now.

Hayes waits on me hand and foot. I try to tell him that I can do things myself, but I think he likes to feel needed.

My students had to complete their final without me, but luckily, they all felt confident with their knowledge of the material before my unexpected absence. I'm proud to say that every single student passed my class.

It's crazy to think that one year ago I had never even heard of Hayes Murphy. I spent last New Year's recovering from a divorce and applying to jobs all over the Midwest. I never thought my life would take me to where it has today, but there isn't a thing I would change because it's all led me to the wonderful man I love.

Hayes brings me a champagne flute and sits next to me on the couch. He's dressed in his usual sweatpants with no shirt attire that he frequents in my condo. He spends more time here than he does his own house, but that's nothing unusual. We have more privacy here, as we always have.

I snuggle into his warm chest, wearing one of his T-shirts, my legs covered in a blanket. We're getting ready to watch the ball drop in New York City.

He places a gentle kiss on the top of my head and squeezes me a little tighter than normal.

"What's that for?" I ask.

"What's what for?"

"You know what. You're squeezing me like I'm about to run away or something."

"I can't love on my girlfriend for no apparent reason?"

I smile. "You can love on me all you want."

"Good," he says. "I plan to do that for the rest of my life."

He says that a lot. The rest of his life.

The rest of our life.

I have no doubt that Hayes is the man I will spend forever with.

He squeezes me again.

"Hayes, is everything okay?" That's when I look up to meet his gaze.

His green eyes bore into mine. I love the way he looks at me, like he's taken back every time he sees me. Like I'm the only person in the world.

"Everything is more than okay," he whispers. He kisses the tip of my nose, then my forehead. "I love you, Rayna," he says. "Since the moment you walked into that bar, I've only had eyes for you. Your beauty is unmatched. You're easily the most beautiful woman to ever walk this planet, and I'm in absolute awe that you're mine." He rubs a finger along my cheek bone, over my lips, and down my neck until it lands on my chest. "But what's in here, this is what I love most. Your heart. The way you love. The way you care. Everything that makes you, you. That is what I love the most about you. You gave me a chance, even when the odds were against us. You gave me the chance to love you the way you deserve to be loved, and I promise I will love you that way forever."

He kisses my lips gently before he moves his arms out from around me. He stands up off the couch and reaches into his pocket. Before I know it, he's on one knee in front of me, our eyes level as I remain seated.

"I knew I was going to fall in love with you after our first night together. I remember thinking to myself, *I want to give her the world.* It feels like a lifetime ago now, but that thought has remained the same. I want to give you the world, Rayna." He opens the box, revealing the most stunning princess cut diamond ring inside.

My hands immediately move to my mouth, the happy tears falling as I experience one of the best moments of my life.

"Rayna Lynn James, will you please make me the happiest man in the world and be my wife?"

My eyes are so fixated on Hayes that I almost forget to answer. The beauty behind his gaze, the love, the adoration, the truth, it's all enough to cause hysterical tears to run down my face. I throw my arms around him, crying into his neck because I can't believe how happy I am right now. "Yes," I whisper between sobs. "Absolutely yes."

He kisses me so fiercely, with so much love.

Ten, nine, eight, seven, six... The countdown on the TV continues until the clock strikes midnight.

"Happy New Year, Ray. I can't wait to make you my wife."

"Happy New Year, Hayes. I can't wait to be your wife."

Epilogue

Hayes

East Valley won another state title, and I was drafted that June to pitch for the Kansas City Royals. Rayna and I were both thrilled to be staying in the Midwest, though it did mean she'd have to find a job elsewhere. After everything she had been through, she was okay with leaving East Valley. East Valley brought her to me, but other than that, there were things she'd like to leave behind.

We moved into our new home at the end of June, after I had already been training with the Royals for a couple of weeks. We found a beautiful farm-styled home with a lot of land. Once I saw the impressive three-story, six-bedroom house with a wraparound porch, I knew we had to have it. After all, I planned to make Rayna a mother very soon.

One of the benefits to now playing for the MLB, was the vast access to healthcare available to us. After a few appointments with a fertility specialist, there were no longer any uncertainties about with whether Rayna and I would be able to conceive. Though if we were faced with the same predicament she was in her first marriage, I'm certain I would have handled things differently. There's nothing I wouldn't do for Rayna, and I'd make her a mother one way or another.

Jason and Kevin enjoyed their summer post-graduation without the added pressure of school and the team. Kevin was in talks with a minor league team, while Jason went back to school for a graduate degree in business. Jason and Emily still seem to be going strong, and I couldn't be happier for the two of them. Rayna was able to meet Emily in early January at the surprise engagement party I threw for her.

My first season playing professional ball went by fast. My team made it into the second round of play-offs where we lost against the New York Yankees. Our team is full of young players, so we're predicted to go far in the upcoming seasons.

Rayna decided to wait before she went back to teaching. With everything happening in our lives, a new home, a new city, and my consistent traveling schedule, she thought it best to settle down before applying for a new teaching position. Instead, she focused on the interior design of our new home, which she had a lot of fun with. And because of her flexible schedule, she was able to travel on the road with me. She didn't miss a single game of the nearly one-hundred and sixty games we played. She is my biggest cheerleader and my absolute best friend. I still can't wait to make her my wife.

Today is New Year's Eve. It also happens to be our wedding day. I proposed to Rayna one year ago today, and come midnight, she will officially be Mrs. Murphy.

We lucked out with today's weather. It's a beautiful winter day here in Kansas City. The sun is setting beautiful beyond the trees, and though it's a chilly forty-five degrees, it could always be worse. We decided to get married at home, turning our immense amount of land into an enchanting winter wedding venue. Rayna found an elegant canopy tent, its transparent siding allowing for the night sky and stars to shine through on our guests. Twinkling lights hang from above, as well as several other light fixtures that illuminate overhead. The seats are set to face the north, where the moon shines through. There are floral arrangements hanging above each table as well as a sea of rose petals that lead to the alter where Rayna and I will say our vows.

As the last of the guests trickle in, Jason, my best man, walks into one of the guest rooms in the house where I was told to get ready so I wouldn't accidentally run into my bride before it's time.

"You ready?" he asks.

I give him a wide grin. "I've never been more ready for anything in my life."

"Then it's time."

Jason walks with me outside and into the makeshift venue. I walk down the aisle, over the hundreds of soft pink and white rose petals. I first see Coach sitting there, alongside his wife and kids. Then I eye Dan, the man I thank every day for keeping the love of my life alive. He's one of our very good friends, and I couldn't imagine this day without him here. I see Kevin, Emily sitting on one side of him, while a random girl I've never seen before sits on his other. It must be his date — he had mentioned something about bringing a date. My parents are sitting in the front row, Sam and his girlfriend close by.

I pause at the end of the aisle, adjusting my tie and turning to the intimate crowd of people here to celebrate our love. Jason takes his place next to me, and together we wait for my beautiful bride.

By now the sun has set and the nighttime sky lights up the space just as much as the twinkling overhead lights. Music starts to play, indicating that it's time. Our guests rise, anticipating the arrival of the bride.

Then I see her. And I'm instantly taken back by her beauty.

Her father escorts her, her arm tucked into his as she wipes away the tears that are already forming with her free hand.

When our eyes lock, I think back to every moment I've ever had staring into those hypnotic turquoise eyes. From the first time I saw her at the bar, to the day I realized she was my professor. From her insistent need to avoid me, to her inability to stay away. Every single time I've made love to her, told her I love her, held her in my arms. And now to this day, the day she walks toward me in a beautiful white satin gown, preparing to give me her world so that I can give her mine. Everything has led up to this day, to this *moment*.

It's everything.

She's my everything.

From this day on, I'm going to give her the world.

The End

Thank you so much for reading *Give Her the World*. Please take a moment to visit your favorite retailer to write a review.

A letter from the author

     First off, thank you so much for reading *Give Her the World.* I wrote this book during a time in my life when I was really trying to escape. Sometimes, we need a distraction from the life we are living. When I find myself needing to get away, I'll bury myself in reading and writing.

     Rayna and Hayes are a dream. We all hope for a love like theirs. A love that makes you smile, makes life easy, makes you not worry. We search for that happiness that makes us never feel alone.

     I love being able to write for not only myself, but for each of you. Thank you for continuously supporting me. If you haven't already, check out my other novels *See You Never* and *Rocky Love.*

With love,

Delaney Lynn

Made in the USA
Monee, IL
23 December 2022

23457551R00144